"DEAD RINGER"

By BARB NAGEL

To Nancy

Barb Nagel

This book is dedicated to all my family, friends and my RWA chapter members for their patience, understanding and faith in me. A special thanks to Judy for her dedication and assistance in editing.

Chapter 1

How much longer could she continue running? Her lungs felt ready to burst. She could feel every beat of her heart, pounding so hard that she was sure it was beating outside her chest. Her feet felt numb, but she plunged forward, stumbling, snagging her flimsy nightgown on the brush in the woods. She was tired. She needed to rest, but she pushed forward until a searing pain gripped her left side, intensifying, until she had to stop and lean against a tree to draw an agonizing breath. She shivered as the water from the earlier rain dripped from the leaves and limbs, soaking her gown. Fog had moved in making it, impossible to see two feet in front of her. Yet, she had to continue. It was a matter of life or death. The sounds of pounding footsteps and heavy breathing were getting close, too close. She feared she could not outrun them. She needed to hide, but there were only trees, trees everywhere. She heard something in front of her and crouched behind a tree, with her hand over her mouth to stifle a scream. Her eyes began to adjust to the darkness. Were they circling? She could not tell. If she stayed behind the tree they would find her, and her life would be over. She squeezed her eyes as tears ran down her cheeks. Why did they want her dead? What had she ever done? Get a grip on yourself, she thought, you have to keep your wits about you. She had no idea where she was or going, only the need to get away. She heard the sound of steps as her pursuers crunched through the leaves on the ground; they were getting close. She had to keep running no matter how her lungs burned.

These people wanted her, and would not give up until they found her and destroyed her. Well, she was not going to make it easy for them, she thought, and slid out from behind the tree and started running again She'd gone about ten feet when she slipped and fell, causing a searing pain shoot up her right ankle and leg. She pulled herself up only to trip again; this time she found herself rolling down a hill. Her head hit something and then came utter blackness. She lay there covered in brush and leaves, hidden from her seekers as they moved by.

Chapter 2

The woods opened up before him as he caught sight of his home: a rustic log cabin that he had built himself and finished a few months before. He still had a few things to complete, but it was all his and paid for. He'd taken on the task a few years ago. He gazed at the two-story nestled on the plateau of a pine-covered hill, with its breathtaking view of the surrounding hills and valley. A sparkling clear river ran through the valley below his home. He loved the peace and quiet. He hadn't once missed the city with its busy streets, and everyone in a rush. That was not the only reason he left.

He had been happy with that life back then. He'd had a great job as one of the city's top detectives. Best of all, he had a loving wife and a warm, cheerful home. Life had been great then, like the sun shining on a bright summer day. Now all was black as the night skies. After five years of marriage, his beautiful wife Mary had died of cancer. It took a year for him to realize he was not happy with his work anymore. Mary used to listen while he reviewed his cases, when they took long walks together, and over loving, quiet, candle-lit dinners. They had a wonderful marriage, short as it was. They had planned on children making their family complete. Sickness took precedence; he lost interest in his job, in life in general. He knew he could not go on like this. It was then he decided to leave law enforcement. He always wanted to write. Mary had encouraged him to do so, but he never took it seriously.

Now here in the peace and quiet of the hills and trees, he had started his first book on criminal justice. He hoped to write a few criminal novels, using some of his old cases. He looked over again at his place. A light was on in the kitchen. He could've sworn he turned it off before he left earlier that afternoon to go hunting. Then he saw the tracks. Big boot tracks leading to his back door! He dropped the two dead rabbits he was carrying. With rifle aimed, he walked up the steps leading to the wrap around porch. He slowly approached his back door and listened for a sound, any sound. Not hearing any, he quietly opened the door, wanting to surprise whoever had invaded his home. The place looked empty. Had he really left the light on? He never locked the door. No one ever bothered him here in the dense woods. He started to lean the rifle against the wall, when he heard footsteps. He aimed the rifle down the hallway that led from the kitchen. "Glad you've made it home."

"Damn it Matt, you scared the shit out of me! I almost shot you, thought you were an intruder."

"Well, I'm not. Now put that rifle down."

Rip leaned the rifle against the wall and smiled at his old friend. "I'm sorry, Matt. I saw the light on and--hell, I forgot. The detective in me took over. I'm sorry; I should've guessed it would be you." Matt was his closest neighbor and did pop in from time to time.

"Were you out hunting?" Matt asked.

"Yes, I got two rabbits, which I left outside. I'd better bring them in before some animal gets hold of them." He turned and headed out the door, calling back to Matt, "Were you out hunting too?" He heard yes and then Matt's words faded as the wind swept them away.

"It was damn cold out there today. A sure sign winter is just around the corner," Rip said as he placed the rabbits in the sink. The rabbits could wait, he thought, he needed a cup of hot coffee. He turned to make some when he saw that Matt had already done so. "Thanks for the coffee."

"I knew you'd want some as soon as you got back."

"How long you been waiting?"

"Not too long. Rip; did you hear what I said about hunting?" Matt followed him into the living room where Rip stood by the fireplace rubbing his hands together.

"I see you kept the fire going too, thanks. To answer your question, yes, I heard you, and you said you went hunting. I guess you didn't get anything or you would be bragging." Rip knew that Matt was a better hunter than he was; he had lived his whole life in these woods. Rip would be what one called a novice. Then he really looked at his friend.

"Matt, are you okay? You look pale and you are not acting like yourself. You seem a little nervous. You have been twisting that mangy hat of yours in your hands ever since I arrived. What is the matter? Did you shoot more than your limit?"

Matt put his hat back on his head. He grinned, and showed two missing teeth on the bottom. "I feel fine. You know I eat what I kill. Today was just not my day for rabbits. I did get something though."

"What are you saying? Tell me you didn't shoot a deer. You know the season does not open for few weeks."

"No, I'm not stupid."

"I'm not saying you are stupid. But admit it, Matt; you have been known to kill animals out of season."

"Yes, but only when my stomach starts to growl. A man has to eat. Then I go out and get me food."

"Matt, stop with the double talk, will you. Just come out with it." He was getting on his nerves. First, he came home to find Matt in his home and now double talk. He had to admit he'd never seen Matt so nervous before. Not even in front of the conservation officers.

"Do you have to talk so loud? Shush it down a bit." Matt put his index finger on his lips.

"You're going to wake her up."

"Did he say wake her?" Rip shook his head. He was about to ask him to repeat it, but before he got a chance, Matt continued, as he stood twisting his hat.

"I know you're going to be upset, but your place was closer and nicer than mine..."

"Matt! What the hell are you talking about, your place or mine?"

"The girl I found in the woods."

"Whoa! Stop right there. Let me get this clear. You're saying you found a girl in the woods?" Matt nodded as he held his head down. It took Rip a few seconds to realize what his friend had just said. Then, turning to him, he said, "Well, why didn't you say so in the first place? Where is this girl?"

"I put her in your spare bedroom."

"You did what?"

"I put her in...."

"I heard you, but--." Matt backed away and looked shaken. "Matt, just show me."

"I didn't think you would mind. She was unconscious and her body a mess. She needs a little cleaning up. She was wearing some silky thing that's all torn and muddy. She looked half-frozen when I found her."

Rip slowly opened the spare bedroom door, and stepped in. The light from the hall filled the room. Rip noticed that Matt had put on the night light.

He approached the bed with Matt at his tail. He didn't know what to expect, but it was not what lay in front of him. The person on the bed definitely was no girl. The person on the bed was a grown woman. He guessed her to be in her early to mid thirty's. He saw the small gash on the right side of her head above the temple. He leaned over her and saw that it wouldn't require stitches, but from the size of the bump, she would have one hell of a headache when she woke up. He whispered to Matt to get a clean damp cloth and a butterfly bandage from the medicine chest.

He gently cleaned the cut and placed the bandage over it, all the while worried she'd wake up. He started to pull the covers back when Matt grabbed at his arm. "Matt, I want to see how badly she's hurt." Matt let go.

Matt had been right, the women wore practically nothing and what she did wear was so transparent it was as if she wore nothing. He noticed her swollen right ankle, but it didn't look broken. Small abrasions and scratches covered her body. Her feet too were cut and muddy. She had not worn shoes. The injuries were not life threatening and they could wait. He'd take care of the worst cuts and leave the rest alone.

She looked like Sleeping Beauty lying there. Her face was void of any lines or expressions, very relaxed. Her brunette hair flared out onto the pillow where her head rested. Her facial features were delicate and perfectly proportioned except for the bump that would eventually go away. The body under the covers matched the rest of her, perfect. Rip stared at the woman and wondered, what were you doing out in the woods at this time of year dressed like this? He motioned for Matt to leave, and they backed out of the room. He needed more information from Matt before she woke up.

Once in the kitchen, Rip poured himself another cup of coffee and sat at the table. He looked over at Matt, who stood twisting that damn hat again. "Matt, sit down. I want you to tell me how you came across this woman and how she ended up in my house injured."

"I don't——I mean, you sound and look angry. I'll go and come back tomorrow after you've cooled down." Matt turned to leave.

"Like hell you will," Rip said loudly, then remembered the woman down the hall and said in a quieter but firm tone. "Matt, I just want an explanation. Of course, I'm upset, it's not every day that I come home to find a strange woman in my house, battered and bruised.

"You would've done the same thing, if you had found her," Matt replied, taking a seat across from Rip.

"Okay, so tell me."

"I was out hunting, and not having seen any rabbits, decided to try the river's lower ridge. I was almost there when I heard what sounded like deer running through the woods, and twigs snapping. I saw a flash of something, and then it was rolling down the hill in front of me. It came to a sudden stop when it hit a small boulder. I knew then it was a person. I hurried over, and that's when I saw her head bleeding. I noticed her chest going up and down and realized she was alive. I tried to wake her, but was out cold. I looked around to see if she was with someone, there was no one. Then, I heard some sounds off in the woods. I called out, but got no response. I couldn't leave her there, so I draped her over my shoulder and started for my place, then decided your place was closer. In the back of my mind, I thought you would know what to do, you being a retired cop and all."

Running his fingers through his hair, Rip leaned back in his chair and asked, "You sure no one else was around?"

"I'm sure. What I don't understand is why she was out in these dense woods, miles from the nearest town or city, dressed like she was?"

"I have no idea. We will have to wait until she wakes up and ask her."

Chapter 3

Warmth engulfed her, where before she'd been freezing. She slowly opened her right eye and then the left. A ceiling fan came into view. It wasn't moving. Where am I? She lifted her head and quickly lay back as a horrific, piercing pain shot through her head. She closed her eyes, and the pain subsided. She slowly opened her eyes again, but lay very still. She glanced from side to side at her surroundings, but nothing looked familiar.

She didn't recognize the bedroom, with its oversized wood furniture. Moving slower, she sat up. Her head still throbbed, but not as bad now. She noticed an open door at the far end of the room. She could see it was a bathroom. Where was she? She pulled the navy blue comforter away, and looked at herself. She cringed and slid deeper under the covers. Stifling a cry, she bit into the blanket. Then lifting the covers again, she began to shake. Where were her clothes? Where was she? Tears ran down her cheeks as she realized she didn't recognize the body under the covers. She turned her hands as she gazed upon them. Whose hands were they?

As she slid slowly from the bed and started to walk, she had to grab the side of the bed, for her right foot hurt. Lifting it, she hobbled her way to the bathroom. She flipped on the light switch and slowly made her way to the vanity and the mirror. Looking in the mirror, she had to grip the edge of the vanity to keep from falling. She didn't recognize the person who stared back at her. Who was she?

Then she heard a noise, footsteps. She wanted to run. Where could she go? She quickly made her way back to the bed, bouncing on one foot. In bed, she pulled the covers up to her neck and closed her eyes tight as she heard the door open. She knew someone stood by the bed. She could hear them breathing. She was afraid to look, but knew that she had to peek and attempted to open her eyes. A few minutes passed and hearing nothing, she slowly opened her eyes. A man stood by the bed. She pulled the covers up over her head. Her hands were trembling. Who was this person?

She pulled the covers down to her neck. Rip didn't want to frighten her any more than she was already from the look in her eyes. "Don't be afraid. I'm not going to hurt you. I'm glad to see you're alive. I'd begun to think you were going to sleep forever." She didn't move, but just kept staring at him and clutching the blanket to her. "How are you feeling? You have a small cut and bump on the head, but it will be gone in a few days. You are lucky. With that fall you took, your injuries could've been worse." She pulled a hand out from under the blanket as she continued to stare at him and touched the bandage.

"Who are you? Where am I?" He was smiling at her.

"I'm Robert Walker, Rip to by friends, and like I said, you are in my house."

She gazed into his face, a square face with dark brown, almost black eyes. The eyes that stared back at her were gentle. Yet she still feared him. She did not know him.

Holding the comforter up to her neck, she sat up and leaned against the headboard. "Did you do this?" She continued to hold her hand to her head.

"No, you fell."

"Where are my clothes?" She'd get dressed and leave. Leave to where she did not know. She had no idea where she was or who she was. She again looked at the man standing beside the bed. He was still smiling. Should she trust him?

"Listen, you don't need to be afraid. I want to help. A friend of mine saw you falling down a hill. You hit your head on a boulder and passed out. He brought you to my house. As for the bruises and other marks on your body, I have no idea how you got them. You asked about clothes, you're wearing what you had on when he found you."

She shuddered and felt her face flush, knowing that she wore almost nothing. "Thank you for caring for me." She touched the bandage. She had no choice but to trust him. After all, he had bandaged her wounds. "You wouldn't happen to have any clothes I could wear, would you? I'm sure your wife has something."

"I'm not married." He saw her eyes glance from the door and then back to him. He smiled. "I live here alone. If you look in the closet over there," he pointed to the double sliding doors, "I'm sure you can find something in there to wear.

"Mr..."

"Please call me Rip."

"I know you told me that I'm in your home, but where is home?"

"A small town called, Buford. Since you've been asking all the questions, I have one. Who are you? What's your name?"

Her name, he asked. She thought about it and realized she not only didn't recognize herself, she didn't know who she was let alone know her name. She felt tears welling up in her eyes and brushed them away. She looked directly at him and said. "I don't know."

"You don't know who you are?" She shook her head. The blow to her head must have been worse than he'd anticipated. "That's okay; a blow to the head does that sometimes. I'm sure you will have recall in a few hours." She nodded. "I'll leave you to clean up and get dressed. I suppose you are hungry. I'll fix us some lunch. When you've finished dressing come into the kitchen, it's right down the hall from this room."

In the kitchen, he opened up a couple of cans of stew and put it in a pot on the stove to heat. With it heating, his thoughts turned to the woman in the other room.

After Matt left last night, Rip went in and checked on her again. Her forehead felt a little warm. He was also about a fever. He was also worried that she had a concussion, how severe, he didn't know. The nearest hospital was over fifty miles away and the local clinic closed. He had read somewhere that rest was the best cure for a concussion. The fever however, bothered him; he had to do something. He sat on the edge of the bed and placed a damp cloth on her forehead. As he gazed upon her, he saw a beautiful woman. He wondered who she was and why someone had abused her. When he saw the marks around her wrists and ankles, he'd not said anything to Matt, but was very concerned. The burn marks looked as though a rope had caused them. How could anyone abuse a woman like this?

As he continued holding the damp cloth to her forehead, he felt compelled to talk. He had not sat and talked to a woman since his wife died. He talked to her about how he'd built the place; that it had been his dream for years. He talked about the peace here. He spoke about anything and everything that came to mind. She had the face of an angel as she lay there sleeping, a true sleeping beauty.

With a towel wrapped around her damp hair, she stepped out from the shower. She stood in front of the vanity mirror and examined her body. She tried to think, to remember how she had gotten so many bruises and cuts, and those marks on her wrist and ankles, where had they come from? She couldn't remember a thing upon waking up and finding herself in this house. She couldn't even remember her name. With a towel wrapped around her body, she went to the closet in search of something to wear. Well, what had she expected women's clothes, she thought, seeing nothing but men's attire. He stated that he lived alone.

The sweatpants had to be double or more her size. Thank goodness, for the pull string or they would have fallen off. She found some scissors in the vanity drawer and cut the legs to fit. The flannel shirt hung below her knees. She had to roll the sleeves up. Well, she thought, looking in the mirror, it would have to do. She brushed her hair and let it hang down to her shoulders. One thing she needed and could not find was a toothbrush. She made a mental note to ask. She turned as she heard a knock on the door. "Yes?"

"Lunch is ready."

"I'm not hungry." Now why did she say that? Her stomach ached for food.

"You should eat. Besides, you could use a little more meat on that body of yours, but suit yourself. You can't stay shut up in that room forever." Rip smiled as he sat at the table. She'll come, he thought, dipping his spoon into the stew. He could understand her apprehension.

She glanced down at herself, meat on her body indeed! She looked fine except for the bruises. Her face got warm as she remembered that he'd seen her. Had his hands really been on her body? How could she look him in the eye? He was right, she couldn't stay cooped up in here, and food sounded wonderful. Her stomach ached at the thought. Yes, she needed food.

"It smells good," she said, walking with a limp into the kitchen. He sat reading a book. He didn't look up or acknowledge her presence. "I'll just help myself." She waited, but still he said nothing. "Did you hear me?" She asked a little more loudly.

"Yes, I heard. You don't have to yell. Help yourself to whatever you want. You might have to re-heat it though."

He said all that without looking up from the book. She sat at the table with her re-heated food. The silence was maddening. "That book must be very good."

"Yes."

"Good, because I thought you were being rude on purpose." She continued to eat. She heard the book close with a snap. She sneaked a peek at him. He sat with his arms folded across his chest. He has a broad chest, she thought, and noticed the dark hair that sprouted from his shirt. She quickly moved her eyes to meet his gaze.

"I always read when I'm at the table." He had started the habit since being alone.

"Well, I think it's rude, especially when you have someone sitting right across from you.

Rip smiled and leaned forward, resting both arms on the table as he stared into her beautiful eyes. "So you're a lady of edict? That's a start. Anything else you know?" She shook her head. Well, I'm sorry if I was rude, but it's rude not to come to a meal when called, also."

"I'm sorry."

"So am I. Now would you like some more stew?" He saw that she'd finished.

"I can get it." She got up and made herself another bowl and when she turned, she noticed he was leaning back on his chair with his arms folded over his chest, smiling at her.

"What?" She asked sitting down with her refilled bowl.

"I was only trying to be pleasant."

"I know, but you have done so much already. I can at least help myself," she smiled, "even though I hobble a bit. Thanks for the food, it's good. I really wasn't hungry at first, but once I smelled it—-well my stomach knew better."

"The food was nothing. I opened up a couple of cans and voile, you got stew." She smiled. "You should smile more often, it's becoming."

"Really, well I wouldn't know." She looked down at her bowl of stew.

"Your memory will come back. It's just a matter of time before it does."

"I want to know everything now. I should be on my way and not be burdening you anymore. Do you have a phone?"

"What for, you have no one to call?"

"You're wrong, Mr. Walker. I need not burden you any more. I will call a taxi and find a hotel to stay in until my memory comes back."

Rip wanted to laugh, but this was no laughing matter. He knew she was serious. He also knew he couldn't let her leave. He couldn't stop her, but he could reason with her. "Listen, first, you're not a burden: second, there isn't a taxi around for at least fifty miles. You're out here in no man's land, as the saying goes." She started to interrupt, but he continued. "Third, as for a hotel, or motel, they too are not near, and fourth, you have no clothes or money." He leaned back in his chair as he watched her ponder what he said.

She wanted to cry. This man sitting across from her was right. She had nowhere to go. She looked at this stranger and knew he was all she had. She tried to smile as she answered, "I guess you're stuck with me for the time being, however long that will be."

Rip replied, "That is, if you remember to come when a meal is ready."

"Or what, you'll kick me out?"

"No, not as drastic as that, but the next time I say a meal is ready. I mean it's ready, not one-minute later.

He was smiling and showing his deep dimples. She grinned and said, "A man who is always on time, I see."

"Yes, usually unless it can't be helped. I have always been a man who likes promptness."

"I will try to remember that," she said. She glanced around the kitchen and really noticed it for the first time. It was a nice, big kitchen with lots of oak cupboards, and an island in the middle. A kitchen anyone would love. The floor was oak like the bedroom. She felt him watching her. She picked up her bowl and went to the sink to rinse it out. She glanced out the above the sick and saw the woods that stood some hundred feet or so from the house. A rabbit darted across the yard, in front of the window. "Oh! Look there's a rabbit," she said all excited. "I saw them once at the petting zoo." Now how did she remember that? What zoo and city had that been? She wondered, as she felt his arm brush hers.

"Look, there it goes again," he said point to the rabbit as it scurried back across the yard and headed to the woods.

She watched the rabbit disappeared into the woods. "You have a wonderful place here. It seems very peaceful. Do you have any neighbors? I don't see any houses near by."

"There are a few, but they're not close by. The nearest is about a mile up the road. Matt lives there. He's the one who found you."

"I thought you found me. I am in your house."

"Matt brought you here; my place was closer. You will meet him later today. I know you're curious as to how this happened. He can explain how he found you. Maybe that will help jar your memory."

"I hope so. It is maddening not knowing who you are." She touched the bandage on her temple. "I can't begin to thank you enough." She glanced at the clock on the wall and saw that it was two in the afternoon. "Rip, what day of the week is this? I seem to have lost that too."

"Tuesday, why do you ask?

"Shouldn't you be at work?"

"No, I'm retired from law enforcement. I'm what you call a novice writer. I'm in the process of writing a book on the laws of criminal justice."

Retired, and a retired cop no less. A cop, she'd never have guessed. "You don't look old enough to be retired. How old are you? What I mean is…?

"I know what you mean. I was tired of my work. I wanted more out of life so I retired. In answer to your second question, I'm forty-two," he grinned and asked, "How old are you?"

Rip didn't mean to offend her, as he saw tears develop. "I'm sorry; it's not polite to ask a woman her age.

"I know, but--oh, this is awful!" She wiped her nose on the sleeve of her shirt. "I don't," she stuttered. "I don't know a thing about myself. The only thing I know is that I woke up here. Everything else is a blank. I don't know who you are. I've only your word. You could be a murderer for all I know. I'm so frightened. I want to trust, you but...." She couldn't stop the tears. He handed her a box of tissues. "Thank you," she said through sobs, as he sat staring at her. She wondered what he was thinking.

Rip sat waiting for her to calm down. What next, he thought. She didn't even know her name. She had amnesia. What was he going to do? It wasn't her fault. She needed reassurance.

"You really don't know who you are?"

"No," she said looking at him with swollen, red eyes. "I don't know what to do."

He looked over at her and couldn't help but warm to her. If she only knew how silly she looked dressed in his clothes. Then he noticed that she'd cut off the pant legs of his favorite sweatpants. He started to say something but thought better of it; she had enough problems. Rip realized he'd have to get her some clothes appropriate for a female. He made a mental note to do so. She needed a name. He couldn't keep saying. Hey you.

"What would you like to be called? I mean, pick a name," Rip suggested.

"I don't want any old name. I want to be called by my name."

"You know it's not every day a person gets to pick their name. I've always liked the name Richard, but I'm stuck with Robert Walker. That's why you're lucky. Pick any name that comes to mind." Rip smiled, hoping to make her feel better.

She liked it when he smiled; it made him look more relaxed and handsome. Not that she could compare him to others, she couldn't even picture another male, let alone another female. She just knew that he caused butterflies in her stomach when he smiled. He wanted her to think of a name, but none came to mind. "What do you think my name should be? I can't think of any."

Rip's wife's name had been Mary; that wouldn't do. "My late wife, Mary, always said if we'd had a daughter she'd like to call her Cindy."

"Like Cinderella?" What made her say that? She thought.

"You remember Cinderella?"

"I don't know. It just came out."

"I read about trigger words earlier in this book." He pointed to the book he was reading when she came into the room. "It says here in the book that a person may get amnesia from a hard blow to the head, and that certain words or sayings can bring memory back."

"Like the name Cindy made me think of Cinderella?"

"Yes, do you know who Cinderella was?"

"No, I'm sorry, do you?"

"She's a character in a fairy tale that most little girls like to read. It's about a poor girl in rags, who is invited to a ball and meets a prince and they fall in love. She leaves without telling him her name, but drops a glass slipper. He goes in search of her, looking for the love of his life."

"Just like me. I don't know who I am. So maybe my true love will come looking for me. Tell me, did the prince find her?"

"Yes, and they lived happily ever after."

"Maybe you're my prince and have come to rescue me."

Rip laughed. One thing for sure, she had an imagination. "I'm sure there is someone out there looking for you right now. In fact, tomorrow I'll go into town to see what I can find out."

"Can I go with you? Maybe someone will recognize me."

"We don't know yet whether recognition is something we want. Matt found you running in a nightgown. We don't know why. Don't forget, I was a detective, and a darn good one. You stay here and in a few day's we'll go into town together. We need to get you some clothing, too."

"I don't have any money for clothes. How am I going to pay?"

"Don't worry about that. I want you to concentrate on getting well and getting your memory back. Now let's clean up this mess. I like a clean kitchen."

"Yes sir." She laughed and helped clear the remainder of the table. "If I can't pay for my clothes, the least I can do is help around here. Do I wash or wipe?"

"I don't care, do what you normally do."

"Rip, I can't remember ever doing dishes."

"Cindy, why don't you just wipe."

"Good, I'll wipe. Rip, I like the sound of Cindy, that is, for now, until I remember my real name. I may even like Cindy better and decide to keep it instead of my own name."

"Well, Cinderella, let's get these dishes done." They were laughing when Cindy suddenly stopped. Rip saw how pale she'd gotten; she looked like she'd just seen a ghost. She was pointing with her finger. Rip saw Matt peering through the window of the outside door. "Cindy, he's a friend of mine," he said, taking her hand in his and with the other, opened the door for Matt.

Matt stepped in and moved to the side. "I knocked, but you two were laughing so hard you didn't hear me. Maybe I should come back another time." He turned to leave, but Rip blocked him.

"No, come in, stay awhile. We'll all go into the living room and you two can get acquainted." Rip saw that Cindy's coloring had returned to normal.

Cindy sat at the end of the couch with her feet curled under her, and looked from Rip, who sat in the overstuffed chair, to Rip's friend, who sat in a leather chair opposite him. She had a plain view of them in case--in case of what she thought. She had no place else to go.

"Now isn't this cozy?" Rip hoped to make light of the situation. They both seemed tense. He couldn't ever remember Matt acting so nervous. "I think introductions are in order," Rip looked from one to the other. "Matt, this is Cindy, well, that's the name she's picked. Cindy, this is Matt Pearson, an old and trusted friend. He's the one who found you and brought you here." Rip gave Matt a look that said this is your doing.

Cindy looked over at him and gave a weak smile as she whispered thank you. She kept her gaze on him. This old man with a beard had found her. Matt sat gazing back at her. He had a few missing bottom teeth, but he seemed nice enough. She looked into his eyes, and saw nothing but gentleness. This man definitely meant her no harm. He reminded her of someone she knew. Then he spoke and his voice held nothing but concern for her.

"You look a lot better than when I last saw you. You're even prettier than I thought."

Cindy lowered her eyes and felt heat rise to her face in embarrassment. She'd looked at herself in the mirror earlier, and what had stared back at her wasn't anyone she knew, and as far as being pretty, well, that she didn't know. Heck, she didn't know a lot of things. She said, "Rip says you found me. Would you care to tell me where and how?"

"You don't remember?" Matt asked, sitting up straighter in his chair.

"No." She turned her attention to Rip.

"Matt, we picked out the name Cindy. I couldn't keep saying, 'hey you'. She doesn't remember anything. Go ahead and tell her how you found her."

When Matt had finished, Cindy didn't know anymore than she had a few minutes ago. "You didn't see anyone else? I mean, I certainly wouldn't have been out there all alone in my nightclothes for no reason."

"I didn't see or hear anyone, but I heard sounds. I could take you to the spot where you fell. Would that help?"

"Yes." She looked to Rip and asked, "Can we go now?"

"That's a good idea, it might help jog your memory, but I think we should wait until you're a little stronger."

"I feel fine. I don't see why we can't go now."

"Okay, but not today. It'll be dark in an hour or so. We'll go tomorrow." Rip had wanted to check the area himself, look for any clues, but he didn't want to leave her alone.

"I heard we're in for a storm," Matt said. I went into town this morning for supplies and bought you some staples, too. I've got them in the truck."

"Good idea, but I didn't hear anything about a storm. Then I haven't had the radio or television on for the last few hours. I listened for a report of anyone being missing, but did hear of any one. Did you hear anything while in town?" Rip looked over at Cindy. She was engrossed in what they were saying. She glanced anxiously at Matt.

"I put my radar to work. I went to every building: there aren't that many in Buford, as you know: two taverns, a hardware store, a pharmacy, a beauty/barber shop, a grocery store, gas station and lumberyard, where most of the people in the area are employed. I listened, but not a soul talked about a missing person. The only talk I heard was about the upcoming storm, which is supposed to dump at least a foot of snow. Everyone figures it to be the last one of the winter, as April is just around the corner."

"You didn't...?" Rip started to ask.

"Rip, don't you trust me? I didn't mention her." He turned to Cindy.

"Why wouldn't you mention me? Is there something the two of you aren't telling me?" Cindy's eyes went from Matt to Rip.

"No, but we don't want to put you in danger, either."

"Why? What would make you think I'm in danger?" Cindy asked. "If I am in danger, why haven't you gone to the authorities?"

Rip saw how her face had paled. They were frightening her. He needed to explain. "Relax, Cindy. We mean you no harm. Our concern is for you. When Matt first saw you, you were running, and then you suddenly tumbled down the hill, where you finally stopped by hitting a boulder. It's what you were running from that concerns us, and the fact that no one has inquired about you."

Rip got up and knelt before her. "Do you have any idea why you were running?" He attempted to cup her hands in his to comfort her, but she jerked her hands away. Rip stood and walked to the window. "Cindy, we need you to think really hard. Try and remember something, anything that could help us find out your true identity."

Cindy sat staring at her hands. When Rip's hands had touched hers, a picture flashed before her of a different pair of hands. They had long skinny fingers, and wore a big flashy gold ring on the right ring finger. Those hands would cause her no harm. She didn't know how, but she knew. She looked over at Rip, who had gone back to his seat. She looked at his hands resting on the arms of the chair. His fingers were long, but had more meat on then, and he wore no ring. What had all this meant? "I'm sorry, Rip. I don't remember. I'm a little tired. I think I'm going to go and lie down for awhile."

Rip watched her walk away. She looked like a lost child, and so small in his oversized clothes. He turned to Matt and said, "She'll sleep for awhile. I don't know what spooked her when I went to touch her, but something did. It was as if she though I was going to hurt her. Matt, are you sure you heard nothing in town?"

"No, and I even went back to the spot where I found her. It's about a mile west of here. You know the spot, that old logging road they used for timbering. There were fresh tire tracks, but nothing out of the ordinary. A lot of people use that road as a shortcut into town."

Rip knew the area and the road. He had used it as a shortcut himself. "See anything else?"

"Yes, I could see where a vehicle had pulled off the road. There were at least two sets of men's boot tracks. They looked like two men had gotten out of the vehicle and walked around it, and stopped by the front right tire. There were many footprints in the area. I got the impression that they had a flat tire, and changed it there. I found the tire they left alongside the road."

Matt had been a hunting guide in the area when he was younger. He still did it every now and then for fun. His skills at reading signs were impeccable. "That's good. Do you have any idea what kind of car it was?"

"I couldn't swear, but by the tire span, my guess would be an SUV. But there's more. There was a third set of footprints, small ones. The tracks were made by a barefoot person, a lightweight person, who was running."

"Cindy," Rip said. "That's it, Matt. She was running from whoever was in that vehicle."

"I guessed as much and followed the tracks until I lost them. The person, if it was Cindy used her smarts and covered the tracks with leaves. That didn't fool me, though. I found more prints further on and continued to follow them until I came upon the spot where I found her. I went back and checked the tracks left by the vehicle. The two other sets of prints followed her. When they lost her track, they went the opposite way that she'd gone. I followed them and they circled back to the SUV."

"Damn Matt, why'd you wait to tell me this? Damn it to hell man, I've been racking my brain over this."

"I'd planned to tell you when I first got here, but when I found out she had amnesia, well, I thought it better if I just told you. I was going to tell you when we got the supplies out of my truck. Rip, what are you going to do?"

"Me! You mean us. You're in this right along with me. There is one thing that bothers me. Why didn't they keep looking for her?"

"Maybe they weren't familiar with this area, or they spotted me and got scared. I'll tell you one thing, if I had not come along, she'd be a goner. She would have frozen to death and the animals would've had a feast."

"You're right, Matt, by the sound of it, Cindy is in some sort of danger. I mean, what woman in her right mind would be running in the woods, in the dead of winter wearing only a flimsy nightgown? She had to be running for her life. What I don't understand is why nothing is on the news. Don't you think that's strange?"

"Yes, but maybe she's not from around here. I mean, look at her. Her skin is soft and milky. Women around here have tough skin, and a weathered look, and consider her attire. Women around here wear flannel to keep warm. No, this woman is definitely a city slicker." Rip walked over to the picture window; a few snowflakes were coming down and the sky had clouded over, all signs that the storm would be here shortly. Those signs were not as bad as those signs Matt had just mentioned he saw. What Matt said led him to believe that Cindy was in danger. What kind, he didn't know. However, he wouldn't let her handle it alone.

Chapter 4

Rip sat in his favorite chair, a brown leather recliner, for a long time after Matt left. He kept going over in his mind what Matt had said. Matt had been right, Cindy couldn't be from around here. He'd considered that briefly; Matt only confirmed his thinking.

The townspeople had called him a city slicker when he'd first come here. That had been true. He'd lived most of his adult life in the city, but he'd spent his childhood here. His dad worked for the Conservation Department here. When Rip turned sixteen, his dad got a promotion and that took them to the city. He always loved this area. They would camp every chance they got. He built this home on the exact spot they pitched their tent. It sat on the highest hill around, offering a panoramic view of a river that ran through his property where he fished. He had a beautiful view of the river from his large picture window. He planned to build a dock, but first he had to build steps leading to the river. He had everything—-no, not everything. A lump developed in his throat at the thought of his beloved wife. She'd been more than a wife; she'd been his friend and companion. He lost a lot with her death. She was unable to bear children. It was something they accepted. They had each other. He glanced towards the door where Cindy now slept. He knew Mary would want him to help her in every way possible.

Rip closed the book he'd been reading on amnesia and stared at the fireplace where he'd started a fire after Matt left. So far, the book hadn't told him anything he didn't already know. Amnesia could be temporary, lasting a few hours or days, to even weeks. Then there were those cases, which lasted on for months, even years. A chill ran through him at the thought. He hoped hers would be short term. She could stay here if she wanted, but he couldn't force her. With that settled in his mind, Rip lay back in the chair and closed his eyes. Soon he was fast asleep and found himself dreaming of her.

He dreamed about how she looked when he first saw her. In the dream Cindy, unbuttoned his shirt and ran her fingers through his chest hair. A ripple of pleasure shot through him. He felt newly awakened. Mary's face floated before him. She spoke, "Rip, you are young. I will always love you, but I want you to go on with your life." Then she faded. Rip placed his hands over this beautiful woman's small, round yet firm breasts. She moaned and kept saying his name, Rip, and Rip, please, Rip. Then something touched his shoulder.

Rip woke with a start. He found himself staring into the face of the woman he'd been dreaming about.

"I'm sorry to wake you." She removed her hand from his shoulder, her hand cooling from the electricity she'd felt at touching him. "You were sleeping so soundly."

When she first walked into the room and saw him asleep, she stood there watching him. The lines on his face were relaxed; he seemed so peaceful in his sleep. She liked this look. In fact, she liked looking at him. He certainly was handsome.

"If you didn't want to wake me, why did you?"

Yes, she liked him better when he slept. She took a few steps back as she asked, "Do you have a dog?"

"No. Why?"

"I heard a dog barking outside my bedroom window."

Rip glanced out the window and saw that the storm was now in full force. "It's probably a wolf you heard. There are lots of them in this area. Don't worry."

Oh! She wanted to shake him. What did he take her for, an imbecile? Well, she wasn't. She stood with her arms crossed over her waist. Her right foot began to stamp impatiently as she said, "I may have amnesia, but I do know a dog bark when I hear it. You haven't even looked out my window."

"Okay," he said, getting up from the chair and grabbing his coat and hat, he opened the door to howling wind and blowing snow.

Cindy waited. It seemed like he'd been gone a long time. It didn't take that long to walk to her window. She started for the door just as it opened. Snow covered him as he stood there staring at her. She waited and he didn't say anything. Gee, he was getting on her nerves! Why didn't he say something? If it wasn't a dog, why didn't he say so? Then he spoke, but it wasn't what she'd expected.

"Boy, it's freezing out there! I sure could go for a cup of hot coffee. Moreover, I'm sure this little fellow is thirsty. Get some water and add a little milk. It can't be more then a few hours old."

Cindy watched as Rip reached into his coat to pull out a small ball of fur. "A dog," she squealed. "I told you I heard one!" She reached out her hands, seeing the small ball of fur. "Here, give her to me." She reached over and took the small bundle from him. "Oh, she is so cute." She poured some water and milk into a bowl. When she put the little dog down, it almost devoured the bowl. She turned to Rip. "I think you owe me an apology."

"I don't think so," he smiled.

"Well, I certainly do."

"We were both right."

"Rip, quit playing with me. I'm not stupid."

"I didn't say you were. You see, it's a wolf, a wolf cub. A small cub sounds a little like a dog. We both were right. For your information, it's a he, not a she."

"I see," she said, watching it finish drinking. "There, little one, you'll feel better now." She reached down, picked him up and cuddled him against her neck. She turned to Rip. "You wouldn't happen to have an old blanket and something to make a bed with?" He didn't answer. He stood leaning against the archway frame. "Well," she said. "Do you?"

"Listen, you can't keep it. He's a wolf cub. The mother will be back looking for him."

"What if you don't find the mother? You can't seriously be thinking of putting him back out in that snow storm. He will die."

"I'm not that heartless. I didn't send you back out when you needed help."

"No." Cindy lowered her head and dropped her eyes to the floor. "Well then what? What are we going to do?"

"As soon as the storm lifts, I'll go out and see if I can find the mother. Until then you can take care of him." He turned and left the kitchen.

"You're mine! Did you hear that, little one?" She sat at the table and began brushing its fur with her fingers. "I'll take good care of you."

"Here, use these," Rip said, setting a wooden crate and small wool blanket on the floor at her feet.

"Thanks," she gathered up what he brought. With it, she made a bed up for the cub, by the fireplace.

Later, they sat in the living room watching the cub play with an old ball Rip found. They laughed as he rolled around with the ball between all four paws.

Rip glanced over at Cindy. She looked so young and happy. It was nice to see her laugh. Damn, she is pretty, he thought. Then he noticed her staring at him. "Would you like me to freshen up your coffee?"

Cindy watched him go to the kitchen. He could be so pleasant one minute, and such a bear the next. She preferred his nicer side. The cub came waddling over to her with the ball held in its mouth. He dropped it by her feet, and she reached down, picked it up, and gave it a little toss in the air. She watched the cub catch it and begin to play with it again. What would happen to him if they didn't find its mother? Would Rip let her keep it? "Come here, Little One, come here," Cindy called.

"I think you should give it a name. You can't keep calling it Little One."

"Like me, lost and abandoned with no name. Does that mean if we name him we get to keep…?"

"Cindy, let's wait and see what happens after the storm. If I can't find the mother or another pack of wolves that will take care of him, then we'll keep him until he is big enough to take care of himself."

"Thank you!" Cindy jumped up from the couch and gave Rip a bear hug and kiss on the cheek. "Thank you, thank you!" Then she realized what she'd done. She'd kissed him. She backed away as her face flushed from embarrassment. "I'm sorry Rip; I don't know what got into me. Please forgive me."

"No apologies necessary; in fact, I liked it." He touched the spot she kissed. "Show's you're human. Have you thought of a name?"

"Yes, how does Bandon sound? It's short for abandoned," Cindy smiled. She felt happy just to have something, even if for a short time, that belonged to her. She reached down and picked the cub up and asked, "How do you like the name Bandon?" The cub licked her hand showing his pleasure.

"Well, I guess that's settled," Rip laughed. "Bandon it is." Bandon barked again and they both laughed.

The lights flickered. Rip noticed that the wind had picked up. He hoped the electricity would stay on. He had a generator, but hadn't tried it out yet. "It looks like this storm is going to be a big one," Rip remarked, sitting in his recliner.

"This is a strange tasting coffee you've made," Cindy said, taking a drink of the brew he handed her earlier.

"It's hot chocolate. I had a taste for it and thought you might--here, I'll get you some coffee."

"No, I like it. It's wonderful and hot, especially with the storm outside." The lights flickered again. "I hope the lights stay on."

"Yes, well, one never knows. Matt said the storm could last a few days, and seldom wrong. He's lived in this area his whole life. It's like having your own private weatherman."

"So you've known Matt a long time?"

"No, I got to know him about the time I started building this house. I'd say it was a little over two years ago. Matt helped me a lot. He worked right alongside me."

"You built this house!" Cindy thought that amazing.

"Yes, it was something my wife and I always dreamed of doing someday, but then she died of cancer."

Cindy watched Rip as he stared out the window. She hadn't given much thought about him being married. He wore no ring. She didn't know what to say, but had to say something. "I'm sorry Rip, if I'd known--."

"That's okay, I've adjusted. Now enough talk about me. We need to talk about you, find out why you were in the woods running. That's what we should be thinking about."

"I know, but how can I when I don't know where to begin?" She got up and went over to a tall wooden cabinet that sat in the corner of the room and opened it. "You've got a television? Here I thought you had locked yourself away from the world."

"I may want to live in the woods, but I'm no hermit. You can watch it if you want."

"That's okay. You are right we need to talk about me."

"Do you remember anything at all from your past?"

"No, but I do recall certain things, like this television, cars, types of food--general things."

"Maybe a good nights rest will help." He went to the picture window and gazed out into the night. The storm had gotten worse. They'd have at least a foot of snow by morning. He looked at his watch. It was late, time for bed. "I'm going to bed," he said, turned and headed for the stairs that led to his bedroom. "We'll talk more in the morning." He reached the top of the stairs and turned back to her. "Have a good night's rest."

"You too," she said, and headed to her room.

Chapter 5

Cindy awoke early, after a restless night's sleep. She dreamed she was in a dark room, bound by rope. She didn't see anyone, only darkness. She shuddered, and noticed how cold it was as she shivered. She pulled the blanket up tighter around her neck. A glance at the window showed it continued to snow. How long would it last? She heard the back door slam. Rip! Had he gone outside in this mess? She got up; it was as if she was walking on ice. She could see her own breath. She pulled the blanket around her and opened the door, only to step into Rip's path. He carried arms full of wood. "Is something wrong with the heat?"

"Yes, but don't worry, I've got a back-up generator. I've not tried it out yet, so no showers, only sponge baths. I have to find out how much energy it will give us. Heat and water use energy. I suggest you stay in bed until I get the place warmed."

She shut her door and leaned against it, she was in his way now. A man alone wouldn't worry about heat and water.

She dressed, in his cloths again. She hoped that he would go into town soon and get her something decent to wear. Dressed she headed to the living room. Rip sat in front of the fireplace holding Bandon in his arms. "Good morning," he said cheerfully.

"I want to help and we need to talk."

Rip smiled and looked at her outfit, his clothing. He had to get her some feminine attire. "I don't think you're quite dressed for the work. Here hold Bandon and keep him warm. I've got more wood to bring in. We can talk afterwards."

Cindy sat on the couch, the blanket wrapped around her and Bandon while she waited for Rip to return.

"Okay," Rip said, returning with another pile of wood. That should last us awhile. I had trouble with the generator, but it's running good now. The place will be warm and toasty soon. I'll make us some coffee."

"Oh Rip, let me. I should've thought."

"No, you stay there. I'll get it."

"Thanks," Cindy said, taking the hot cup of coffee from him a few minutes later.

"Now, what is so important?" Rip sat in his chair.

"I think I should leave. I'm just a burden to you. I'm sure you wouldn't be worried about the heat if I wasn't here."

"Of course I would. I don't want my pipes freezing and I don't want to freeze either. Hard telling when the electricity will come back on, sometimes it takes days. As for you leaving, don't be foolish. There is a storm blowing outside, besides you have nowhere to go. Why the sudden need to leave?

"Because---I want to go and find out who I am, where I belong. I won't find out sitting here in the woods."

What had gotten into her? He saw the dark circles under her eyes. She hadn't slept well. "I don't think you understand...."

"I understand that I can't sit around here and do nothing. You won't even let me help around here. You can't hold me here."

"That angered him. He was doing all he could to make her comfortable. She needed rest to get herself well. But, she was right, he couldn't hold her here. If she wanted to---"You want to leave?" She nodded.

"Fine, I'll get the truck warmed up. I don't like this, not one bit, but I'll take you wherever you want to go in the storm."

Cindy watched him leave. He really doesn't want me here, she thought, and cuddled Bandon. "I've been abandoned just like you," she said. She began to cry since she didn't know what else to do. Rip didn't want her here, she knew it now. Then the door burst open and Rip came barging in as he stomped his boots and removed his coat and hat.

"The truck won't start. Therefore, you'll just have to wait until after the storm. I'll get Matt over here to give me a jump. Then I'll take you to the nearest town. What you do from there is of no concern of mine." He didn't look at her, but at the sound of muffled crying, he glanced over at her. "Now what, you said you wanted to go, or is that a lie too?"

"I'm crying because you don't want me here. I'm scared and you don't care."

Rip ran his hands through his unruly hair. He never understood women. "Listen," he said. He walked over and sat beside her on the couch.

"No, you listen," Cindy stood and wiped her eyes with her shirtsleeve. "You say you want me here, but then when I ask to leave, you jump at the chance to get rid of me. Maybe I should have let those people catch me, then I wouldn't have amnesia and---I would know who---." Then the room began to spin and she felt herself falling.

"Cindy, please wake up," Rip said, placing a cold towel on her forehead. He watched her eyes flicker and then she tried to sit up. "No, don't try to get up."

She read concern in his eyes. "What happened? One minute I was talking and then, nothing."

"You fainted; I caught you, laid you on the couch, and you weren't talking, you were yelling. I don't want you to think about that. I want you to lie here and rest. I've got more wood to bring in. I don't know how long the power is going to be out. Then we'll talk more, and this time I promise to really listen."

When Rip finished gathering the wood, figuring he had enough to last through the night, he looked over to where Cindy lay on the couch. A smiled creased his face; she lay sleeping with Bandon curled alongside her. He let her sleep. He read that sleep was a good healer. He turned the battery radio on in hopes of hearing something about a missing woman. Nothing, the weather was the talk of the day. He'd been right. They were expecting a foot before the storm subsided. He decided to read. He got out his book on amnesia. He'd read a few chapters when he heard Cindy mumbling, something about needles and someone not being that her sister.

He waited, but she said no more; her breathing, rushed before, returned to normal. He stayed by her side, kneeling and thinking. "Are you praying for me?"

Rip smiled. "No, I'm asking for your forgiveness. I can see where someone might get bored with nothing to do around here, especially in the winter, cooped up in the house.

She sat up, pulled her knees to her chest and wrapped her arms around them. "I wasn't very nice either. I didn't want to make you mad. I guess I didn't explain myself very well. I don't want to be a burden. I want to feel useful, like helping with the wood, but…"

"Cindy, I'm sorry," he smiled. "I don't want you getting pneumonia on top of everything else. Let's say we start all over. What do you say?"

Cindy began to laugh; she couldn't help herself, he looked so funny kneeling before her. "You're forgiven, but please get off your knees. You don't know how silly you look." She reached out her hand as he stood. They shook hands and said in unison, "deal!" They laughed and Bandon barked, which made them laugh harder.

Rip stood staring at her; maybe he'd lost his touch. He'd always been a good judge of character, a trait that had helped make him a good detective. He'd never let an attractive woman hinder his thinking, and Cindy was certainly gorgeous. He hoped he wasn't deterred now. "Rip?" Cindy asked, bringing him back to the present.

"Yes!"

"I really want to tell you how I feel."

"Shoot, I'm all ears." Rip took a seat next to her and rested his arm on the back of the couch.

"You really were a detective? How original. Is this how you interrogated the people you arrested? No, don't answer that," she grinned. "Don't look so smug."

"I'm not."

"Then why do I feel like I'm under a gun?"

"Relax Cindy, I won't bite. I just want to be attentive, that's all. Now…"

"Shoot," she said and laughed. "Okay, let's be serious." She turned around and faced him. "There isn't much to tell. First, I know all the basic things of ordinary life. In fact, I know a lot, but most importantly, I still don't know who I am or where I came from. I don't know if I've got a family or if I'm married or divorced or what. I don't think I'm a fugitive. Anyway, I hope not. You know what--?" She suddenly began to cry, she couldn't help it, as the tears came. She sobbed. "I'm afraid, Rip, and I don't know where to turn. If you don't believe in me, I have no one.

Do you understand? I need your help, but only if you truly want to help."

"Cindy, look at me." He reached out, lifting her face with his thumb and gazed into her watery eyes. "I want you stay, and I want to help. Furthermore, I don't think you are a burden".

"Did you hear that Bandon?" She hugged him. Then she reached over and kissed Rip on the lips, "Thank you."

Rip touched his lips. Her lips were as soft as he guessed they would be. He knew she'd been excited and the kiss had only been a friendly gesture, but the touch of her lips sent different signals to his body. He would have to remember that she was a guest in his home. The house had warmed, thanks to the generator and fireplace. "You warm enough?" He asked.

"Yes." She tossed the blanket to the side. "When do you think we can go into town? I want to get started on finding my identity."

"As soon as the roads are passable, I'll go." He saw her start to get on the offensive. Before she got the chance, he continued. "Finding out your identity is important, and why I need you to tell me whenever you remember something, big or small. Is that a promise?"

"Yes." Bandon began licking her face. "You're going to be good luck," she hugged the cub. "Where do we start? Do we call the authorities and all of that?"

"Cindy, I don't want to frighten you, but since nothing has been on the news about you——well, I think it best we keep it between us three for now, you, Matt and me. That is unless you want to go to the authorities?"

"No Rip; you're all the authority I need. I trust you. I truly do."

"Good, then you'll rest for today; you've been through enough for one day. Tomorrow will come soon enough."

'Tomorrow,' Rip had said. She had that to look forward to, or did she? She wanted to know the truth, but she feared it also. Was she married with children? She didn't even know her age. Did she have parents and siblings? That and a lot more bothered her, especially since Rip said there hadn't been anything about her on the news. Maybe she had no one. Was that possible, to have no one? Well, tomorrow they'd begin. How, she didn't know, but things couldn't stay as they were. She pulled up the covers and turned the lamp out, thanks to the generator. She needed a good night's sleep. She fell into a deep sleep and dreamt.

She found herself sitting in bed, with knees folded. She didn't recognize the bed or the room. A big room, with pastel pink walls and white provincial furniture: a dresser, and a glass top dressing table covered with an array of female products, perfume, makeup, and a small jewelry box with a rose carved on top. The bed covering was a white satin comforter. She saw a set of French double doors that opened onto a large balcony. There was another closed door, with a brass knob. It was this door that she walked to and stood in front of before banging on it, screaming. "Let me out! Let me out!"

"Cindy, unlock the door," Rip yelled, as he pounded on the door. "Cindy, what's wrong?" Still no response came from the other side of the door. "Damn it, Cindy, open the door, right now." Still nothing happened. He didn't know what else do. He had to get in there, to find out why she kept screaming. "Move," he said to Bandon as he pushed him aside with his foot. He took a few steps back and then rammed his body into the door. The door and part of the frame gave way and stood hanging from the bottom hinge. He looked around, ready for what he didn't know. Morning light shone through the window blinds, casting shadows around the room. He turned his gaze to the bed where Cindy lay. He approached the bed and saw that her body was wet with perspiration. She lay quiet, but he was sure he heard her screaming. It surprised him that the noise of breaking the door down had not awakened her.

Rip slowly lowered himself onto the bed and sat beside her. He touched her arm, which was clammy to the touch. "Cindy," he said quietly, as he patted her arm. She surprised him by jumping up, and beating his chest with her fists, while yelling, "Leave me alone! Leave me alone!"

Rip grabbed her wrists and held them. He noticed that even though her eyes were open, they held a blank stare. "Cindy," he said calmly. Rip prided himself on not hitting a woman, but this called for drastic measures. He gently shook her, no response. He gently slapped her across the cheek with the palm of his hand.

Chapter 6

"Why'd you hit me?" Cindy cried, putting her hand to her cheek. She backed away until she hit the headboard.

"You were screaming and beating on my chest. I couldn't get you to stop, so I slapped you. It worked he said grinning."

"Why was I screaming?" What were you doing to me?"

"I did nothing. Listen Cindy, you were screaming. I knocked the door down to get into the room." She looked at the door.

"I—the door, it's ruined." The door hung with the frame splintered into pieces. "You did that?" It showed her that the man definitely wouldn't let anything stand in his way.

"You were dreaming, but I didn't know that from the screaming you were doing. I thought——well, never mind. Look, you're all wet from sweating." She glanced down and he smiled as she pulled the covers up tightly around her neck, but not before he got a look at her breasts. Did she always sleep in the nude? Then he pictured that body next to his, warm and sultry. His body started to respond. He got up and went to the window. He needed to distance himself from her. "If you feel up to it, you should get dressed," he said, continuing to gaze out the window with daybreak on the horizon and the storm still in full force.

"But the door, it's ruined."

"It can be fixed. I was more worried about you than some door. Now that I can see you're all right, I'll leave you to get dressed. I'll wait for you in the living room. Then we'll talk about your dream. Find out why you were screaming."

She sat on the edge of the bed after he'd left the room. She didn't want to think about the dream. She shuddered, as it all came back to her. She'd been in a locked room. "No!" she yelled, and then realized she'd said it loud enough for Rip to call from the other room. "You okay?"

"Yes, I stubbed my toe." She lied. "I'll be along shortly." She glanced at the remnants of the door and shook her head. The man had used brutal strength to knock it down. The door was made of solid oak. "Rip, I'm truly sorry about the door," she stated while padding into the living room. The warmth from the fireplace was cozy and inviting. "Are you sure it can be fixed?"

Rip was adding more logs to the fireplace. "I built this place. I'm sure I can fix a door frame." Then he looked up at her. She looked awful. There were bags under her eyes and she stood shivering. "Here," he said, going to the couch where he retrieved the afghan. "Cover up with this; you look cold."

He wrapped the cover about her as they sat, with only a few inches between them. She felt her body warming.

"Good, you're nice and warm now. "I'll go and fix us some breakfast. Is there anything special you'd like?"

"No, whatever you're having. I'm really hungry though."

"That's a good sign, shows you're getting some strength back. Breakfast coming up," he said and headed to the kitchen.

In the kitchen, he stood cooking bacon and eggs as he thought of the promise he'd made to her, that he would help her find her identity. He knew he couldn't just let her walk away. She still wasn't completely cured and he wasn't a doctor. Oh, he'd helped with her outer wounds, but the inner ones in her head, that was another story. Maybe he should take her into town, turn her over to the police. They'd make sure she got the medical attention she needed and help find out who she was. But, she'd asked him not to call the police, that she only wanted his help. How could he turn her down, especially when she looked at him with those beautiful eyes? He put the food on their plates and while doing so, knew he would find a way to help her. He hadn't been able to help his wife. He hadn't been able to stop the cancer that ate at her. He smiled and called Cindy to eat.

When she entered the room, he noticed again how beautiful she was, even dressed in his clothing. He'd have to watch his step since they'd be working closely together.

After they'd eaten, they sat in the living room, relaxing with a second up of coffee. Bandon lay on the floor by the fireplace, his eyes going from one of them to the other. Rip broke the silence. "I think we should get started on discovering your identity. Are you ready? This isn't going to be easy on either of us."

"I'm ready. Where and how do we begin?" Cindy put on a brave front, not wanting him to see how nervous she truly felt. She feared the truth, yet the drive to know it outweighed all else.

Rip walked over to the couch where she sat and said, "Good," as he sat at the opposite end. He reached over and touched her shoulder. She didn't flinch at his touch, which was a beginning. He needed her to trust him, to trust him fully. "What I've gathered so far is you've no recollections of life before waking up here, am I correct?"

"Yes, I've tried, but it is all a blank."

"The dream you had, do you remember it, any of it? It might give us a clue, a starting point." She closed her eyes.

"But it was just a dream. I don't see how…"

"Let me be the judge. I want to hear it all, no matter how minor or insignificant you may think it is. I don't want you to leave anything out."

Chapter 7

They sat quietly, each with their own thoughts. She felt a lot calmer after telling him her dream, especially knowing that he believed her. She'd had total recall and hadn't left anything out, right down to the nightgown she'd worn. She even told him about the flashback she'd had when he tried holding her hands. Rip sat quietly staring at the fireplace. She wondered what he could be thinking. She found herself gazing at his lips, lips that she suddenly wanted to touch, to be kissed and wondered if they'd be as soft as they looked. Then she felt his hand on her arm.

"Cindy, are you all right?"

"Yes."

"You looked like you were a mile away. I bet you didn't hear a word I said."

Embarrassed and not wanting him to know what she'd been thinking, she said, "Sorry, I was wondering when the weather would break so we could go into town for some decent clothing for me. Not that I don't appreciate you lending me yours, but..."

"I promise, as soon as the weather breaks, we'll get you some clothes."

"Great! Now what was it you were saying?"

"I was saying that I think you're off to a good start, remembering. I think you want to remember. It will just take time. I lay in bed last night thinking about your amnesia. I handled a case about ten years or so ago where a woman had been raped and had blocked the whole incident from her memory." He saw her face turn ashen. He quickly said. "Of course, I don't..."

Cindy felt her stomach surge. She wanted to vomit. She took a deep breath and replied, "Rip, you can't mean--I mean, I don't think I was--you know, violated. Wouldn't I know?" She looked down at herself and shivered. Oh, why couldn't she remember? She didn't even know if she'd ever had a relationship with another man.

"Cindy," Rip reached over and put his hand on her shoulder. "I didn't mean to upset you. What I'm trying to say is that there are a lot of different kinds of amnesia. This woman had a dramatic shock to her body. Sometimes it takes another shock to retrieve the memory, and you have had a shock yourself, the blow to your head, and by the bruises on you, I know you've been physically abused." He felt the tension in her body relax as she asked, "Does this woman have her memory back?"

"Before I answer that, I want you to understand something: every case is different. There are no two alike. Some take days, weeks, even months. We've only touched the tip of yours, but you will get it back. It's a slow process, but like I said, I'm in it with you till the end."

"I'm glad Rip, because I don't think I could handle this by myself." If she'd dared to admit it, she was afraid, no, more like terrified of what she didn't know. "Rip, what if I did something bad, really bad, will you still stand by me?"

Rip reached over, and taking her hands in his, pleasantly surprised that this time she didn't pull away, said, "Cindy, I've always been a good judge of character, and you definitely are the victim. What we have to find out is why."

Cindy felt relieved at his words. She wasn't a bad person. She realized that he held her hands and she wasn't afraid. In fact, she liked his touch; it gave her a sense of security. She looked up at Rip, their eyes made contact. Cindy couldn't pull her eyes away. It was like she was having her first crush. She found herself melting, as she leaned forward, her eyes not leaving his for a second. She was inches from his face, such a wonderful face, one she wanted to touch. She reached up and then suddenly the eyes turned evil, deep and dark. She turned away. She'd seen those same eyes in her dream.

"Cindy, are you okay?" Rip asked, seeing the sudden change in her. She was shaking. "Please, tell me what is wrong. Is it something I said or did?" Rip couldn't think of anything. They'd been gazing at one another and then the next moment, she looked at him like he was a monster.

"I'm okay. I guess I'm just a little jumpy." She didn't want him to know that his eyes had turned evil. "Hey," she said, wanting to get back to the discussion at hand. "You never told me; did the woman get her memory back?"

"Yes, she did. Her lapse lasted three months. I don't want you to think yours will last that long, but hers did. It took the shock of seeing her abductor in a lineup."

"I hope it doesn't take that long. I don't know if I can wait till then. Isn't there some way, we can hurry it along? There has to be something we can do."

Rip didn't know how she felt, but he could take a wild guess. Not knowing your own identity had to be devastating to one's sanity. "Yes of course there are things we can do. What we don't want is to rush. We have to go slow. Sometimes, it's best to let things take their own course."

"What you're saying is that we need to wait?" She didn't want to; she wanted to get the ball rolling.

"No, we don't have to wait."

"So when do we start?"

"You've already started with the dream. I'm sure other things will come to mind. We'll just have to take things as they come." Then the lights flickered a few times and came on brighter than they were before. "Good, the electricity's on."

"How can you tell, I thought the generator…?"

"Yes, but it's only a backup for when the power's out. When the lights come on this bright, it means the electricity is on. I'm going to go out to the shed and shut the generator off. I won't be gone long, but I'm going to have to shovel my way there."

Cindy sat for a while after watching Rip leave. Bandon jumped up on her lap and she absently began petting him. "Guess you wonder where your mother is?" Cindy asked Bandon, at which he looked up at her. "Yes," she continued rubbing his soft coat. "We have a lot in common, you've lost your mother and I've lost my memory. We are both indebted to Rip for taking us into his home." Bandon gave a yelp, which made her laugh. Then she remembered the mess in the kitchen. She thought of Rip as she finished wiping the last of the dishes. She felt drawn to him; his good looks and masculinity pulled at her very core. Yet the sight and touch of him made her uneasy. Earlier, when she'd leaned into him, she'd been compelled to kiss him, but hadn't.

"Boy, its cold out there," Rip stated as he bounded in the back door. Then he whistled, seeing that she'd cleaned up the kitchen.

"I thought, since you're going to be helping me, the least I could do is the dishes." Embarrassed, she turned and looked out the window above the sink. "It looks like the snow has stopped."

"Yes and the winds have died down. I got the truck started. Thought I could start digging a path to the main road, but first I wanted to get a thermos of coffee. Would you mind making some? I want to put on warmer clothes."

"Coffee coming up," she replied as he headed toward the stairs. Yes, this man would take care of her. Then, he'd taken care of many other people in distress. What made her think she was special? He probably thought of her as a case study. Still, she found herself drawn to him. She liked him and felt a tingling whenever he was near. She wondered how old he was. She'd seen streaks of gray in his hair, but that didn't always tell one's age. She didn't even know her own age, but did age really matter? She continued to think of him. She wondered if he had any family. He'd said his parents and wife had died, but hadn't said anything about siblings. Then he returned, and taking the thermos from her said thanks, and out the door he went.

Cindy watched him from the window until she lost sight of him in the woods. She guessed the road went through the woods. She went into the living room with Bandon following at her feet. She grabbed the book on amnesia that Rip had been reading. She'd been reading it for about an hour, finding the book enlightening, when she heard a gunshot. Bandon jumped from her lap, and she dropped the book onto the floor. All kinds of thoughts were racing through her mind. Was someone hunting? Had someone shot at Rip? Had he blown a tire?

"Cindy, are you all right?" Rip came into the living room when she hadn't answered his calls. She sat staring at nothing, yet looked like she'd seen a ghost. He gently touched her arm and said, "Cindy?"

"Rip, thank God you're all right. I heard this bang, it sounded like..." A picture flashed before her. She saw a car swerving. The driver lost control and hit a tree. Then the vehicle came to a stop. She saw it all from a view in the back seat. Two men got out, leaving their doors open. Then she was running. Someone was calling, but she couldn't hear what they were saying.

"Cindy, it's okay." He knelt down and pulled her against his chest, as she was shaking. "I'm fine, but I can't say the same for Bandon's mother. She wasn't in good shape. I had to put her out of her misery."

"You shot her? Couldn't we have had done something, like take her to a vet?" She reached down for Bandon as a lump developed in her throat.

"Cindy, she was a wolf. She'd gotten injured and once an animal in the wild is hurt or near death, other animals begin to feast on them."

"Stop, I don't want to hear anymore."

Rip moved away and she pulled Bandon into her lap. "That's okay; we'll take care of you." She stared up at Rip.

He leaned over and patted Bandon on the top of his head. "Looks like you've got a new mother," he said, giving Cindy a smile.

"Thanks Rip."

Just then, they heard a motor. They both jumped up and went to the window. Matt was getting out of his truck. Rip threw open the door.

"Matt, I didn't think I'd see you for a few days. It's a good thing I plowed the lane. In fact, I just finished a few minutes ago."

"My lights came on and I thought I'd check and see if yours were on. My phone isn't working yet. Is yours?"

"I haven't checked. Cindy, will you check for me? I need to put more wood on the fire."

When she left the room, Rip turned to Matt. "It wasn't the lights or the phone that brought you here."

"I just came from town. I got our mail."

"Did I have any?" Rip asked, and noticed that Matt stood twirling his hat. Just then Cindy called out, "The phone is working. I think I'll go to my room for awhile so you two can talk about whatever it is men talk about."

"Matt, why are you so nervous?"

"Do you think she can hear me?"

Rip glanced toward the bedroom. He'd have to get that door fixed. He heard soft music coming from the small radio he'd put in there. "No, she is listening to the radio, why?"

"It's probably nothing, but there were two strange men in town. I've never seen them before."

"Matt, there've been strangers in town before, and with the storm, it probably brought in more than usual."

"These men were different. Any man in his right mind wouldn't drive five miles off the main highway to our small town without a good reason."

"What was different about them?" Matt had piqued his curiosity.

"These men were from the city. That isn't what bothered me. As you said, we do get some city slickers here now and again. No offense intended. But these guys were inquiring about a map."

"So, they wanted a map. They were probably lost and needed to get back on track."

"No Rip; they wanted a different kind of map. They wanted a map of the area with its homes and cabins."

"Did the postmaster give him one?"

"Nope, Old Henry told them he had no such map, told them they'd have to maybe go to the county municipal courthouse to get one. Said he doubted they'd get much help there either. The men asked how far away the courthouse was. Henry told them, and then they left. Now tell me, Rip, why would two men want to know where everyone lived?"

"Good question, unless they were some developers wanting to buy out some property. What did Henry think?"

"He said he didn't like the looks of them two, that they reminded him of the bad guys on television who wear black suits. Old Henry showed me a map after they left. It showed where everyone lived. He said he didn't like any big shots snooping around his town."

"Good for Old Henry."

"Who's Henry?" Cindy asked as she entered the room. They both turned and smiled at her. Rip answered.

"He's our town postmaster. You'll get a chance to meet him. When you do, he'll talk your leg off. Likes pretty women to talk to."

"Rip, cut it out, you're making Matt blush." Cindy came over and put her hand on Matt's shoulder. "How's my favorite person?" She saw Matt's face redden deeper, if that was possible. He already looked like a beet.

"Thanks for asking, Miss Cindy. I'm doing fine. I must say, you look a lot better than when I first seen you. You didn't look so good. Now you got color. Rip taking good care of you?"

"Yep, but he can be a slave driver, now that he's got a woman in the kitchen," Cindy said, grinning.

"Oh, Cindy did the dishes. I don't call that being a…."

"I'm kidding. I have to earn my keep around here. Anyway, I wanted to do them. Just like right now. I'm going to cook for my two favorite people. You want to stay for supper. I'm sure I can find something in Rip's kitchen."

"Yeah, Matt, why don't you stay," Rip said. "While Cindy's fixing us something to eat, you and I can talk." Rip gave her a wink.

"Talk about what?" Cindy asked, wondering if they would continue talking about her. She'd heard her name mentioned earlier, but it seemed they'd stopped when she entered the room.

"Just man talk," Rip smiled, giving her a light shove in the direction of the kitchen. He wanted to find out more about the two men.

Chapter 8

"What do you mean, you can't find her? Damn it, I told you two not to let her out of your sight. I want her found. Is that clear?"

"Yes sir, Boss," they both said in unison to the skinny man behind the big walnut desk. "We'll do our best," continued the tall heavyset man. The other man, dark skinned, with a pitted face and not as tall or quite as heavy just stood there.

"I want better than best! I want her found! You won't get one cent until she is, and your life won't be worth a plugged nickel either. Do you understand?"

"But Boss, she just vanished. We scoured the area, but found nothing. Some animal could've gotten hold of her. Besides, they had a big snowstorm up there in the mountains. She couldn't have survived such a storm."

"Then bring me a body, anything, to show me that she's dead. I have to know. I can't have her suddenly showing up here, not after all the planning I've done so far. I don't intend to spend the rest of my life in jail over some bungling on your part. Now get out there and do something."

The bigger man sat rubbing his triple chin while the other man just stared at the man behind the desk. He may be black and not as rich as the boss hoped to be someday, but he wasn't anyone's dog, and right now that's what he made him feel like, a dog. "Boss?" He asked.

"Yes, what is it Jake? I thought I made myself quite clear."

"Yes you have, but Hank and I need some expense money. What I mean is that we have to eat and need gas money, and such."

"What did you have in mind?"

"Well, we thought we'd stay in that burg of a town they call Buford. There is a small rooming house. From there we could scout the area, and it's not small; there are a lot of hills and mountains. You know, act as if we're interested in the purchase of property for hunting purposes. That will cost money."

"Hank, is that the plan?"

"Yeah, sure boss, that's our plan, just like Jake said." They didn't have a plan, but Jake's idea sounded great. Hank just didn't know how much mountain climbing he could do.

They watched as the man they called Boss reached into his top drawer and pulled out an envelope. They called him boss because that's what he wanted to be called. Said only his friends could call him by his name and they weren't his friends, just hired thugs. Well, they'd find that woman and get their money, and be done with him. They didn't like what they were doing, but they needed the money to pay off gambling debts. They had to find her, because if they didn't, they were dead, either from the boss or the people they owed money to.

"Here's a couple grand," said the skinny man. "This should do, but it will be deducted from your final pay. Now get out of my sight."

They started to leave when he said, "Stop! Don't use that door, leave through the back."

The intercom came on, and Stella, the receptionist, said, "Mr. Osgood, Mr. Bradford would like to see you in his office as soon as possible."

"Tell Mr. Bradford I'll be along shortly. I've a few calls to make." He let go of the intercom button, wondering what his future father-in-law wanted. He'd been lucky to get this job. Of course, the man's daughter had a lot of input. In one month if everything went as planned, she'd be Mrs. Mark Osgood. Boy, that had a nice ring to it, he thought, and picked up the phone and dialed.

"Hi honey, I thought I'd let you know that we still have a problem. I don't want you to worry; I'm working on getting it resolved. In fact, nature may have taken care of it. My men are checking it out as we speak." He ended the call and headed to Mr.

Bradford's office, wondering what the old man wanted now. He probably wanted to discuss the wedding to his precious darling. He smiled, thinking that soon the obstacle would be out of the way, and with it, his plan of being rich would come true. They had to find her.

Chapter 9

"Matt, I'm concerned about that woman's safety," Rip said, nodding toward the kitchen. "I'm going to need your help with this."

"When it comes to Cindy or whatever her name is, I'll do what I can. I am concerned, too. I mean, she is a lady. One can tell at a glance, she's got style."

"Why Matt, if I didn't know better, I'd say you have a crush on her."

"You've got to admit Rip, she is beautiful. Unless you have blinders on, and besides, I'm old enough to be her grandfather. But that doesn't keep me from admiring her. I think that woman has spunk. I mean, most women would be hysterical not knowing who they are; not her, she's got guts."

"That she does." Rip reflected on how she reacted when the lights went out. She hadn't panicked; she'd taken it in stride. Beautiful, that she was, but he wasn't about to let on to Matt. "She's caring and tender too, Matt. She takes care of that wolf cub, which she's named Bandon, like he's a baby. I know one thing, the lady needs our help."

"Count on me, but what about the book you're writing?"

"It'll have to sit on the back burner for now. Besides, I have the rest of my life to write. Cindy's problem is in the present and has to be resolved."

Cindy found the makings for spaghetti and had the noodles boiling. She liked puttering in the kitchen. Did she like cooking?

She really didn't know, but she felt comfortable doing it now. She could hear the men's voices coming from the living room, but couldn't make out what they were saying. They were her two favorite guys. In fact, the only guys she could remember. Rip and Matt were all she had now and she needed them to help her find her identity, unless by some chance she got her memory back. She thought of Matt. If he hadn't found her, what would have become of her? If only she could remember why, or from what she was running, and in a nightgown, no less. Rip, he didn't have to let her stay here. He could have taken her into town and turned her over to the police. Why hadn't he? She wondered. What motive did he have for letting her stay? Then Rip called from the other room.

"Whatever you're cooking in there sure does smell good."

"I hope it tastes as good as it smells," she hollered back. She turned to see Rip leaning on the frame of the archway to the kitchen. "Anything I can do?" He asked.

"Yes, you can set the table while I drain the spaghetti noodles." Cindy didn't see Matt. "Did Matt leave, after I made all this?"

"I'm here. Let me drain those noodles," he said, coming into the kitchen and taking the pan from the stove to the sink.

Cindy smiled at Rip and pointed to his head and at the same time pointed toward Matt. Matt had taken his hat off and slicked his hair back. She bet in his younger days he had the women chasing him. Rip smiled back at her in acknowledgment. They both laughed when Matt turned around and, snapping his suspenders, said, "Well, dinner is ready."

"I don't know about you Rip, but that's the best spaghetti and garlic bread I've ever eaten," Matt said, as he leaned back in his chair and rubbed his small belly. "Yes ma'am, you are one good cook, Cindy. Where did you learn to cook like this?" Then he realized the irony of what he said. "I'm sorry, I didn't mean…"

"That's okay, Matt. I'm glad you liked the meal, and as for cooking, I guess my mother must've taught me. I just don't remember."

She got up and carried her dish over to the sink. Her mind began to spin. Did she have a mother? Was she worried about her? What about her father?" Tears stung her eyes. She needed to get hold of herself. She reached for Bandon's bowl to focus on other things. Bandon came running. She looked down at the little mite and wondered what he was thinking about not having a

mother. Then she remembered what Rip had said. Wolves were
meant to live in the wild, to hunt, kill and eat. She knew a time
would come when she would have to let him go, just as there
would come a time when she'd have to leave here. She gazed out
the window as the sun began to set, but she wouldn't be leaving on
a black, dark night, although the snow was casting a radiant light of
its own, so bright it could light a path. What path would she take?
She liked it here. She couldn't think of any place else except that
room in her dream, and she didn't want to go there.

"Cindy, did you hear me?" Rip asked for the third time.
"Matt is leaving."

"I'm sorry Matt, I guess I was daydreaming. I don't know
if I've thanked you for what you've done, but I want you to know
that I really appreciate everything."

"Gee, Miss Cindy, you don't have to thank me. I did what
any decent person would do. I want to continue to help, too, so if
there is anything I can do, just let me know. I must be running
along now. Thanks again for the dinner."

Cindy and Rip sat and relaxed by the fire, drinking coffee,
after Matt left, they cleaned up the kitchen. Afterwards, the turned
on the television set in hopes of finding some information on her
disappearance.

"I guess no one is looking for me," Cindy said, wiping the
tears from her eyes with the back of her sleeve. "It's been three
days. Wouldn't I be missed by now?" she asked Rip.

Rip felt such pity for her. Her eyes looked like two pools
of water. He watched as a tear dropped from one eye. It brought
a lump to his throat, as he thought about how terrible it must feel
knowing that no one missed you. Why wasn't there some news
been out about her being missing? Why? That worried him. Yet
he wouldn't let on to Cindy. "Don't cry. I'm sure there's a good
reason. Maybe you went on vacation and they won't be looking
for you until you're due back." That, Rip thought, was the most
likely scenario. The thing that kept gnawing at him though, was
what was she running from?

"That's it, Rip," Cindy said jumping up and grabbing
Bandon. "You hear that, Bandon?" she asked, hugging the bundle
of fur. "I'm on vacation somewhere. That's why no one is looking
for me. Oh, Rip you don't know how relieved I am. How long a

vacation do you think--I mean, how long a vacation do people generally take?"

He didn't want to burst her bubble. He started to say as much, and then thought better of it. He'd rather have her in a positive frame of mind than negative. "It all depends on what kind of vacation one takes and how much money one has to spend. The average is one to two weeks and it's only been a few days." Her eyes lit up as she smiled at him. "Cindy, I'm sure with some rest, your memory will come back. You've had a severe blow to the head."

"You're right; I guess I'm just impatient, but I just want to know now. You can't imagine what an awful feeling it is not to know anything about yourself."

"No, I'm sure it's frustrating. I give you credit, you've been quite calm about the situation."

"What other choice do I have? I could throw a fit, but what good would come of that? No, I'll have to trust that my memory will come back, and soon."

Rip hoped so, because he worried about her safety. She was safe here in his home. She would want to leave sometime, whether she got her memory back or not. Would the problems or people she'd been running from still be lurking out there, wanting to do her harm? From what Matt had said and what Rip had gotten out of her, she'd been running for her life. Rip knew he couldn't stop her from leaving or doing whatever she wanted. Yet why did he feel the need to protect her? He watched her lying on the couch with Bandon cuddled up next to her, as they slept. Cindy looked so innocent and beautiful lying there. Rip felt a stirring in his loins, an emotion that hadn't been rekindled since his wife's death. Yet when he looked upon Cindy——no, he wouldn't go there. Hell, he didn't even know her age. He had to remember to keep his distance and control himself. He'd do his damned best to protect this beautiful creature, but at the moment all he wanted to do was strip her of her clothes, to ravish her body with kisses and bring her to the point of desire that only a man and woman can enjoy when united as one. "Is something wrong?" Cindy asked, jarring Rip from his daydreaming.

"No, I'm going outside to bring in more wood. I was about to tell you, but saw you were sleeping. Now go back to sleep. I'll be quiet as a mouse." Rip reached down and patted Bandon on the head as he said, "You watch over her, and don't let any harm come to her." To which Bandon gave a small yelp. "You're in good hands, Cindy," he said, then turned and headed toward the kitchen.

"Boy, I guess you rate," Cindy whispered in the cub's ear as she rubbed her face against its fur. "You got a pat, and all I got was 'go back to sleep' as if I were a child." Well I'm not. Why didn't he see that? The man had taken her into his home, given her virtually the clothes off his back and fed her. What more did she want? Damn it, she wanted him to notice her as a woman. Then what, she thought, as he came into the room, his arms full of wood. She watched him bend over in front of a wooden barrel where he placed the extra logs. Rip's shirt had pulled loose from his pant's waist. She stared at his lower backside that led toward a nice firm butt. Her eyes traveled further down to the muscles of his thighs, which were pulling on his jeans as he squatted over the fire. "There," he said, turning toward her. "That should last through the night."

"I thought with the power on, we wouldn't need to worry about firewood?" Cindy inquired.

"True, but I don't heat this place with electricity, I use propane gas. I try to conserve and supplement the gas with the wood, since I've plenty of old rotten trees on the property. The more wood I burn, the less gas I use and I get rid of the old wood lying around."

Cindy liked that, though she didn't know why, but she seemed to like a man who was conservative with money. She wondered where she got that idea. Maybe she had to scrimp for every penny. She laughed and said, "A penny earned is a penny saved." Now where had she heard that before?

"I see you've got a sense of humor. Nothing like a good nap to refresh one's memory, because I'm sure you had to have heard that saying from someone somewhere." Rip removed his hat and brushed his hand through his hair. "Yes, Cindy, I do believe rest is what you need."

No, it isn't, Cindy thought. I want—oh, what's the use, he'd never see her as a woman. "Come on, Bandon, let's go to bed and get some needed rest." Cindy got up and with Bandon in her arms, walked by Rip with her head held high. "Maybe you can fix this door tomorrow," she called from the room.

Rip stood looking after her and shaking his head. They had a wonderful dinner with Matt. Everything, he thought, had been going great and then this attitude. What had he done? Maybe he needed to watch his back with her. Hell, he really didn't know a thing about her. She could be a--no, no a murderer. No, she was confused and--yet why be rude? He would keep a close eye on her.

Cindy sat up with a jerk. That pounding! She turned her gaze to where that terrifying noise came from. "What are you doing, besides waking me and bursting my eardrums?"

"Fixing the door like your highness ordered."

"I didn't order, I asked, but I didn't ask for it to be done at the break of dawn, can't you see that I'm sleeping?" Cindy started to lie back down. Men, she thought.

"You're awake now." Rip suppressed a grin as he continued to pound the finishing nails into the frame.

"Only because of you," she said and pulled the covers up over her head. Oh, how he infuriated her. One minute he treated her like a girl and the next--"I'm up. Are you happy now?" She yawned then stood alongside the bed.

Rip snickered, he didn't mean to, but he was sure she didn't realize she was standing in nothing but her birthday suit. "I'm always happy to see a woman in her..."

Cindy glanced down at herself. Her body chilled even though a rush of heat went through her. She stood in the nude. Realizing her dilemma, she jumped back into bed and pulled the covers up over her head.

"Cindy, the door is fixed. It's near noon and I've got to run into town for a few things. I thought you might like to tag along, but if you want to sleep all day, that's fine too." He smiled as he shut the door. Then he called out, "Cindy, don't be embarrassed. It isn't like I haven't seen you without much on."

Cindy pulled the covers tighter around her. He'd seen her, touched her. She shivered at the realization. He must have seen and touched her when he mended her wounds. She pictured his strong hands. Were they tender or rough when they touched her? She peeked at her body as the thought of his strong hands on her caused a warm sensation.

Rip bent down and picked up Bandon who had begun to whine. He carried him upstairs to a spare bedroom that served as his office. He checked his e-mails. He saw that he had one from a longtime friend, Sarah. They'd worked together on many cases.

They kept in touch by e-mailing every so often. He made a note on a post-it to e-mail her later. Halfway down the steps he saw Cindy emerging from the bedroom. She wore the same outfit she had worn yesterday. He wanted to laugh, but pressed his lips together for control. She definitely needed some new clothes. He smiled as he reached the bottom step. "So, are you going into town with me?"

"That depends."

"On what?"

"I need to know if…" Darn, she couldn't say it. It was just too embarrassing. She wrapped her arms about her waist. What would she do if he admitted to violating her? What could she do? She had no proof. Besides, where would she go?

"Need to know what, Cindy?"

Darn him anyway, she thought. He stood there so smug. Well, she had to know. "Did you, or did we do anything? Darn it Rip. I need to know if you took advantage of me." She gave a sigh. There, she said it. She'd been looking at the floor the whole time and now raised her head to see him smiling. "I don't see anything funny. Just answer my question."

"First off, I can't believe you would think that of me. Haven't I treated you with the utmost respect?"

"Yes, yes you have," Cindy again looked down at the floor. "It's just that I've got to know." Then she felt him in front of her, felt his hand as it cupped her chin and brought her face up to his. Their eyes met. "Cindy, I only took care of your scraps and cuts, that's all," he said. Their lips were only inches apart. She suddenly felt the urge to touch his lips, to feel them against hers. "Well, shall we go?" Rip asked as he stepped away, bringing her back to reality.

"Yes," Cindy replied, taking the jacket he handed her.

"This will have to do," Rip said as he helped her with the jacket. "Once in town we'll have to get you some clothes. Not that I don't like what you've done with my clothes, but I can't have you going around cutting them all up," Rip said gently, with a touch of humor.

"Can we take Bandon?" Cindy asked.

"Not this time. We'd have to leave him in the truck. We'll take him for a ride some other time."

Chapter 10

They drove in silence and Rip thought back to the question Cindy had asked. It wasn't like he hadn't wanted her, he had. Touching her soft and firm body, he was reminded of how long it had been since he'd been with a woman. He looked over at her now in those oversized clothes and felt a surge of desire. Hold on Rip, he thought. You have a job to do. Yet, it didn't stop him from having the want.

To get his mind on something else, he asked, "Cindy, are you hungry? You missed breakfast and its lunch time. The hotel serves great food; Martha and Frank, friends of mine, own it. Besides, it's the only place in town where food is served. Don't get me wrong, though, Frank is the chef and a good one."

Cindy had to admit she was hungry, as her stomach growled. "Food sounds great."

Rip pulled the truck to a stop in front of the hotel. "You'll like Martha and Frank."

Cindy smiled as they entered through the heavy, wooden doors. The aroma of food made Cindy hungrier than she thought she was. A warm feeling embraced her upon entering the charming room. Tiffany chandeliers hung from the ceiling for lighting. Red and white checkered tablecloths covered six tables. A small "L"-shaped bar stood at the far end. A mirror on the wall behind it ran the length of it, and behind it stood a very pretty woman, with a face that reminded her of a china doll she once had. "I had a doll like…." She started to say before Rip cut her off.

"Cindy, I'd like you to meet Martha and Frank," Rip said as Frank emerged from a door to the left of the bar, "They run this establishment."

Cindy reached out her hand and met theirs in greeting. "Hi, I'm glad to meet you. Rip says you make wonderful meals here. I look forward to trying one." Cindy suddenly felt conscious of her outfit. She still wore Rip's clothing and knew she looked shabby.

"Cindy is a longtime family friend and has come to help me with my writing. She does most of the typing. I picked her up from the airport last week, and the airport misplaced her luggage. We came into town to purchase some clothes. Mine don't seem to fit so well," Rip gave a small laugh and patted her on the back. "Right partner?" he asked, gazing fondly at her.

"Right, and right now your partner's hungry," she smiled and gave him a small slug on his arm.

"Well Frank," Martha said. "Let's fix these two starving people our special of the day, which is hot roast beef sandwiches, mashed potatoes smothered in mushroom gravy, and a salad on the side. I'll even throw in a piece of my homemade apple pie."

"Sounds great, Martha, you've got my mouth watering," Rip said. "We'll take a seat by the window."

"I'd like to use the ladies room before we sit down," Cindy said.

"Follow me," Martha gestured with her hand. "It's this way. We'll let the two guys chat."

When Martha came out from behind the bar, Cindy noticed that she was pregnant, and by the looks of it, she was near her due date. "When are you due?"

"In a month if the doctor is correct. I know the first can come at anytime. I just hope everything goes well. Frank and I have waited five years for this. We're so excited. Maybe after you eat you'll have time for me to show you the nursery. We live upstairs. This makes it convenient running the hotel and restaurant. We do have some land just west of town where we plan to build a home someday."

Cindy liked this woman. She was warm and friendly, and anyone could tell that by the way the two looked at one another, that the two of them were very much in love. She hoped that a man would look at her like that someday. They reached the bathroom, and Cindy thanked her. "I'd love to see the nursery, if not today, then another time."

"So you'll be here helping Rip for a while?"

"Yes, for as long as it takes."

"Rip is a wonderful guy. He's gained the respect of the people in our small town. He's well liked."

Well, she liked him too, she thought as she returned to the table and the meal that Frank had set before them.

She ate heartily hardly stopping to take a breath between bites. "Well, what do you think of the food?" Rip asked as they finished their meal.

"The meal was great. Your friends are nice. I like them. They're very down to earth. In fact, Martha invited me upstairs to see the nursery."

"Cindy, we should get going. We need to get some clothes for you, and I've a few errands to run. I'll bring you into town again and you and Martha can visit all you want." He saw her chin drop, but he wanted to get back before dark, and they still had a lot to do.

Two hours later Cindy sat in the truck as Rip went into the post office to get his mail. She considered the packages in the cab of the truck. She purchased some jeans, sweaters, a nightshirt, and undergarments. She also got a pair of tennis shoes and boots. They went to the drug store where they purchased a toothbrush and some make-up. Rip wouldn't let her see how much the bills were, saying he would find a way for her to pay him back. How, was the big question? Because if he thought…. Cindy suddenly slid down in her seat. That's the way Rip found her.

"Cindy, what are you doing?" Rip asked, as he opened the truck door and saw her squeezed down on the floorboard. Her pale face stared up at him. She looked like she'd seen a ghost. Then he noticed her shaking. Every part of her body shivered.

"Are they gone? Please tell me they're gone, Rip."

"There isn't anyone around. What are you talking about?" Rip hurriedly climbed into the truck.

"Two men, one is heavy and the other, skinny and black. Are they still standing by the hardware store?"

Rip scanned the area. "I don't see anyone. They must have moved on. Now get up before you get stuck down there." How she managed to do it, he couldn't fathom.

"If you're sure they're gone." Cindy slowly maneuvered herself up on the seat while she gazed out the windows. She trusted Rip, but she needed to see for herself. Her eyes searched the front of the hardware store, then all the other shops. The two men were nowhere around. Had she imagined it? With the loss of her memory, could she be losing her mind too? She turned to Rip and suddenly felt very tired. "Can we go home now?"

Rip backed the truck out and headed toward home. He saw that her face had gotten some of its color back, yet she continued to stare out the windows. "Cindy, what are you afraid of?"

"I know you don't believe me, but I saw those men. I don't know why, but I fear them. It was as if I'd seen them before, but I don't know where. I just know."

Rip didn't want to frighten her anymore than she already was. He too was concerned. The two men, from Cindy's description, sounded like the same men Matt had seen asking questions. Were they the ones who'd been chasing her and were looking for her? He asked in the post office if they'd received any new wanted or missing reports. They hadn't. The small town didn't have any local police. The nearest police station was twenty miles away at the county courthouse. That would be his next stop, but not today.

Rip sat at his computer long after Cindy had retired for the evening. He couldn't seem to write. His mind kept going back to the problem at hand. Old crimes didn't seem as important as the present situation he found himself in. He didn't question Cindy on the way home about the men who had caused her fear. Instead, he opted to have a light conversation. They talked about Martha and Frank. Cindy seemed to have made a friend of Martha. He was pleased, as Cindy could use a woman to talk to besides old Matt and himself.

Thinking of women, Rip decided to e-mail Sarah, his old friend from his last workplace. She had finally made it to the rank of detective last year. She'd make a good one. He always wondered why the department had taken so long to see that. Rip wanted some answers and hoped she'd be able to oblige. When he clicked on the send button, Rip leaned back in his chair, to wait.

Chapter 11

The man behind the desk looked over at the two men who sat squirming in their chairs. What did they mean they couldn't find her? They had been gone for days and all they had to report was that they couldn't find her and they'd run into a snow storm. What did he care about some storm? He bit down on his lower lip to keep from lashing out. He needed them, and they knew they wouldn't get paid until they accomplished what he'd sent them to do. Find her. It had been their fault that they'd lost her in the first place. They hadn't drugged her enough. It had been a simple order. Drug her and take her to an undisclosed place and keep her there, drugged of course, until they heard further instructions from him. He had no alternative but to go to plan B, but first they had to find her. He'd work on an explanation about her absence, in the meantime, but finding her meant everything. He turned his attention back to the imbeciles in front of him. "Now listen up you two. I don't want to hear anymore excuses. Get your bloody asses out there and find her." They sat staring at him. "Damn it, if you want your money, you'd better get moving! Give me a call when you've something, and it better be soon. Now get, he screamed." He watched them leave through the side exit door. He couldn't take a chance of anyone seeing them. Damn them and damn her. Where was she? He had a lot at stake and wasn't about to let anything or anyone stop him from getting what he'd been working so hard for. His plan had to work.

Chapter 12

Cindy woke to the smell of food, her stomach growling. Her last meal was at the hotel. Getting back to the house, she told Rip goodnight even though it was only six o'clock. After hanging up her clothes, she lay down and was soon asleep.

Her sleep was anything but peaceful. She tossed and turned, as pictures of those two men, she'd seen earlier kept coming into view. They laughed at her and then they spat at her. These scenes kept repeating themselves until the aroma of food and something wetting her face woke her up.

She opened her eyes to gaze into Bandon's furry face. "You smell it, too?" She stroked his head. "Well, come on let's see if my partner has fixed enough for all of us." Cindy started to get out of bed when there was a knock on the door as Rip called out, "Cindy, are you awake?"

She called to him, "We'll be along shortly. Bandon and I are starved." Then she remembered her dream and the fear of seeing those two men. To be so frightened she must know them. She banged her forehead with her right hand. "Why can't I remember, Bandon?" Bandon didn't care; all he wanted was food. "Okay," she said, patting the wolf on the head. She dressed in a pair of jeans and a sweater, one of the outfits she'd, no, Rip had bought. She pulled her hair back and tied it with a band. With a quick splash of water to the face and toothbrush to the teeth, she was ready. A glance in the mirror surprised her. She had to admit, she looked good. What would Rip think?

He answered her question with a low whistle when she entered the kitchen. He wore a smile as he set the food on the table, and announced. "Breakfast is ready m-lady, and I must say how attractive you look this morning in your new duds."

"Thanks to you, I still don't know how I'm going to repay you. I've no money." Cindy pretended to empty her pants pockets.

"I told you not to worry. I'll find a way for you to pay. Now let's eat before it gets cold."

Cindy had taken only a few delicious bites when she said, "Since I'm your partner, I think I could type. It looks easy enough. Wouldn't I be entitled to be paid?" She saw Rip's forehead crease. "What I mean is, work for the clothes on my back." She waited for him to say something; when he didn't, she asked, "So?"

"Cindy, eat your breakfast."

They sat in silence for a while then Rip asked, "Cindy, would you like to talk about those men you saw yesterday?" She nodded. He reached across the table and, taking her left hand in his, said. "I believe those men triggered your memory. It might not have been those two, but they could resemble people you knew. I think you're starting to remember things. That's a good thing, but it worries me too because you were afraid of them." This morning she looked rested and had time to think. "Do you think these men or someone resembling them could be who you were running from?"

Cindy got up and emptied the rest of her omelet into Bandon's bowl. She watched as he consumed it in two gulps. She refilled her coffee cup and returned to her seat. She felt Rip's eyes following her. She looked over at the man who said he would help her. He'd shown her nothing but kindness and seemed to care, not to mention his good looks and the way every time she got near him her body reacted in ways that were familiar, but not quite. She felt warm and giddy, which caused her heart to beat at a rapid pace, as it had when she'd seen those men, only with Rip, it wasn't fear. She wanted to get close to Rip, to have him hold and comfort her, not run and hide.

With the coffee cup held in both hands for stability, because, just the thought of those men made her skin crawl, she answered, "Rip, I know I scared the daylights out of you yesterday.

I'm sorry. It was something I couldn't seem to control. One minute I was watching people go by, mothers with their children and men going from one place to another, and then they were there. I didn't see where they'd come from, they were just there. All of a sudden, I couldn't breathe; it was like I was choking. I started to shake. I knew I had to get away, but if I'd left the truck they would have seen me. I didn't know what else to do, so I scooted down and hid. I was afraid even to peek. That's how you found me."

Rip reached over and, taking the cup from her hands, held her hands in his. He noticed she began to tremble. "Cindy, look at me." She was staring at her coffee cup. "You're safe, they're gone. You're in my house."

She looked up. "I know that I'm afraid of them. Yes, them, and no they don't resemble anyone, because I've nothing to compare them with. I don't know if they are the ones I'd been running from. I have the feeling that they mean me harm. Why, I don't know. I wish to God I did." She started crying.

Why did she always cry? Why wasn't she strong? Had she always been afraid or cried a lot? She heard Rip move his chair beside hers. He placed his arm around her shoulders. She leaned into him until her sobs subsided. He lifted her chin with his thumb. Their lips were inches apart. Cindy again wanted to touch his lips, and wondered if they would feel as soft as they looked. She felt herself leaning toward them and then he suddenly pulled away.

"Now that you're feeling better, we'll get these dishes done and then if you feel up to it, ride out to the area where Matt found you."

Cindy kept her eyes on the road and surrounding terrain as they drove down the country road. Rip pulled off to the side of the road, but left the engine running. "Is this the spot?"

"Yes, but it looks like all the rest, a patch of woods with trees. "I'm sorry, Rip."

"Don't be sorry. We'll just sit here awhile, maybe something will click."

A half-hour later, he turned to her. "Cindy, do you think if you got out and walked around, it might…?"

"It's worth a try." She already had the door open before he finished. They were silent while on the drive out to the spot where

Matt said a car had pulled off the road. She trudged up and down the sides of the road. Nothing! She was about to give up when she heard a bang. The sound came from inside her head. Then like a movie screen, it played before her. She was in a car. The car swerved and she fell against the side of the car. A man cursed and then the car stopped. She remembered the car being black as she ran from it, and then she heard someone calling her name. Her eyes squinted in hopes of remembering, but again there was nothing. She turned around and came back to the truck where Rip sat waiting. She got in, saying, "This is the spot." Then she told him what she recalled. He said reassuringly, "Cindy, it'll come. You have to be patient."

They left the spot and drove around as Rip showed her his property lines. They rode past where Matt lived. They stopped, but he wasn't home. Rip said he probably was out hunting. Cindy liked the area. It had everything from woods to plains and rolling hills, and even steep mountains. The river, she liked best, frozen now, but she could picture its flowing stream of cool water as it ran through the hills. She looked forward to seeing it in the spring when all the wildflowers would be in bloom. Rip said they were plentiful. Would she be here in the spring? She studied Rip, who had been talking about a big fish he caught last fall. She liked listening to him talk about life here. When she left, and she would, because he had his life and she had hers, whatever is was, she knew she would miss this place, and him. She had feelings towards him that were more then friendship. She was falling in love with him. She felt he only thought of her as a case. She knew it wasn't good that she had feelings so for him. She could be married with children. No, she couldn't let her feelings be known without knowing the truth. She looked over at him as he continued to drive, telling her this and that about the area. Yes, she thought, gazing at him. I need to get my memory back, and soon. "A penny for your thoughts," Rip said, turning and smiling at her. It was that smile and gentleness that drew out her feelings. It reminded her of someone. Damn, if she could only remember. Smiling back, she answered him.

"Not much for your penny, I'm afraid. I was thinking how lucky the people are here. It's so beautiful and peaceful. Is it always like this?"

"Yes it is, especially on my property. On state property, we get hunters who come from the city during deer season, but other than that, I'd say the winters are fairly calm. In the summer, it gets a little more crowded with campers. People bring their families out for a week of camping to let their children know what it's like living in the rough. We get hikers. They take the state trails that run through the hills and mountains. You'll see once spring breaks."

Cindy could only hope so, as they pulled into his drive. "Home sweet home," Rip said as he got out and opened her door. She could hear Bandon barking as they neared the back door. "A good watchdog," they said in unison.

Rip wanted to write and headed toward the stairs to his room. Cindy played with Bandon for a while and then decided to explore the small pantry off the kitchen. She found a can of mixed vegetables, some potatoes and with the package of stew meat she got from the freezer, she had the makings for a meal. She put the meat in the microwave oven to defrost, thankful that the kitchen had all the modern conveniences. She cut the potatoes, opened the can of vegetables and added them all to the browned chunks of beef. She felt pleased with herself as she lowered the heat and put a lid on the pot. The meal would be ready in an hour and a half.

Cindy went into the living room. She liked the open balcony that circled half of the living room. It gave a panoramic view of the home's interior. Rip had his door closed. He needed his privacy, especially since she had invaded his home, she thought. She turned on the television to see if she could find anything interesting to watch. She settled on a talk show, where women were complaining about their husband's infidelity. Had Rip been disloyal to his wife? No, he'd spoken highly of her and said how much he'd loved her. She couldn't picture him as being unfaithful. Then it hit her. Was she being untrue? With that, the telephone rang. She heard Rip answer it from upstairs. She couldn't hear what he saying. He talked for about five minutes. Then all got quiet. The door opened and Rip came to the railing.

"Hey, I smell food."

"I decided to fix supper, since you're working so hard. Hope you don't mind."

"No, that's great."

"I just mixed a few things together. I hope you like it?"

"Well, from the smell, I'd say you've done a good job."

"Let me know what you think after you've had a taste."

"How long before it's ready? Do I have time for a quick shower and shave?"

"A good half hour, so take your time."

Cindy busied herself with setting the table. She sampled the vegetable beef stew and found it to be quite tasty. She enjoyed preparing the meal and wondered if in her life, the life, locked in the back of her brain somewhere, someone else had enjoyed it too. She felt Rip's presence before he spoke. She looked up to find him leaning his shoulder against the archway frame. A very masculine man, which showed in the tight fitting jeans he wore. His shirt was unbuttoned, showing a small patch of hair that covered his magnificent chest. He strolled over to the stove and lifted the lid on the stew. "It looks and smells wonderful."

He sure does, she thought. He smells wonderful. That cologne he wore, she remembered it. "Rip"--she couldn't finish. Her head felt light, like she was floating, and the room seemed to blur. She was falling and couldn't stop. Rip, no, not again.

"Cindy, Cindy, wake-up." Rip pleaded, placing a damp cloth on her forehead. Then her eyes fluttered. He reached for her hands, which felt damp and clammy. She pulled her hand away, fully awake now, and propped herself up with her elbows. "What happened?"

"You fainted. I caught you or you would have fallen on the stove. I carried you in here."

Cindy then realized she was lying on the living room couch. "I fainted, how? How long was I out?"

"Not long, a few minutes at the most. One minute you were standing there and the next you called my name. Then you started to fall. "Do you know why?"

"I think--come closer."

"Cindy, I don't think this is the time or the...."

"Appease me, Rip. Now lean a little closer." As he got closer, she sniffed at his neck. "That's it."

"What's it?" He continued to lean close. Hell, if he had his way he'd smother her with kisses and it wouldn't be just on the lips. Her whole body would feel his lust as he kissed her in the most private of places. Soon her body would be begging for more than just leaning closer.

"Rip; come back from wherever it is you've gone."

"I'm sorry." Rip leaned back. "What did you say?"

"I asked you what kind of cologne you are wearing. It's a scent I remember."

"I don't see how my cologne would cause you to faint." Maybe it was the combination of food and his spice cologne. Then he remembered reading somewhere where women who were pregnant sometimes fainted at such aromas. "Could you be pregnant?" Damn, that's all he needed, a woman with amnesia and with child to boot. She was smiling at him. This is not funny, he thought.

"Rip, that's it, the smell. I don't know why I fainted, but I know I've smelled that before. It was close up, not from far away. Whoever wore it, I had been close, very close to this person."

She thought about his last question. Was she pregnant? That she didn't know. She couldn't remember having had sex with anyone. "Rip, I don't think I'm pregnant. You would think I'd know if I was, but I don't. If I am, that means I'm married and I've a husband out there somewhere looking for me. Oh Rip, if only I could remember."

"Cindy, don't worry, it'll come back. Everyday you've remembered something. Mark my words, one day you'll wake up and it'll all be there."

"I hope you're right." Then another aroma reached her. "Rip, the stew, it's probably burnt."

"No, its fine, I turned it down when I got you the damp washcloth. Would you like to eat? I'll turn it back up."

Chapter 13

The next morning, Cindy woke up to the sound of Rip talking to someone. She could hear Rip, but not the other person. Getting up, she opened her door and peered into the living room. He sat in his favorite chair talking on the phone. "You mean there isn't one missing person report that matches her description, not even slightly? Come on, Sarah, there has to be." He was talking about her. Who was this Sarah person on the other end of the line? Who was this woman? Were they close, like did he date her? These thoughts were going through her mind as Bandon came up and started dancing in a circle. She ignored him. She was too intent on what Rip was saying. "Whoever she is, I'm having a hard time believing that not one person has come forward. Hell, she was running for her life. Someone was chasing her. That much we know. Okay, just keep on looking and if you hear anything, let me know." Then Cindy saw Bandon running toward Rip. He jumped on his lap. She saw Rip glance around, then say. "Listen, I've got to go, she must be up, and the cub just came running in here. Bye."

Cindy came strolling into the living room. "Who was that you were talking to?"

He was going to lie, but when he looked into her face, she had that look; a look his wife had when she asked a question and already knew the answer. Why did women always have the upper hand? Well, it was no use lying. She'd find out sooner or later and he figured she already had heard part of the conversation.

"Someone I used to work with, Sarah. I called her the other day. I wanted her to check on any missing person reports with your description."

"And?"

"She didn't find any. That is, unless you've been missing for over a year."

She knew he felt helpless, if she'd only remember. Maybe Rip had been right; she was blocking everything out because she was frightened. She'd hidden like some criminal when she saw those men. Would another blow to her head, jar her memory? She looked up at Rip. "Rip, what if I banged my head on something?"

"Cindy, let's not go there. Besides, you've already had a small concussion; another hit on the head would not be good. No, we'll just have to wait. I was thinking before you got up, that we'd take a ride over to Matt's. I'll show you a short cut from the way we went the other day. What do you say? Want to get out of here for awhile?"

"Give me ten minutes to change out of these night clothes."

He watched her go bounding off with Bandon at her heels. He hadn't wanted her to hear him talking to Sarah, but in a way it had turned out for the better. He'd asked Cindy to be up front with him and he needed to do the same. He was about to e-mail an old friend he knew who worked in the district attorney's office in Chicago, when he heard a vehicle coming up the lane. It wasn't Matt's old truck; he didn't recognize the sound.

Gazing out the window, he saw it wasn't a truck, but a black sedan with two people in front. He turned to see if Cindy was coming, just as the doorbell chimed.

"Yes, may I help you?" Rip asked opening the door to stare into the faces that matched the description Matt and Cindy had described. There was no mistaking them, as the one certainly needed to lose weight and the dark-skinned man was dressed as if he'd just stepped out of a fashion magazine.

"Are you, Mr. Walker?" The fat man huffed, straining the buttons on his coat.

"Yes, that's me. Why do you ask?" The other man was gazing over my shoulder.

"Live alone?" He asked as he looked in.

"You know you ask a lot of questions for someone I don't know. Who are you? What do you want?" Just then, Bandon came charging up and stood between his legs. Rip reached down and picked him up. "May I ask what brings you two out here into no man's land?"

"That's precisely why we're here. You see, the man we represent is in the market for some property around here. Your spot would be perfect for what he wants, with the river running through the land. We were wondering if maybe you were thinking of selling it or a parcel in the near future."

"No, I just built this home, for privacy, I might add. I'm a writer and like to be left alone. That's why I picked this place. Not many people around, as you can see." Rip motioned with his hand at the terrain, "nice and quiet." He hoped Cindy heard him talking as she had earlier and would stay put. He would bet his life on it that these two men weren't in the market for land.

"Now if you two will excuse me." Rip started to shut the door when the tall skinny one put his foot in the door. "Please, if you change your mind, we'll be in town for a few days. We're staying at the hotel, I'm sure you know which one, as there is only one." He smiled, showing perfect white teeth. Perfect like the rest of his clothes. Rip bet his suit cost at least a grand if not more, and the shoes he wore definitely weren't cheap.

Rip watched them pull away. These men are trouble with a capital T. He turned to see Cindy standing there pale as a sheet. He rushed up to her for fear she would faint, something she seemed prone to do.

"I'm okay, Rip. Those two men, they were the same ones I saw yesterday. Why were they here?"

Rip took her hands in his and guided her to the couch. They sat side by side, as he turned toward her. "Cindy, I know you're terrified of them. If only you could remember why."

"It's not like I haven't tried. I can't help it if…."

"I'm sorry; I didn't mean to upset you. It seems I'm either making you cry or faint." Then she started to laugh, and she continued to laugh and then suddenly she began to cry. "Cindy, please, I said I was sorry."

She sniffled, "It's not that. It's those two men. Why did they come way out here? What do they want? I should leave you, go to the police, and turn myself in."

"Hey, they've gone. They said they were looking to buy property for a client."

"Do you really believe that? Do you, Rip?"

He looked over at her red swollen eyes. "I've no reason not to believe them. Of course, I will admit they seemed a little shady. I've nothing else to go on." He saw the look of fear in her eyes. "Cindy, I know you're afraid of them. For what reason, I don't know, but I can't go around accusing people of things when I've got no proof. Now come on, let's go for that ride."

The three of them were bouncing down a bumpy lane in Rip's truck when a deer ran in front of them. Bandon began to bark and tried to get out the window. Cindy began to laugh, a joyous laugh, which Rip found refreshing. He made a note to have her laugh more often. It agreed with her. "Well, there's Matt's place. A little rustic, but he calls it home."

Cindy studied the old rustic cabin. Smoke poured out from the stone chimney. "Does he know we're coming?"

"No, he doesn't have a phone. In fact, old Matt doesn't have any of the modern conveniences."

He saw her face wrinkle up. "He has no bathroom? How does he--you know, do his thing?"

Rip pointed to a small shed that stood about ten feet from the cabin. "There. It's what they call an outhouse."

Cindy may have lost her memory, but she was sure she'd never used an outside toilet, or outhouse, as Rip called that small building. It didn't look big enough for even one person.

She saw Matt coming out the door. He must have spotted them coming. She smiled. He didn't have much, from the looks of his place, but he had a big heart. "Hi, Matt," she waved and stepped from the truck, when Rip brought it to a stop. Bandon went bounding off toward a rabbit that had gone scurrying in front of them. "Hey, he found a rabbit," Cindy said.

"Yep," Matt said as he called after the wolf, "You leave my friend alone, Bandon. That old rabbit has been around for years, the meat would be too tough to eat. Besides, I look forward to seeing it every morning."

"Come here, Bandon, you don't want old Matt getting mad at you now." Rip picked Bandon up. "Sorry Matt, he's only doing what comes natural."

"Well, what brings the two of you over here? I haven't had as many visitors in the past ten years as I've had today."

"There didn't happen to be two men in a big black sedan stop by?"

"Yep, they visit you too? They said they were looking for property to buy. My guess is they were just nosing around. What do you make of it?"

Hearing that they had visited Matt made Rip now know for sure that Cindy's life was in more danger than he first realized. He was about to ask Matt more questions when Cindy came up behind him and they entered the cabin. Then Cindy stopped and he all but ran into her. She was staring at Matt's bear rug in front of the fireplace. A look of fear crossed her face. She had more to fear than a dead bear rug. "It's okay Cindy, it won't hurt you."

She turned and smiled at Rip. He knew that he'd never let any harm to come to her. He knew he couldn't sit idle and wait for her memory to come back either, not with those men hanging around. He had to get a picture of her to Sarah.

Rip turned to Matt. "I hope we're not bothering you. I thought it would be a good idea to get Cindy out for a while. She's been cooped up in the house. Besides, she wanted to see your place."

"It's not much," Matt said. "But it is home to me."

"I think it is nice and cozy," Cindy smiled, still looking at the bear rug. She couldn't imagine anyone wanting to or having the nerve to go after such a big animal. "You must be a great hunter, Matt."

"Why, thank you. I like to think of myself as one of the best."

Rip saw Matt giving him the eye. "Cindy, don't be getting him started. He will burn your ears with his tall tales."

"Tales, my foot, you're just jealous that I've gotten more rabbits than you this year."

"The year isn't over yet."

"Hey, you two, I thought we came for a visit, not a comparison showdown.

"Cindy's right. We had decided to come over here when those men stopped by."

Matt looked from Rip to Cindy. He didn't know how much, if anything, he should say in front of her. They were the same two men he saw in town earlier. When he looked again at Rip, he gave him the go-ahead sign with a nod. He never got a chance to say anything, as Cindy spoke up.

"I'll bet it was the same two men who came to Rip's house a little while ago. Did one happen to be short and fat and the other tall and black with a pitted face?"

Matt's eyes went to Rip. "Yes. Matt knew this wasn't good. "They said they were looking for property for a prospective buyer."

Rip glanced from Cindy to Matt. "Yes, they said about the same, but I didn't believe them. I told them I wasn't interested, and then they left. I don't like any of this. First, they asked questions in town and now they're out questioning the people in the area. Cindy saw them for the first time in town yesterday. They frightened her. She seems to have ill feelings about them."

"Did they see her?" Matt asked. How their lives, Rip and his, had changed in just a few days! Their lives had been so tranquil, each doing their own thing. Matt hunted and trapped. Rip spent most of his time working on his book. Matt wondered if Rip ever had a case similar to the situation they now found themselves in, in finding Cindy. If only she could remember. It sure would make things simpler. He wondered why anyone would want to cause her harm. A pretty thing like her should be out having the time of her life.

"No, they didn't see me. At least, I don't think so. I slid down in the front seat and hid." Then she pointed to a mounted animal head above the fireplace. "What is that?"

"A twelve point deer. It's my pride and joy. I got it about five years ago. I'd been tracking it for a few years. I finally outsmarted the old buck. You can touch it if you like."

"No thanks. I'd rather keep my distance." Cindy noticed other animals, a raccoon, a duck, and a variety of fish, all mounted on the wooden walls. She observed the cabin to be quite small. The living room and kitchen were one room. The fireplace served as the main focal point, not to mention the deer head and bear rug that caught one's eye as they entered the cabin. A wooden ladder led to an open loft, where she could see an old wooden bed and dresser. That had to be where Matt slept. She saw Matt watching her, a big smile on his face.

"These are my prize catches. I usually don't trophy hunt. I hunt and fish for food." Cindy could see the pride in his face as it glowed when he looked from one animal to the other. She'd been going to ask him how he could be so cruel as to kill them. Yet, who was she to cut down the way one lived or survived. Wasn't she herself just trying to survive?

Matt served them all coffee. Cindy had finished hers as Bandon began barking, wanting to go outside. "I'll take him outside, let you two visit," she said.

Rip waited until she shut the door then turned to Matt. "We've got a big problem on our hands. It's bigger than I first thought. These men, whoever they are, aren't looking for property. They're looking for Cindy. They know they lost her in this area and are checking every house to see if they can find her or see a sign that she's been around. You get that feeling or is the detective in me playing with my imagination?"

"No, I mean, it isn't right," Matt replied. "I can't ever remember anyone coming around asking about property. They usually go to the county seat and check for property for sale. I think it's fishy too, but what are you going to do?"

"What am I going to do? You mean us. You brought her to my place, or have you forgotten?" Not that he was angry about it. Matt had done the right thing. It was just that he didn't like those men being so close. He'd have to keep watching over his shoulder at all times. He wasn't used to that, not here in the country. He'd been used to the city with its many hiding places. Here they were in the open. "Cindy," he called, going to the door.

"Yes?" She turned, smiling at him. "Is Bandon about done out there? You aren't dressed for the cold."

"We were just coming in. Come on, Bandon, the master calls." She really didn't think of him as master, but it felt nice to have someone care. She only had on a lightweight coat she had just purchased, rather Rip had, and she was beginning to get cold. Yet it felt so good to be outside. She jumped and laughed as a rabbit scurried by, which caused Bandon to take off after it. "Bandon, come back here!" She went running after him. He ran behind the cabin to the small building that Rip called an outhouse. The rabbit had gone into a hole behind it, and Bandon stood there barking. She picked him up and turned only to run smack into Rip. She looked up into his eyes. They seemed angry. He grabbed her by the shoulders. "Don't run off like that again. Do you hear me?" She pulled away.

"I'm not a child. You have no right to order me around. Besides, I was only getting Bandon who'd run after a rabbit." She spun away in a huff, still holding Bandon, and walked away. She hadn't gotten two feet when she felt him grab her arm. "Get in the truck. We're going home."

"I don't have a home to go to, or have you forgotten."

"Damn it, Cindy, you know what I meant. Now get in the truck. We're going back to my place. I'll say good-bye to Matt." He watched her stomp off and once in the truck, she slammed the door.

Cindy sat staring out the side window on the way back to the house. He didn't say anything and she certainly didn't feel like talking to him. She gazed out the window and watched the trees as they blurred past. She could see that the trees had started budding and knew that spring wasn't far off. Would she still be here then or would she have her memory back and be--where? She glanced sideways at Rip. He kept his head and eyes straight ahead. He held his jaw stiff, and seemed to be biting the inside of his cheek, by the looks of it. She wondered what he was thinking and what had caused his anger. What had she done? Nothing, she had just taken Bandon outside.

"Rip, please talk to me. Tell me what I did that was wrong?" Before he could answer, the truck stopped and she saw they were at his place.

"Cindy, I'm not mad. I'm concerned for your safety. Now go on in the house and take Bandon with you. I'll be along shortly. I've a few things to do outside."

Rip watched her enter the house. He then went about checking out a hunch he had. He walked around the house. Sure enough, there were footprints, and they weren't his! He saw where a vehicle had pulled off the side in his lane. There were tracks leading to the house. The men had come back and had been snooping. The tracks led to the shed and back to the house. He hiked to where Cindy's window was and saw that she had her blinds pulled shut. A sigh of relief washed over him. They hadn't seen anything. He hoped that their curiosity had been satisfied and they wouldn't be back. Yet in the back of his mind, he didn't think so. He needed to be more careful in the future.

Rip hadn't meant to be so angry at Cindy. If they'd been out there and seen her, they could have--he didn't want to think of that. He wanted to pull her tight against him, and not to protect her, but hold her with passion. Only he couldn't do that, she might already be taken. He had to keep his emotions in check; something that wasn't' going to be easy, living with her. Besides, even if she had no one waiting, what made him think she felt anything towards him? Well, for now he would take care of her. He headed toward the woodpile and grabbed an armful of logs for the fireplace. He always liked a fire, even with the furnace going.

Cindy went to her room after getting out of the truck. She shut her door and turned the lock. She wondered what he was doing outside, and then thought, why did she care? She'd stay in this room until her memory returned. She lay on the bed and patted a spot for Bandon to join her. With Bandon beside her, she suddenly felt exhausted as her eye lids got heavy. She fell asleep and found herself dreaming of a man in bed with her. The man had his arm draped over her mid section. She couldn't see him, but the arm was covered in blond hair. She wasn't afraid of this person, but felt comfortable and warm. Then he started to turn around, but she woke before she got a chance to see his face.

She sat up with a start. She so wanted to see the face. It's a beginning, she thought, maybe next time she'd know him. She must have slept a while since the room was black, and with the blinds closed, she had no light. She felt for Bandon and found he still slept at her side. She thought of the dream again. She'd been in bed with a man, a man who had blond hair. That meant there was someone in her life. He must be very worried about her. She forgot her anger at Rip. She hurried from the bed, and rushed into the living room. He sat sipping a glass of wine.

Rip looked up as she came into the room. He didn't see any anger in her expression and decided not to bring up the afternoon's events. "Get a good rest?"

"Yes, and I had a dream. I dreamt I was in bed with a man with blond hair." Then she realized what she'd said, and her face flushed, as she looked at her bare feet. Here she was rushing out to a man she hardly knew and telling him about dreaming of sleeping with a man. What must he think! That she was some hussy, or worse. She'd been so excited, thinking it had something to do with her past, when in reality it could be nothing more than a dream. "I'm sorry Rip. I mean…." Hell, she didn't know what she meant. She stood there staring at her feet.

"Cindy, that's good news. Did you recognize the person?" The thought of her in bed with another man caused a knot in his stomach. It bothered him to think that she could be in love with someone. It would only be natural for her to have someone. What had he been thinking? That she'd been living a life of chastity? One look at her and one would know better. She probably had many suitors. Hell, she might be married. He needed to keep that in mind.

"No," she continued. He had blond hair. I woke up before I saw his face. It probably means nothing." She wished that she'd kept her mouth shut.

"Listen, it could be important. I want to hear anything that you remember and that includes your dreams. We can use any clue you have and right now, we don't have much of anything to go on. Don't forget, we're in this together." He meant it, no matter how mad he got at her.

"Cindy, come here and have a seat. We need to talk."

"I thought that's what we were doing." She made her way over to the couch and took her usual seat. Then she remembered how angry he'd been at her earlier. "That is before you got mad at me." Bandon starting barking at the door, and she got up to let him out.

"I'll let him out. You stay put, please." Well, at least he said please, and that is a start, she thought. She waited while he let the cub out and then he returned, but he didn't sit in his usual chair, he sat next to her on the couch.

"Cindy, I want to apologize for the way I acted this afternoon. I wasn't mad at you, but rather at the situation. I should have explained. It's just that with those men running around, I don't think it's safe for you to be out in the open without someone with you. To be truthful with you, I don't think it's a good idea that you be out at all."

"Not out at all? You can't mean that. I mean, I'd go nutty just sitting around here."

"Think about it for a minute. You are terrified of them; otherwise, you wouldn't have hid when you saw them. Besides, the fact that you're not on any missing person lists that I know of, only shows me that whoever is looking for you doesn't want the world to know you are missing. Why that is, I don't have the foggiest idea. For the time being I think it best that you stay hidden." He saw how her body tensed and her jaw tightened, something she did when she didn't like what he said. "It's not an order, but a request, Cindy. I'm only saying this for your safety, and mine."

His safety, she hadn't thought of that; but of course, if someone meant her harm, with him protecting her, his life was in danger also. How stupid of her not to think of that before now.

She locked eyes with him and saw nothing but sincerity and caring. Where had she gotten the impression that he wanted to control her? He wanted to protect her and was doing the best he knew how. "You're right, Rip. I'm being selfish. I'll do as you ask, but can I ask you to do something for me?"

He knew they were back on friendly terms again. He never liked having a disagreement with his wife either. He liked the making-up part. They would kiss, and make-up and go to bed. He looked over at Cindy, but she wasn't his wife and they couldn't kiss and make-up. Not that he wouldn't like to at this moment. He wondered what her lips would feel like. Would they be soft and sweet as he pictured them? He heard her talking. "I'm sorry, Cindy. What did you say?"

"I asked if you'd let Bandon in. He's out there barking. I'll start supper, I'm hungry. What would you like me to make?"

"Nothing, it's already fixed. I made some chili." Rip spotted Bandon barking at the woods. He felt a chill run up his spine. Were those men out there? Then he saw a rabbit. "Bandon, come here boy, and leave the animals alone." Turning to Cindy he said, "He is definitely all wolf."

Rip walked to the edge of the woods and picked Bandon up. When he turned, he saw Cindy standing in the doorway. The light from the room behind her gave her an amber glow. Damn, it was going to be hard to keep his hands off her.

Rip handed Bandon to her and shut the door. Their hands brushed ever so lightly, causing his pulse to race. She too must have felt something for she blushed and quickly turned away. Could he hope that she held warm feeling for him in her heart? No matter what her feelings, he would protect her from whoever waited for her. "Cindy, I think it best that we keep the blinds pulled down on all the windows, even the big window facing the river." He knew that with a good set of binoculars someone on the other side of the river would have a full view of their activities. He built the place for its magnificent view of the countryside. Nevertheless, he pulled the drapes closed. He hated that they had to hide, but it wouldn't be for long, he would see to that.

They sat in silence by the fireplace eating their bowls of chili and listened to the wood crackle and spark, both lost in their own thoughts. Cindy broke the silence by saying, "I'm sorry to have brought all this on you."

He set his empty bowl aside and layback on the floor with his arms folded behind his head. How could she believe it to be her fault? The fault lay in the hands of the ones who chased her. He rolled over on to his side and faced her. She sat with her knees pulled up, where she rested her chin. "Cindy, don't take the blame. It's those who want to do you harm who are the root of the problem. Not you. I'm thankful that Matt found you and saved you from whatever those men had planned for you." As Rip said that he realized he truly meant it. She had awakened feelings in him he thought were gone for good. He hoped he wouldn't lose her.

"But I've caused you nothing but worry and trouble, not to mention putting your life in danger. Your writing, you haven't done any since I came here." No matter what he said, she knew his life had changed drastically since her arrival. Maybe she could help. "You told Martha and Frank at the hotel that I was here to help you." She wanted something to do besides sit.

How he would love to have her here for just that purpose and maybe more, but first things first. "Cindy, we first need to think finding out who you are and what you were running from. Then, if you'd still like to, and if your life permits, you may help me with my writing." Somehow, he knew that wouldn't happen. She had another life and it hadn't included him. She'd find that life, and they'd both go their separate ways. He reached over, and on impulse, gave her a light kiss on the cheek. "Now let's call it a night. Tomorrow is another day, which may bring light to your memory."

Cindy watched him go up the stairs to his room. She sat there for a long time afterwards. She touched the place on her cheek, which still held the warmth from his kiss. She knew he meant in a friendly manner, but nonetheless, it had sent chills up her spine. She had welcomed it and more if he'd been willing. She couldn't remember ever feeling so excited or moved by such a small kiss. Her body reacted to his slightest touch. She liked Rip more than she wanted to admit. Pleasant dreams, Rip, she thought and turned to Bandon. "Come on, Bandon, let's call it a night."

She undressed in the dark, a suggestion from Rip. Once in bed she lay wide-awake, unable to sleep. She wasn't tired. Bandon lay on the rug by her side. Poor thing, she thought, he's had a rough day chasing after rabbits. She tossed and turned, hitting the pillow with her fist. Then she heard the sound of crunching snow.

She bolted upright in bed. She heard it again. "Shish," she whispered to Bandon. She slid from the bed onto the small carpet piece as she heard the crunching again. Someone or something was outside her window. What should she do? She didn't want to open her bedroom door for fear the hall night-light would show her silhouette. Maybe if she opened it just enough for Bandon to get through.

On hands and knees, she crawled to the door. She stretched her arm until her hand felt the doorknob, and very slowly turned it, opening the door a few inches. She lay very still and pushed Bandon through the opening. "Go get Rip." Through the small slit in the door, he stood there wagging his tail. Please, oh please, Bandon, then she said it again. "Go get Rip." Then Bandon took off. She slowly shut the door and leaned against it with arms wrapped around her knees. What if Bandon didn't go to Rip?

Rip lay in bed reading. Sleep evaded him, and a good book always helped. He'd even put on the radio in hopes that it would help him sleep, but tonight nothing seemed to work. His mind kept picturing the woman who lay in his guest room, a woman who had changed his life. She'd brought mystery with her and meaning back into his life. He'd had a wonderful marriage and had looked forward to growing old together with his wife. When she'd been taken away from him, he'd given up hope of ever being happy again. Now that had all changed, and it was because of the woman who slept downstairs, a woman who probably belonged to someone else. He reached over, shut the lamp, and radio off. He stretched out and stared into the darkness. When this was all over, he didn't know how he would bring himself to let her go.

Almost asleep, Rip suddenly sat up in bed at the sound of scratching. Mice, no, he'd never been bothered with them before. Then he heard it again, accompanied by a whining sound. He listened harder and realized it came from his door.

He opened it to find Bandon standing there. "How'd you get out?" He reached down to pick him up, and headed for the stairs. "Oh, you want out?" Rip grabbed his robe from behind the door. "You're going to have to learn to control that bladder of yours." Then he wondered why Cindy hadn't let him out, she usually did. He went toward the front door, but Bandon took off down the hall. What the he…, he thought noticing her bedroom door closed. How had Brandon gotten out? A feeling that something wasn't right caused a chill to race through his body. He listened by her door, but could hear nothing. He turned to leave, but hadn't gotten two feet when Bandon began to whine. "What is it, guy? Is something wrong with Cindy," he whispered.

Cindy heard Bandon's whine, and slowly opened the door a crack. Relief washed over her at the sight of Rip. She didn't want to open the door any further, but whispered, "Rip, I think someone is outside my window." He bent down and quietly said, "Stay put and don't move; I'll check it out."

Cindy resumed her previous position, but this time the fear had been relieved. Rip would take care of whatever was out there. Then it hit her. How stupid of her! She'd put him in danger. What if those men were out there? What if he got shot? She couldn't just sit here and do nothing. She stood and forgetting about the light went charging out the door only to run straight into Rip. "I thought I told you to stay put."

She sighed and leaned into him. "Thank goodness you're safe. I wasn't thinking, letting you go out there alone. I mean, you could have been hurt or worse, killed." She buried her face in the folds of his robe.

"Cindy, I'm fine." He pulled her away and held her at arm's length.

"I'm sorry. I don't know what came over me." She felt embarrassed and wondered if he could tell with only the night-light on.

"You were afraid, that's understandable." Rip saw her eyes as they sparkled in the dim light. She'd felt so good in his arms. His body reacted, causing a pleasant sensation in his loins. Then he pulled away. He had to, for he might have done something he'd regret later. "Cindy, you're safe. There's nothing outside or by your window."

"Are you sure? I mean, of course you are, but I heard it and so did Bandon. It sounded like someone walking in the snow."

"Oh, there was something out there, a pack of wolves." He saw her look down at Bandon, who stood between them both, glancing from one to the other. "Yes, don't look so surprised. I told you they were around here. Where do you think Bandon came from? They're searching for him; they've probably found where I buried his mother and have found his scent around the house." She bent down and picked up Bandon. "They can't have him."

"Cindy, I've told you before. There will come a time when you will have to let him go. He's from the wild and will someday want to return." He saw the disappointment on her face. "For now, he's yours. He'll let you know when he's ready to go. Right, Bandon?" He patted him on the head. "Now that I'm awake, how about I make us some hot chocolate?"

They sat in the kitchen sipping their drinks when Cindy began to cry. She couldn't seem to stop, the tears just came. Then she felt Rip's hands on hers. "Cindy, why cry now? You're safe. It's all over with."

"That's just it, it isn't. It will never be. We'll have to hide and be afraid of everyone. That's no life. I'm so sorry," she continued to sob.

"Cindy," Rip pulled her from the chair. They now stood face to face. He reached over and tilted her head with his thumb on her chin. He wiped a tear away with his index finger as it ran down her cheek. "Don't cry; this situation will not go on forever. I've got a connection in Chicago and she's checking some things out for me. Now dry those tears so we both can get some sleep. You're going to need it if you want to help me with my book." He saw her face light up.

"You mean it, I get to help?" When he nodded, on impulse, she reached up and kissed him on the lips, then gave him a big hug. "Thank you, thank you. I can't wait! I promise I won't disappoint you. See you in the morning, partner."

Chapter 14

"I told you to call, not show up here. It's dangerous for me to be seen with the likes of you, but since you're here, what have you got?" He looked first to Hank and then to Jake. Hank spoke first.

"We checked the area out, and went from house to house, which wasn't an easy task as they've just recently had a snow storm."

"I don't give a damn about the snow, just tell me what happened and be quick about it. I've a meeting to attend and I can't be late. With the old man out of town, I'm in charge." In charge, how good that sounded. Someday and someday soon, he'd be in full charge. That was the plan, but first they had to find her.

"Let me tell him," Jake said to Hank. Jake continued. "First, we asked in town if strangers had been around. We didn't want them to become suspicious so we told them that we'd heard others were in the market for land and wanted to know if we had competition. They seemed satisfied with that, and told us that they hadn't seen any strangers. After that, we decided to go from house to house looking for her. We knocked on every door; even those that looked like no one lived there. Most were hunting cabins or summer places. We saw nothing. We tried, really we did, Boss."

"Well, that's not good enough. I want you both; to go back there and keep your eyes and ears open. Listen to what the people in town are saying. Anything out of the ordinary, I want to hear about. She's bound to show up. She can't stay in hiding forever. Now get the hell out of here."

"What are we supposed to do? We just can't go there and sit around. That would cause suspicion," Hank said, glancing at Jake who nodded his head.

"I don't give a damn if you stay in your room and watch television and play cards all day. Just do the job I hired you to do. Now, get out of here." They started to leave through the main door. "Use the side door. I've told you before, we've never met."

After they left, he picked up the phone and dialed. "Honey, I'm sorry, but we've got to go to plan B." He could hear the disappointment on the other end of the line. "We've got no choice. The men I've hired haven't found her. When they do, it won't be long and it will all be done. It's just going to take a little longer with this change of plans. We've waited this long, a year, what's a few more days, weeks or months." He knew she was getting tired of sitting around, not going anywhere. "I'm really sorry, honey, you have to hold tight. I don't want anyone seeing you. We have to be careful. No one knows. Everyone thinks she's the only heir. Only we know better. We have the upper hand. Now be good and I'll see if I can't get over there soon, for a few hours. We've come this far, we can't have any slip-ups." He laid the phone down on its cradle. There is so much at stake, he thought. I can't and won't lose. The bitch, he would find her. He could go to plan C, but that plan had too many risk factors, risks he wasn't prepared to take. If only she hadn't found out. Hadn't seen him with….

"Sir, they are waiting for you," his receptionist voiced over the intercom. He glanced at his watch and gathered his papers, and left for his meeting. The meeting was important. He had to show the old man he could do the job. Hell, he could do better than the old fart. The old man had so many old fashioned ideas and was out-dated, worrying about what his creditors thought. To hell with them, they were in the banking business to make money. Someday he would control it, all of it! He'd be in charge.

If only she hadn't wanted to break it off. He'd tried to reason with her, but no, she was going to go to daddy. Well, her daddy had an unexpected trip out of the country for a while. That's when he saw his opportunity, and those two bungling idiots had let her get away. A minor setback, but one he'd figure it out, and he needed to do it soon as the old man was due back in a few weeks. He smiled as he entered the meeting room. He still had time. Had time to come up with an alternative, but first he had to find her.

Chapter 15

Cindy watched Rip chopping wood. The sun was bright today, making it a nice warm day. She laughed at Bandon who went after the stick she threw as he went tumbling over a log. He was still a cub, but soon he'd be grown and he would want to leave her. It saddened her heart, as did the thought that she too would leave here someday. She didn't want to think that far ahead, and turned her attention to Rip. She could see his muscles ripple through his coat as he lifted the axe. She'd noticed those muscles and more this past week. Rip had been true to his word. She helped him organize his files by cases: murder, robbery, corruption, to name a few. He was planning his book in accordance with the crimes he would detail. It was going to be a factual book about law. They had worked side by side every morning. At noon, they would take a break for lunch, which usually consisted of soup or a sandwich. Later, he'd have her relax on the couch while she tried to remember anything from her past. She hadn't gained any memory back. Maybe she never would. Rip said it would take time, but her patience was wearing thin. She wanted to move on. She wanted to show him how much she cared for him. They did everything together as if they were husband and wife, except make love. Someday, she hoped that would be rectified, memory or no memory. Rip turned and smiled at her. She waved.

"Cindy, why don't you go in and put on that pretty dress I got for you? It's such a beautiful day, and you've been cooped up here, I thought we'd go into town for supper."

Cindy felt elated. She had begun to think that life consisted of Rip, Matt, and her. You too, she laughed at the cub as she tossed the stick again for him. "You really mean it? What if those men are...?"

"Don't worry. I think they've gone back to wherever they came from. I didn't see them in town and Henry at the post office says he hasn't seen them either. They probably really were looking for land and seeing that the people weren't selling, moved on to other parts. Now go and get ready. I'll be in shortly. I've got one more log to split."

With Bandon on her tail, Rip watched her leave. She deserved an evening out. Besides, he'd promised Martha that he'd bring Cindy into town so she could see the nursery. Martha's baby was due in a few weeks. He thought it would be good for Cindy to talk to another woman. Her mind would relax, possibly bringing her past into her present consciousness. He turned his thoughts to Sarah and her last e-mail. She didn't have anything new to report, but promised to keep searching. He still wanted to send her a picture. Maybe he could have Frank take a picture of the two of them at dinner. Cindy deserved a night out after all the work she put into helping him this past week. Had it really been a week? It felt like only a few days. With her around, the days were filled with laughter and joking. She filled a void in his life. He dreaded the day it would all end, and end it would; but for now, they were together and going out to eat. How long had it been since he'd taken a woman out to eat? Too long, he thought as he took the steps two at a time.

Cindy let the shower's beads roll over her body as she thought of dinner. She looked forward to seeing Martha again. She seemed so friendly, and Cindy liked her. The baby's due date wasn't far off. Baby, she thought, would she someday have one, maybe two? You could already be a mother! A voice inside her said. A tear ran down her cheek. Yes, she could, and here she stood thinking of going out to dinner. She could have a child and him or she would be missing her, even crying. She quickly finished her shower and dressed. She looked at the dress lying on the bed, a simple yet elegant black sleeveless dress with a 'V' neckline. She pulled the dress over her head and turned to view herself in the mirror. The dress hugged her waist and then flared to just above the knees. She smiled at her reflection in the mirror. The man had impeccable taste. She had to admit she looked stunning.

She stood waiting in the living room, gazing out over the river. Rip said this area was colorful in the warm months with the place covered with an assortment of colored wildflowers. Would she be here to see them, or would she be home. Home, she thought. Where was her home? Sure, she stayed here with Rip, but it was his home, not hers.

Cindy smelled him before he spoke, as he wore her favorite cologne, Old Spice.

"Good, the dress fits and you look stunning. I was concerned when I first picked it out."

"Oh, Rip, it's beautiful." She turned and smiled at him, and then all of a sudden tears welled up. She began crying. She hadn't wanted to cry, but at the sound of his voice, she lost control.

"Hey, I thought you liked the dress. You don't have to wear it. You can change. Why don't you go and put on your jeans. You look beautiful no matter what you wear. I thought that maybe you were tired of wearing pants."

"Rip, it's not the dress. The dress is wonderful. It's a very thoughtful gift." She sniffled and Rip handed her his handkerchief. "Thanks, and that's another thing, I'm always thanking you. You've done so much and what have I done in return, but a little filing. I'm a nuisance and I don't have a home." She began sobbing again, uncontrollably, as her body shook.

What had come over her? Not an hour ago, she'd been happy and couldn't wait to go into town. Maybe it had been a mistake keeping her here. Yet she seemed to enjoy the outdoors. There is the old saying, you can't take a country mouse and make them a city mouse and vice versa. Well, the same went for people and Cindy was a city girl. She may not know it now, but would one day, just as Bandon would realize he belonged in the wild. He pulled her against his chest. Her tears wet his shirt. He didn't mind.

She pulled away and looked into his eyes, where concern showed. If only I could be yours, she thought, and continued to study his face. She wanted to remember every inch of it, because one day she would have to leave. She wanted him etched in her memory. Her tears had dried and she smiled up at Rip. "Let's go eat." She started for the door.

"Now wait just one minute there. You can't go crying all over my shirt and then walk away."

"I'm sorry about your shirt. It's just that I'm so happy and I shouldn't be. I don't know who or what I am."

"Cindy, you've every right to be happy, memory or not. You're kind and caring. Just look how you take care of Bandon. Now let's go to dinner."

Chapter 16

"Have you heard from you're men? Have they found her?"

"No, but I should be hearing from them soon." He'd better, he thought. Time was getting short. He had to find her. He turned to the woman who would be the one to make it all happen. He didn't really love her, but being who she was, he needed her. She was the means to it all, now that the bitch had found him out.

"Honey, how much longer do I have to keep coloring my hair. I've always hated it, that's why I dye it blond." She ran her fingers through the short tresses. I can't believe she thinks this color is attractive. Why she hasn't dyed it. It is so unattractive."

"Not long, sweetheart. Now, what have you fixed us to eat? Talking about food, I see you haven't lost any weight and keeping your weight down is a must. You have to lay off the junk food. You have to be like her. You have to pass the test with the old man or this whole project is for nothing. You got it?"

"I'm trying, but it isn't easy being cooped up in this hole in the wall of a motel. How much longer is this going to take? Tell me, what happens if you don't find her? Will we have to scrap the whole thing? Maybe that would be for the best. We can still be happy. What do you say?"

"No! I don't want to hear that kind of talk again. Don't forget, you are in this as deep as I am. You could go to prison right along with me."

She bit her bottom lip. "I'll behave, do as you say."

"Good, now let's eat."

He watched her set up the small table with the carryout she ordered.

Damn woman, she didn't have two brain cells to rub together. When he'd first started working for the old man, and then met his daughter, that's when the plan materialized.

Chapter 17

They sat drinking a cup of coffee after finishing their meals. Martha and Frank had joined them. "The nursery is beautiful," Cindy said. The both of you have done a wonderful job. "You should see it, Rip. Martha painted a rainbow on the wall."

"I'm sorry I missed it, but I needed to stop at the post office. I'll see it when the baby comes. By the way, have you two found out what you're having?"

"One can find out if it's a boy or girl?" Cindy asked. What did the doctors have, x-ray vision or something, she wondered. Curious, she asked. "How do they do that?" She sat staring at Martha's swollen stomach. It had gotten quiet and she saw the three of them were staring at her strangely.

"You're kidding, right, Cindy?" Martha asked. "I mean, you know that they take pictures with ultra sound. They even give you a copy. I have it upstairs. Here, let me go get it; it will only take a minute."

She started to leave, but Rip laid his hand on her arm. "Martha, that won't be necessary." He didn't know what else to do. Everyone knew about ultrasounds unless you were born in the sticks or had--"Guys, Cindy is recovering from a bout of amnesia. She had a blow to her head. She really came out here for rest. She's recovered most of her memory, but there are a few things-- like ultrasound--that have been lost."

Martha looked from one to the other. "You two don't have to explain anything to us. Do they, Frank? Now I understand why you didn't know what a layette was. Then the four of them began laughing.

When the laughing subsided, Rip turned to Frank. "Frank, would you mind taking a picture of Cindy and me together?"

"Don't mind at all. We bought a Polaroid camera so we could take pictures of the baby and not wait for them to be developed. I'll go get it, it's upstairs."

"If it isn't too much trouble, we really would like a picture."

"No problem, be back in a jiffy."

After the picture taking, they left. Cindy asked Martha to have Frank call as soon as she went to have the baby.

They were headed home, when Cindy remembered she'd left the picture on the table. "Darn it."

"What did you say?"

"I left the picture on the table. What will they think after we asked for it in the first place?"

"Not a problem. We've only gone a few blocks. I'll turn around. I'll only be a minute," he said, pulling up to the curb.

"No, Rip, it's my fault. You stay in the truck and keep it running." She got out before he could refuse.

Frank grinned as she entered the restaurant and approached him.

"Forget something?" Frank said, as he held out an envelope.

"Yes," she smiled and took the envelope. "That happens when you lose your memory." Cindy winked, turned and left. She didn't see the men watching her from a corner table.

Rip looked over at her as they drove home. The interior lights showed enough of her face that he saw her beaming. "You are happy tonight?"

"Yes, very happy. You know Rip. I was thinking," She couldn't help but laugh when he pulled over to the side of the road.

"Have you remembered something? Is it coming back?" He could only hope and then again, if she had, he would lose her.

"No, silly, it's not that. I was thinking how lucky Martha and Frank are. I mean, one can see how much they love one another. Now they have a baby on the way, a product of their love."

He reached over and turned her face toward his with his thumb. "Cindy, you will have all that someday. It is what everyone wants." He wanted it too. He watched as she crossed her legs, causing the dress to crawl up just above her knees. Her legs were smooth and slender. He let his eyes focus on the exposed thigh. His heart raced so fast he could almost hear its rapid beat. He squirmed as his pants felt the pressure of pulsation between his legs. "Are we going on or had you planned on spending the night out here?" Cindy's voice brought him back to reality.

"Yes," he said, pulling back out onto the highway.

Back at the house, Rip helped her with her coat. He stood behind and let it slowly drop from her shoulders. Her perfume and the sight of her bare neck made his body weak with desire. The temptation was so strong he leaned forward and placed a row of ever so light kisses on her neck. He turned her around and as her coat fell to the floor, and pulled her tightly against him. Their bodies meshed, so he felt her very core. He lowered his head to the exposed cleavage and ran his tongue along the tops of each breast. She moaned as he reached with one hand to cup her breasts; smooth and firm as he'd remembered. He ran his tongue across her hardened nipples, causing her to shudder. His body reacted as he leaned his swollen manhood against her.

Cindy's heart beat rapidly as he kissed her neck, and when his tongue reached her breasts she thought she would die from want of him. She could feel his manhood pulsing as she felt the wetness and throbbing between her legs. He now looked at her and could see she wanted the same. When their lips met, she lost all control. "I want you," he whispered, as their tongues wrapped in their need to devour one another.

Rip picked her up and carried her to the couch where they now lay next to one another. He pulled the pins out that held her hair and let it flow about her. In the heat of their encounter, he unzipped her dress, her breasts lay exposed, as she wore no bra. He kissed one then the other as she pushed against him. Her hand found the spot it sought and she rubbed. He thought he would lose his mind with craving for her. He needed her and knew she felt the same as she cried out, "Rip please, I can't take much more." He pulled himself on top of her as she pulled her dress to the waist. He felt the hot spot, all wet and moist, ready and waiting as only a woman in need could be. He stood and started to remove his pants as he gazed at her. Then it hit him, what am I doing, taking advantage of her, not that she didn't want the same as he did at the moment. It was wrong, all wrong. He saw the need, a need he'd been about ready to satisfy. Yet he couldn't.

Cindy gazed up at Rip and wondered why he had stopped. She wanted him; she felt a chill and wanted his warmth. She wanted him now, couldn't he see that. "Rip, what is wrong? You look…."

"Listen Cindy, this is wrong, I shouldn't have started it. It's my doing and I'm sorry. Please, let's just go to bed."

"But I want you, Rip. I don't care that I don't know who I am. I know who I am now at this minute. I'm Cindy, a woman who wants you."

"Cindy, please. It wouldn't be fair to you." He watched her face fall, as she stood and turned her back to him and headed for her room in silence. If you only knew how much I want you Cindy, he thought. "Good-night," he called to her. "It was a pleasant evening," he whispered and then turned and went to his own room.

Cindy lay in bed staring into the darkened room. Her body still tingled with desire for him. He said that it had been a pleasant evening. She smiled. It truly had been a wonderful evening. Rip is right, she thought. She didn't know who she was or anything about her personal life, but that didn't mean she didn't want him. She wondered if she'd still feel the same once she found out her true identity. If only she could remember. She could try until she turned blue in the face, and she still wouldn't know. She beat on her pillow with her fist to relieve some of her frustration. Bandon jumped on her bed and stared at her with those big black eyes. "It's okay," she said, cuddling him next to her. "We are two abandoned souls."

Chapter 18

"This had better be good," he said angrily into the phone. "I've told you not to call me here at the office." Damn fools, he'd worked too hard for them to mess it up now. Not that they hadn't already. Plan 'B' had to work. He wasn't about to spend time in prison over their screw-ups. Why had he hired them anyway? He knew why, because he'd needed someone fast and they were available. "We've got her, Boss," Hank's voice rasped over the phone.

He leaned back in his chair as relief washed over him. With the old man due back in a few days, he was nervous. The old man would want to know where his precious daughter was. Why she wasn't there to greet him. On vacation, he'd tell him. Maybe they could still use plan 'A' as he originally hoped. "Where have you got her?" He asked Hank. He wanted to hear in the mountains, as he planned.

"Well, we don't actually have her...."

"What the hell? One minute you have her, and the next you don't. Which is it?" Imbeciles, he thought. He felt his blood pressure rise.

"We know where she is; we saw her this evening. She appeared to be just fine."

Well, he didn't give a damn how nice she looked. "Where the hell is she? You know if she goes to the police, I'm a goner, and you will go down with me. Now quit babbling about how she looks. When she's dead you tell me how she looks." Cold and still, he thought, and gone

"We saw her talking and joking with the hotel manager where we're staying. It seemed like they knew each other."

"Did she see you?"

"No, we don't think so."

"I don't want you to think so. I want you to know, because if she saw you—well, never mind, just get her and do your job."

"We're sure she didn't see us. She didn't look our way."

"Is she staying at the hotel?"

"No, we watched her get into a pick-up truck with some guy."

A guy, well, that figured. She'd never been able to take care of herself, her daddy saw to that. Pampered wasn't the word for it; she asked and Daddy provided. Money had never been a problem. He wondered how she'd been doing without any money. He had checked the banks and her credit cards, she hadn't touched them. This guy, who ever he was, had to be taking care of her. "Who is this man?"

"Oh come on, Boss, give Jake and me some credit. We followed them to this guy's place. It's close to the spot where we lost her."

"I don't want anymore mess-ups! Do you hear me?"

"Don't worry, Boss, we've got it under control. We're playing it smart. Jake here asked the hotel owner, 'who's that pretty lady?' "Guess what?"

"What? Damn it man, just get to it!"

"He say's she's there helping this guy with a book he's writing. According to the hotel manager, she's here recuperating from amnesia."

"Are you telling me she has amnesia?"

"Yes, that's what the hotel guy said. Now what do we do, Boss? You want Jake and me to go and get her and take her to where we first had planned?"

"No, let me think." Amnesia, it could work to his benefit. "What is the guy's name, the one she's staying with?"

"Robert Walker; he was a detective, moved here to write a book. He keeps to himself. This Walker fellow is too young to be retired, but that's what we were told, that he's retired. Walker and her sure were friendly."

He's a retired cop. That could be a little sticky, but nothing he couldn't handle. "Hank, I want you and Jake to hold tight. I'm coming out there." He looked at his watch. If he left in the morning, he could be there by early afternoon. "Listen, I should be there around one or two in the afternoon. What hotel are you at again?"

"It's the only one in town. Is there anything you want us to do, Boss? What's the plan?"

"No, just sit tight until I get there." He didn't want them screwing this up too. As far as a plan, he hadn't decided on one yet, but he'd have one before he got there. He would have to play this very carefully. "I'll see you two tomorrow," he said and hung up. He had some hard thinking to do. He buzzed his receptionist. "I've got to go out of town for a few days. I need you to cancel all my appointments, don't reschedule. If they have any questions, tell them I'll be in touch when I get back."

He started to hang up when she asked. "Sir, where are you going? You know, in case Mr. Bradford should return early. You know how he is; he likes to know everyone's whereabouts."

"I should be back before then. If not, I'll worry about that later. Now I've got to run, I've things to do before I leave." He likes to know where everyone is, he mimicked. Well, for once the old man wouldn't have to know.

Chapter 19

Cindy awoke to the sound of birds chirping. She stretched and arched her body, a motion that caused Bandon to jump up on her. "Bandon, you scared me." She pulled him into her arms and rubbed her face in his fur. "I bet you need to go outside."

She thought of last night as she showered, letting the water beat against her face. It had been a wonderful evening until the end of it. She cared for Rip and now knew he felt the same. She could still feel his lips as they ignited her body. They'd wanted each other, the heat and desire had been there. Rip had been right to pull away. She didn't think she'd have had the willpower. She needed to find her identity and then she would be free. Free to show him how much she cared for him; but then she thought, stepping from the shower, I may already be in love with someone else. No, she couldn't be. How could one be committed to someone else and feel as she did toward Rip? She'd so wanted him, to come together and bring them both to the point of ecstasy where they felt as one. Yet she knew he'd done the right thing. If only she could remember. She pressed her hands against the side of her head.

She pulled on her jeans and one of Rip's plaid shirts. Her sweaters needed washing, something she would do today. She brushed her long hair and let it fall about her shoulders. With a dab of lipstick and a quick glance in the mirror, she felt ready to face another day. She had a strong feeling that today would be the day. The day she'd remember. "I'm ready, let's go, Bandon."

"Good mor…." Her words died when she didn't see Rip in the kitchen. He wasn't in the living room either. It was nearly noon. She'd slept most of the day away. She looked up to his bedroom. The door stood open. "Rip, are you up there?" When he didn't respond, she glanced outside. Bandon went out barking. "You run and play, I'll be out shortly." Where could Rip be? Then she noticed the truck missing. He'd gone somewhere, and without her! Well, what she did expect? He couldn't wait all day for her to wake up. She wondered what time he'd left. Why hadn't he awakened her?

In the kitchen, she poured herself a glass of orange juice when she spotted the note held by a butterfly magnet on the refrigerator. "Gone to clear some brush along the river. You were sleeping so soundly that I didn't want to wake you. Cindy, I'm sorry about last night. I shouldn't have taken advantage of you in your condition." It was signed, "your partner, Rip."

Sorry, he had nothing to be sorry for, and what about her condition, amnesia had to do with the brain, not the heart. She'd wanted him just as much. In fact, she still did. She jumped at the sound of a vehicle coming up the lane. Rip, she thought, and went running outside, only to stop short. It wasn't Rip's truck. A shiny, dark black sedan appeared from the tree-lined lane. She squinted against the sun that beat onto the car. She'd never seen a car like that in town. It came to a stop about ten feet from her.

She wished Rip were home. She wanted to run, but knew she couldn't go running from every stranger who approached. He's probably here to see Rip about his book. Rip had said his editor might come by. She waited. It took the person a long time to get out of the car.

The car door finally swung open. Cindy breathed out slowly, not realizing that she'd been holding her breath. A very tall slender man wearing a gray suit stepped from the car. The sun shone bright on his blond hair. She couldn't see his eyes for he wore sunglasses. As he started to approach, he called to her, "Cynthia, oh my God, it is you." Cindy stepped back. He'd called her Cynthia. She took a few more steps back. She didn't know why, but suddenly her throat got tight and it seemed hard to breathe. Her heart began to race as he called to her again. That voice, she knew it from somewhere. Her head began to swim and the last thing she remembered was Bandon barking.

Rip pulled the last of the logs, limbs, and brush that had gathered from the bend in the river. Every year it was the same thing, the melting snow and rain washed them into the river causing a dam, which trapped the fish. He stood, stretched and headed back to the truck. His body ached and it wasn't because of the hard work he'd just accomplished. It still ached from last night. He'd wanted Cindy, still did, but not under these conditions. She could belong to another and that wouldn't be right. He'd have to wait. He knew she'd wanted him. She had said so. He remembered the way she responded. That sweet moist pulsating spot between her legs had been ready and waiting, wanting release. It had taken all his willpower not to take her. His body now responded to just thinking about her. He couldn't wait to see her. He hoped she wasn't too upset with him. He looked at his watch. She'd be up now. This job had taken longer than expected. He put his shovel and ax in the back of the truck. He couldn't wait to get home.

As he pulled into the clearing he spotted the car. A chill ran down his spine. He didn't recognize the vehicle, but knew it to be a rental from the license plates. He pulled the truck to a halt. That's when he saw Bandon tied to a post. They'd never tied him up. He sat there whining. What is going on? He went running into the house, almost breaking the door down in his haste. His main concern was for Cindy.

He stormed in the front door to see a man bent over Cindy, who lay on the couch. Anger and rage engulfed him as he reached out, pulling the man to his feet, and hit him across the jaw. The man fell and went sliding across the floor. "Who the hell are you?" He asked, but the man lay dazed. He turned to Cindy, who looked a pale gray. "Are you all right? Has he hurt you?" Rip knelt beside her. He turned to the man, who slowly got to his feet. "If you've laid a hand on her, I'll...."

"Rip, please, I'm fine,' Cindy said touching his arm. "I fainted and he brought me in and laid me on the couch."

"Please, Mr. Walker, I presume that's your name?"

"Yes, I'm Mr. Walker." Rip didn't like the man already with his high and mighty attitude. "Who are you?"

"I'm Mark Osgood, Cythina's--my fiance'."

"I don't...."

"Please Rip, let him explain." She started to sit up, but the stranger who claimed to be her fiance' said,

"Darling, I think it best that you lay still for a while. You've had a terrible shock."

She felt fine and didn't need some stranger, no matter who he said he was, giving her orders. She sat up with Rip's help.

"Are you sure you're okay?" Rip asked, sitting beside her. "You still look a little peaked." "I'm fine now that you're here." That she was. Whoever this man claimed to be, he made her uncomfortable. He wasn't a bad looking guy. In fact he was quite good looking, in a feminine way; tall, slender and with natural blond hair. He sported a tan, which meant he spent a lot of time in the sun or went to a tanning salon. His hands were well manicured, and she wondered what he did for a living, nothing physical, that's for sure. He had an air of refinement. She glanced from him to Rip. Now Rip, he definitely was a man's man. He was as different from this man as night is from day. Mark seemed fastidious, where Rip reflected earthiness, strength and a caring nature. He was a man she'd come to trust, but how could she have these feelings for Rip and be promised in marriage to this man who stood before them? She looked over at Mark and felt nothing but fear. How could that be?

"I need proof," Rip said. "You can't just walk in here and say things and expect us to believe you. As you can see, Cindy doesn't recognize you. Cindy, do you know who he is?"

She shook her head. "No I don't."

Hell, he could be in with those that she'd run from, Rip thought. He looked over at the man with the fancy suit. No, he wouldn't let her go. He'd said he would protect her and damn it, that's what he planned to do. He'd become fond of her, more than that, he'd come to--he couldn't say that word, but his heart felt something more. He wasn't about to let her leave on one man's word. "I'm asking you to leave." He went to the door and placed his hand on the doorknob. Bandon, who'd broken loose, stood at his feet growling at the man. He didn't like this man either.

"I've found her and I don't plan to leave without her," Mark said. "Cynthia, please, your father will be worried sick if you're not home when he arrives from Europe."

Cindy rubbed her temples. He said Father, she had a father. What other family did she have? She looked over at the man who seemed to know more about her than she did. It was frightening for her to not know her own self. "I don't know," she stammered. "I told you that I hit my head and can't recall anything. If it wasn't for Rip," she smiled at him.

"I'm very grateful," Mark said. "Once you're home, and around familiar surroundings, I'm sure your memory will return."

Had Cindy told him she had amnesia. Rip wondered what else she had told him. He hoped not much of anything. He'd always been a good judge of character and there was something about this man that he didn't trust. What he said might be true, but something about the man didn't seem geniune. "I still want proof," Rip said, his voice carrying a tone of authority. After all, this happened to be his home and he'd remove the man by force if necessary. By the looks of him, Rip didn't feel that would be a difficult task.

Cindy glanced at Mark and wondered if he had such proof that she was indeed Cynthia Bradford. No wonder she'd liked the name Cindy when Rip mentioned it, it truly was her name. Cindy being the short verson for Cynthia. She preferred Cindy. "I've proof in the car," Mark said.

Rip watched him walk toward his car and hoped he'd get in it and drive away, but he didn't. Rip returned to Cindy's side, taking a seat next to her. "Cindy, are you sure you don't recognize this man, even a little bit?"

"Rip, I don't, I've tried. I only know that he makes me uneasy. I don't know why, he just does, that's all. Rip, I'm afraid."

"I said I'd take care of you." He held her hands in his and could feel her tension. He still hadn't figured out how this guy knew Cindy was here at his place. Those men, that's it, they worked for him, but they hadn't seen her, or had they? Maybe the men saw her when they went to town. He'd been careful and scanned the area where they were and not once had he seen them. He then saw the man walking toward the door. He'd soon find out what this man had or didn't have. Cindy gripped his hands tightly. "Relax, let's see what he's got," Rip said. Cindy moved closer to him, their bodies touching. Any other time he would have enjoyed this, not that he didn't now, but he had to keep his mind on this man who'd come to take her away from him. He didn't care what the man had. He'd promised to protect her until her memory came back. She belonged under his care, not some stranger's. "Well, what have you got?" He asked, as the man came to stand a few feet from them.

"If you don't mind," Mark said, placing a briefcase on the coffee table. "I've brought pictures of Cynthia, her father and me. I've even brought our engagement announcement that was in the paper."

Cindy leaned over to have a look at the items in question. The picture sure enough looked like her. She stood in the middle smiling; with her arms around the two men in the picture. One man being Mark and the other, she looked closer. So this was her father. He was a tall man, not slender or heavy, medium built with a head of white hair. He wore a pair of dark-rimmed glasses. He was smiling at her. She reached for the newspaper clipping, another picture of her and this man who called himself Mark. Underneath the picture she read, 'The well-known and prominent billionare banker Mr. Harry Bradford III proudly announces his daughter's engagement to Mark Osgood, who works for Mr. Bradford, at an elegant affair at the Maple Grove Country Club. Those in attendance said Miss Cynthia Bradford's dress of cream satin enhanced her beauty. The May wedding will be one spectacular event with a host of dignataries invited. The lucky groom, Mr. Mark Osgood, a businessman himself, has worked two years for the bank.' Cindy dropped the clipping and turned to Mark. "My father is rich?" She saw that Rip had picked up the article and began reading. She saw how his face suddenly paled.

Rip couldn't help but notice that the pictures looked like Cindy. Anyone could have made them up, but not the picture in the paper.

"Yes, rich and very much loved," Mark said. He handed her the Fortune magazine in which he had pages marked. "Open them, Cynthia, and then tell me that you deny who you are after seeing the pictures."

Cindy opened the magazine so that Rip and she could look together. Pictures of her and Mr. Bradford riding horses together, on a trip in London, on a cruise ship, at numerous dinner parties. All had captions under them, telling about the famous Mr. Harry Bradford III and his beautiful daughter. "Is that really me?" She glanced over at Rip.

Rip had to admit that the pictures sure resembled her, more than that, they were identical. The woman in the pictures looked like she didn't have a care in the world. A happy person, yet he could see sadness in her eyes. He looked closer at the pictures and then turned to Cindy again. He saw that same look now. "Cindy, I want to make a few calls. I want to check a few things out. I won't be long." He smiled, and reached down and picked up Bandon and put him on her lap. "Keep her company till I get back," he said and patted Bandon on the head. He turned and glanced at Mark, "Don't touch her," then headed toward the stairs.

Cindy sat avoiding the stranger and kept looking at the pictures in the magazine, not so much at the woman who looked like her, but at the older man. Was this man her father? If so, why didn't she recognize him or at least have some sort of recollection? She sat rubbing Bandon's fur and trying to make some sense of all this. "Cynthia, I know this is difficult for you," Mark said and started to sit down beside her, but Bandon growled, showing his baby teeth. Mark backed away and sat in the lounge chair. "What kind of mutt is that? I wasn't going to hurt you."

"Bandon isn't a mutt, he's a wolf and very protective of me. His mother died and I'm taking care of him, and I'd prefer that you call me Cindy." She saw his forehead wrinkle. "Did I say something wrong?"

"Wrong, no, but I must say you've changed."

"How is that? I've no recall one way or another."

"The Cynthia, sorry, Cindy I know would never stand for anyone calling her anything but Cynthia. When she walked into a room everyone noticed. She had that air of sophistication that so many women want. She was a goddess of her time, and she loved horses, rode all the time. In fact she loved all animals. She had a caring heart where they were concerned. She cared about a lot of things. Yet one didn't want to cross her, because if they did, they had an enemy for life."

Cindy wanted to know about the elderly man in the pictures. She wondered if there was a mother. "Mark, let's just say I'm the one you are looking for." He started to say something, but she shushed him. "Hear me out, please. How did my father and I get along? Where is my mother? I don't see any pictures of her." She surely had a mother.

"Your father is a very prominent businessman. Well-liked and respected. His work is important to him, as he has taken over from his father and his grandfather before him. He runs a three-generation empire, but nothing, not even his work, is as important as his daughter. She, you, Cindy, are his life. You come before all else."

"My mother?" Cindy wanted to know as much as possible.

"A lovely woman, from what I've heard. I never met her. She died when you, Cynthia, excuse me, habits are hard to change. She died when you were only ten years old. Some sort of heart ailment."

Cindy wondered if the girl in the pictures looked like her mother, for she sure didn't see any resemblence to her father in the pictures.

"Cindy, you must come back with me. I'll take you to the best of doctors. This is no place for you. Look at it, it's so--plain and out in no man's land. Look at you, you are dressed in rags. The Cindy I knew wouldn't be caught in such attire. You are used to the best money can buy. You love lights, glimmer, and an active social life."

"I like what I have on. It's comfortable. I like the quiet here with the birds chirping and watching rabbits and squirrels run about. The air here is refreshing." Which you are not, she thought.

"All I'm saying is that this is not you. You'll never get your memory back if you stay here. You need to come home where there are people who love you and can take care of you."

"Mark, you are wrong about this place, it has character, and Rip has taken good care of me. I don't miss the things I don't remember having. I like it here."

"I'm glad to hear that," Rip said descending the stairs. He stopped in front of Cindy. "May I see you in your room?" He glanced toward Mark. "Make yourself comfortable, we'll only be a few minutes."

"Mr. Walker, I don't think it proper that...."

"Mr. Osgood, please, I've cleaned and bathed this woman. I'm sure I can be trusted with a few moments of privacy." He saw the shock on Mark's face. It turned a beet red. He smiled, taking hold of Cindy's hand, leading her towards her room. If he'd wanted to harm Cindy he wouldn't have waited until some prissy from the city came around to object.

"Rip, what's wrong?" Cindy asked as soon as they entered her room. "Cindy, have a seat on the bed," he said, shutting the door behind them. "Rip, I don't think this is the time for any...."

"Cindy, I wasn't thinking of that, but now that you mention it, it doesn't sound like a bad idea." He reached over to put his arms around her, causing Bandon to jump from her arms. "Rip, really, I'm serious."

"I am too, now sit still. I need to check out something and I can't if you won't sit still." He pulled her hair back from her left ear. He saw the dark brown spot about a half inch in size, behind the top of her ear.

"Rip, what are you doing? You're messing up my hair." She pulled away. "What has gotten into you?" She ran her fingers through her hair. Then he began to laugh. "What is so funny?" She searched his face. "I don't see anything funny, and what that man out there is suggesting is certainly not funny."

"I'm sorry, Cindy. It's just that I have to laugh or I might want to go out there and beat the living shit out of that man before I kick him out of my house. How you could be engaged to him is beyond me!"

Cindy started to say something until she heard his last words. Engaged, he actually said she and that feminine speciman of a man were--no, it couldn't be true. "Rip, no more joking around. Tell me what is going on?"

"You truly are Cynthia Bardford just like he says."

Cindy stared at Rip. He had to be kidding. She couldn't be, yet those pictures. "Rip please, no more pulling my leg. I can't take it. If you thought by saying that, that it would jog my memory, well, it didn't."

"Cindy, I hope I'm wrong, but I just got off the phone with Sarah, you remember me talking about her? The policewoman that I used to work with." She nodded, and he continued. "I sent her that picture of us at the hotel. She recognized you immediately. I guess she's up on all the celebrities. She even described Mark to a tee. She couldn't believe that you were actually in my house. Said I wasn't your type. She also said there hasn't been anything in the newspapers about you being missing. She'd heard somewhere that you'd gone on vacation to an undisclosed place."

Rip hadn't liked what he'd heard from Sarah. In fact, his chest hurt at the thought that her and that man out there could--he had hoped that Sarah was wrong. "I had Sarah do some further checking. That's what took me so long upstairs. I wanted proof, a birthmark, anything that would help. Sarah searched on this new identity database that is open to all law enforcement facilities. A wonderful program that was put into place after I retired. Miss

Bardford's passport described Miss Bradford a dark birthmark on the left side of her head behind her left, upper ear."

"Rip, you're saying that I'm that woman, Miss Bradford?" She ran to the bathroom, slammed the door and turned the lock. She sat on the toilet as the tears flowed. She didn't want to be this Cythina Bradford. She wanted to be herself, Cindy, the Cindy who wanted Rip. She didn't want that man, this Mark Osgood, and all his fancy ways. She wanted…. She didn't know what she wanted. Damn it, why couldn't she remember?

Rip lay back on the bed with his arms folded across his chest. What had he done? He stared at the bathroom door. He'd only tried to make her think and see that she could be this Cynthia Bradford. He knew after seeing the birthmark that she most likely was. Sarah had been positive. She'd said there were a few other avenues that she wanted to check out, but it only had to do with her curiosity about the rich and gorgeous Miss Bradford. Bandon jumped up on his chest and proceeded to wet his face down with his tongue. "Yes, I hear it too," he patted Bandon on the top of the head. Rip went to the bathroom. "Cindy, please stop crying and open the door. We need to talk."

"Go away, leave me alone," Cindy sobbed. How could he just let her go? Didn't he care, not even a little? Then she heard his voice again. "Cindy, please, you don't have to leave." Her heart ached for him. Was it love, or that she felt protected? She only knew that she became excited and flustered when he was around. She heard Bandon whining and scratching at the door. Poor Bandon, she couldn't abandon him. Rip had said she didn't have to leave. Did he mean it, or was it a ploy to get her out of the bathroom? She couldn't stay in here forever; besides, there was that man out in the living room, waiting to take her away. Well, she wouldn't go. She splashed water on her face and slowly opened the door. One look at Rip and she began crying again. "I'm afraid," she said and leaned into him, her face against his chest, as they wrapped their arms around each other. She felt safe and secure in his embrace. "Rip, I don't want to leave."

"You don't have to." He pulled her away from him as he stared into her eyes. He could see the fear. She didn't know that man out in the living room any more than she had known him a few weeks ago. Everyone was a stranger. "Let's sit down on the bed for a few minutes. I want to discuss a few things with you, rationally. I don't want you getting upset, because this needs to be worked out. Good," he said, seeing her nod her assent.

"First off, and don't get on the defensive, but all indications are that you very likely could be this Cynthia Bradford." He saw her cringe a little, but she straightened up and said. "Okay, so if I am, what next?"

He couldn't help but admire her, she might be scared, but she had strength and stamina. Most women would've been undone by now. Cindy took it moment by moment. She'd adopted in Bandon, which showed her to be caring. Now she wanted to know what they would do next. He didn't know, but he wasn't letting her go with this man. He'd take her wherever she wanted to go, Chicago, her home, anywhere she asked. Yet one thing still bothered him, who or what was she running from that day? How had Mark Osgood known she was here? Cindy had asked what next. Well, he had a plan.

Chapter 20

Cindy and Rip returned to the living room, took seats on the couch, and held hands as Rip spoke. "This has all come as a tremendous shock to Cindy, and with her having amnesia, it is even harder. She has told me that she doesn't have any recollection of you or anyone in the pictures that you've been so kind to show us. I have talked to a friend of mine on the police force in Chicago. That's what I was doing up in my room earlier. I described Cindy to her and she did some checking. She is a big fan of Miss Bradford's." Rip grinned at Cindy. He could see her nervousness, but she smiled in return. He turned his attention back to the man, who looked ill at ease, and yes, upset.

"I just wish you hadn't called the police. You see, Mr. Bradford doesn't like that type of publicity. I've forgotten to tell you. Cynthia's father doesn't know that she is missing. He thinks she's on vacation. Cynthia, I do think it best that you pack your bags and come with me, now."

Cindy started to say something, but Rip interrupted. He wanted to let this man know where they stood. He didn't want Cindy to start crying again. "Listen, Mr. Osgood, if that truly is your name," Rip said, seeing the man reach for his wallet. "I-- we will need more proof than a driver's license. What you say may be all well and good, but there is one thing that Cindy does remember." The man's face lost its tan look and paled. Why? Rip wondered as he continued. "You see, she knows she was running from something or someone, and that someone could be you."

There, he'd said it. The man's face, which had been pale, turned red with anger as he stood and marched to the picture window, his back to them. With his hands clasped tightly behind his back, Rip could see the tension in his stance as he gazed out at the woods.

"Rip, what…." Cindy began to say, but he shushed her by placing his index finger over her soft lips.

"Wait," he whispered. A few moments passed before Osgood turned around and returned to his chair, a controlled look on his face.

"You make this very difficult, both of you. I hadn't wanted to do this, but I see no other way."

Rip felt Cindy poke him in the ribs with her elbow. "It's okay, let's hear what he has to say," he whispered. "I'm not letting him leave with you." She smiled up at him as Osgood continued.

"You were running from yourself. You were on drugs. I tried to get you to quit, but nothing seemed to work. You were getting bad, and I was afraid your father would find out. Here we were, planning on getting married in a few months, and you had to start with that stuff."

Cindy put her hand to her ears. Drugs, what is he talking about! She never remembered doing anything of the sort, but then, she didn't remember a lot of things. She looked over at Rip and could see his jaw tighten. She turned back to the man who claimed to be her fiancé. Now he claimed she did drugs.

Rip felt like punching the man, but held his fisted hands tightly at his side. The man had to be lying, and then he remembered how delirious and foggy Cindy had been when she'd first got there. He thought it had been the hit on the head. Could it have been the combination? He saw a look of disbelief on her face. In the past few weeks, as he came to know her, she'd shown no signs of withdrawal.

"You were at a party a few months ago," Osgood continued. "You thought it was the cool thing to do to try it. When I found out, I was furious. I tried to get you to stop, but you wouldn't listen."

Lies, Rip thought, all lies. The man was full of bullshit. His detective's instincts told him the man wasn't to be trusted. "Mr. Osgood, I'm still confused as to why Cindy happened to be here in Wisconsin when she's from Chicago. She was found wearing nothing but a flimsy nightgown."

"Cindy, I'm sorry about all this," Mark said, ignoring this barbaric man. He wanted to punch his lights out, but knew the man could overpower him. He had to be subtle. "Cynthia, you came home late one night all drugged out. We were supposed to be going to a party at the mayor's house, but when I saw how bad you were—well, I got mad and put you to bed. I called a few people and rented a place about fifty miles from here. I hired these people to take you there. I tried to talk you into going on your own, you know, to dry yourself out, but you argued. I had you tied, gagged, and put in a rental car. You were wearing your nightgown, a flowing white thin thing, but I was afraid, with all the commotion you were making that Grace, she's the maid, would come into your room. I wrapped you in a blanket and when all was quiet, got you out of the house. You got away from the men I hired when the car got a flat tire. I only had your best interests at heart. Please, you have to believe me. I meant you no harm. I love you. Please come home." He hated begging, but if that's what it took--he'd do anything to get her away from this man, his life depended on it. If only those men hadn't screwed up, he wouldn't have to be groveling like some fool.

Best interests my ass, Rip thought. He wanted to tear into Osgood. He'd hired them all right, not to help her, but to do away with her. He'd bet money on it, but he didn't have any proof. He turned to the sorry specimen of a man and asked. "How did you know she was here?"

"At the hotel, she'd forgotten a camera or something and one of my men saw her. They've been scouring the area for you. I've been concerned the worst had happened. The amnesia, we can work on. At least you're alive."

Cindy sat looking from one man to the other. If what Mark said was true, then why did she have this ill feeling toward him? She stared long and hard at him, but nothing came to mind. She turned to Rip, her lips curved up into a half smile. She felt comforted and protected with him. She trusted him. He'd saved her life. He could have taken her into town and turned her over to the police, but he'd been willing to help her. She wondered if he still would help. She had an idea.

"Mr. Osgood, Rip, I've not said much, but I've been listening." She picked up the magazine and pictures from the coffee table. "If I am truly this person," she waved them in front of her.

"You are," Mark said. "Can't you see that? Please call me Mark; you've never called me Mr. Osgood."

"Let her speak, will you," Rip stopped him. "Go ahead, Cindy." He encouraged her, but had to admit his nerves were a bit on edge. He hoped she wasn't planning something stupid.

"Mr. Osgood, I mean Mark, I've just met you, not that I don't know you, but I have no recollection of you. I do however know Rip. In the past few weeks, I've come to know and trust him. After all, he saved my life. I may be this Cynthia Bradford. That is something I have to find out yet, something I know I can't do by staying here."

"Good, you've come to your senses," Mark said. Thank goodness, she's come to her senses. He'd thought he might have to revert to drastic measures. He forced a smile at her and asked, "When can you be ready to leave?"

"She's not going anywhere with you," Rip said. "Cindy, you can't be truly thinking of...."

"Please, the both of you, be quiet for a few minutes and let me explain. Then you can argue all you want." When they both sat quiet, she continued.

"I too want to know the truth and find out who I am more than anyone. It's my life." She saw them both nod. "You've been great, Rip, taking me in and letting me stay here, not knowing anything about me." Rip nodded at her while Mark gave her a look of discontent. The fear of not knowing who she was plagued her. Fearful or not, she couldn't go on like this. A lump had developed in her throat because of what she was about to suggest. She didn't want to do this but saw no other way. She sat up and squaring her shoulders said. "I'm going back to Chicago." She saw a look of relief on Mark's face. Rip ran his fingers through that beautiful head of hair of his but didn't say a word. He sat there staring at her as if he couldn't believe what she had said. Her heart went out to him. She would miss him. The thought of leaving him and this place she'd called home for the past few weeks wouldn't be easy, but it was something she had to do to find the truth. She hoped Rip would visit her. She didn't want to lose touch with him. "Rip, I don't know how to thank you...."

"Cindy, I can't believe what I'm hearing. You're just going to leave with this man, this stranger? Tell me I'm not hearing you right." She didn't know what she was doing. She couldn't. Well, he wouldn't let her leave. "Cindy...."

"Please, Rip, let me finish," Cindy said, interrupting Rip. He had to hear her out. "Just hear me out, and then I'll let you say whatever it is you want."

"Go for it, but it better be good," Rip said, because the way he felt, she wasn't going anywhere with this man.

"Thanks," Cindy gave him a warm glance. Her heart went out to him. But she had to do what she knew was right. She addressed Mark. "I want you to leave now, today, this minute. Go back to Chicago."

"But I thought you said you were coming?"

"I am, but not with you. I want you to give me directions, and let me see, today is Thursday, and I'll be there on Saturday by mid afternoon. That's if Rip will take me?"

"Now wait just one minute. I'm not standing for that. Cynthia, I'm your fiancé. This man is a stranger. You must come with me. I won't do it. I won't leave you here with him."

If his eyes could shoot daggers, Rip would be dead, as Mark glared at him. Rip looked over at Cindy and knew she was serious in what she wanted.

Cindy ignored Mark and turned to Rip. "Will you take me to the place that is supposed to be my home?"

"Of course, if that's what you really want. You don't have to go there; we can work things out from here." He saw that she felt she needed to go. He didn't want her to. He'd come to enjoy having her around. The place would be empty without her. He'd come to care for her more than he wanted to admit to himself. "You really want to do this, Cindy?" He had to ask one more time.

"I don't, but I have to. It's the only way I'm going to know if I truly am this Cynthia Bradford. Maybe being there, around familiar things, my memory will return. If it doesn't, I'll just take it day by day." Rip seemed at a loss for words, which surprised her. He usually always had some remark, good or bad. She saw moisture in his eyes. He cared very much that she was leaving, but why, when she'd been nothing but a burden to him? He should be relieved. Could he really care about her?

Mark finally left, after seeing that Cindy wouldn't have it any other way. Cindy and Rip sat quietly next to each other on the couch, each lost in their own thoughts. Cindy held Bandon in her lap as she wondered what lay ahead for her. She would be going to a place and life foreign to her. She wondered if the rest of her life would be that way, charting the unknown. Bandon began to lick her face. She laughed. "I'm going to miss you," she ruffled his small gray ears. She felt Rip staring at her and turned to him. Their eyes met and held until Rip said, "I'm going to miss you too."

He wouldn't see her smile in the mornings or her hair mussed up as she came out to breakfast. He'd miss her laughter when--damn it, why did she have to go? He didn't feel right about this whole situation. This thing about her being on drugs, didn't sit right with him. He watched her now, petting Bandon. No, Osgood was wrong. He needed to call Sarah.

Chapter 21

They'd been on the road for about an hour, with neither one saying a word. Cindy glanced over at Rip, who looked anything but happy. Cindy knew he didn't like this whole thing. Her eyes dropped down to the map on the seat between them. In another few hours, they would be there. She shivered in anticipation.

This silent treatment of Rip's drove her crazy. "Rip, you haven't said a word, not one since we left the house. You've kept your eyes focused straight ahead." She noticed his jaw tighten, but he still hadn't budged. He just continued to stare at the road. She couldn't stand the quiet any longer, she'd scream. She reached over and turned the radio on. The sound of Celine Dion's voice filled the cab of the truck as she sang 'Where Does My heart Beat Now?' She leaned her head back against the top of the seat. Where does my heart beat? She thought and glanced at Rip. Her heart beat for him. If she let her heart guide her, she would've stayed with him. Forget this man Mark, who said they were engaged. She needed to find out the truth about herself. She hummed to the radio as another song began to play, but suddenly all got quiet again. Rip shut the radio off. "Well, at least you're alive. I'd begun to think that a robot sat behind the wheel.' Nothing, he said nothing. They pulled into a small town and stopped at the places only stoplight. This silence had to end. She opened the truck door.

"What the hell are you doing?" Rip said.

"If you'll unlock the back so I can get the bag with my clothes, I'll be out of your hair shortly," she answered. She'd find a bus or something to get her to Chicago. She stood by the curb with her hands on her hips. Rip pulled the truck over. She watched him get out of the truck, and by the way, he walked toward her, she knew he was upset. The crease between his eyes had gotten deeper. She furtively searched for a place to escape to, for she'd never seen him so mad. She spotted a restaurant across the street and started for it when Rip hollered, "Cindy, watch out!" Then she felt his arm grab hers as he pulled her against him. She heard the sound of a horn as a semi flew past them. Rip had saved her life for a second time. She started to say thank you, but didn't have a chance.

"That was a damn fool thing to do. What are you trying to do, get yourself killed? Now get back in the truck and quit acting like some spoiled brat."

Brat, how dare he insinuate. She felt him tug on her arm again. "Now stop this nonsense and get in." He held the door for her, but she didn't budge and stood stiffly with her arms folded over her chest. "No."

"What do you mean no? This was your idea, or have you forgotten? You could have stayed at the house. We could have checked out Osgood and all the things he claimed. We could have gone to Chicago to check this all out. You didn't have to do this, go there alone. Why? What do you hope to gain? You don't know what lies ahead. Have you forgotten that Matt saw you running? Cindy, I don't trust this Osgood character. You don't know what you're getting yourself into. Please think about what you are planning."

She looked at him standing there, handsome as ever, she thought. She had to admit that what she was about to do scared her, but she couldn't hide behind Rip. None of this was his problem. Matt found her and Rip took care of her during her amnesia. She would forever be grateful, but she couldn't stay hidden, and hope to find herself. She knew it was the right thing, going to Chicago and facing the past, in hopes of jarring her memory.

"Rip, please let me do this. I love your place with its tranquillity and fresh air, with its tall mountains, small hills, and rivers. I hope to return someday. That's if you don't mind? This is something I have to do. I'd hoped you would understand and wish me well." The line between his eyes softened and he smiled, not a big one, but a smile. He reached over and put his arm around her. Their eyes met and his held a look of concern. At that second, Cindy knew he truly cared about her.

"Cindy, I do wish you well. I do, and I don't understand your thinking, but I can see that you are determined to go ahead with this plan of yours no matter what I say, so let's call a truce. You get in the truck and I'll take you on to Chicago." He felt her shoulders relax. "Promise to talk? I can't stand it when you are quiet," she said.

They chatted for the rest of the trip about Rip's house. How he planned to build the steps to the river. They talked about his book, Cindy saying now that he didn't have her to worry about; he could get back to his writing. They were on the last twenty or so miles, when Rip turned the conversation back to her decision.

"Cindy, we are almost there. You still have time to change your mind," he said. She shook her head. She sure is stubborn, he thought. He liked women who had a mind of their own. "Well, at least let me drive you up to the house, and before you say no, hear me out. You don't know the area and anything could happen. I'd feel a lot better knowing you got there okay."

She'd planned to take a taxi after he dropped her off at the bus station, but what would it hurt for him to take her to the house? Why didn't she want him to take her to the house? It had been Mark's idea to get a taxi. Why? He said he would be at the house to meet her. She went over the story Mark had worked out to explain her extended absence. She had taken an unscheduled vacation and while on the trip had fallen and bumped her head, causing a memory loss.

Rip turned onto Cambridge, the street Mark had given them. She'd finally given in and let him drive her up to the house. He knew the area. It was where some of the wealthiest and most prestigious families lived. They had guarded gates and sprawling lawns and trees that hid the beautiful three-to four-story mansions with six to eight garages. Some had one or more guesthouses, or additional guest wings.

When he stopped in front of the last house on the road, he faced Cindy. "This is it. Are you ready?" He wasn't. He didn't like the idea, hadn't from the beginning, but what could he do, besides kidnap her? She was looked pale. This whole thing was taking its toll on her. He couldn't imagine what she could be thinking, but if her face was any indication, she was afraid. She faced him and smiled. He couldn't help but admire her determination.

"I can't see the house," Cindy said. She took in the big double gate with sides held by tall, white, cement pillars. Trees lined the endless drive. She spotted rooftops that she assumed were part of the house. Her home, or was it? She looked over at Rip. "I don't remember any of this, nothing looks familiar." She started to open the truck door when Rip spoke. "You don't have to go through with this. I can turn the truck around. Just say the word."

"I've come this far." She shut the door as Rip got out and retrieved her bag from the back of the truck. He followed her to the gate, where she pressed the intercom. A deep voice sounded. "May I help you?"

Cindy looked over at Rip, as he nodded his head. Cindy tried to swallow but her throat tightened. The voice asked again, "May I help you?"

"This is Cindy, may I…," she stammered as her voice broke.

"Miss Bradford, you're back!" the voice sounded, and the gates opened.

Chapter 22

Cindy turned and gave one last wave to Rip as she reached the curve in the drive. He stood by the closed gates and gave a half-hearted wave back. She knew it took all his willpower to leave her there. She'd promised to call him once she got settled and to call everyday thereafter. She watched as he got into the truck. She had a fleeting moment of wanting to run back to him, to go where things were familiar, but it only lasted a few seconds. She needed to find herself and soon, as she missed Rip and Bandon already. With her shoulders squared and bag in tow, she turned and headed toward the unknown.

She walked slowly, not in any hurry to reach her destination. Her eyes feasted on one beautiful scene after another. Small flower gardens graced both sides of the paved driveway, lying dormant, waiting for spring. The gardens were surrounded by sprawling yards that seemed to have no end. The grass had started to turn a deep green, with spring around the corner. She saw birds of numerous species, and squirrels running from trees that were scattered about the property. She continued on another fifty feet and that's when the drive opened up into a circular drive. A house of mammoth size loomed before her. This couldn't be her home. She looked at the address again. It was the one Mark had given her and the voice on the intercom knew her. She came upon the white, three-story house with its six tall pillars, and windows with green shutters. The pillars graced a large porch and in its center were enormous double doors. She noted that the drive continued behind the house, but she couldn't see where it went after that. She began rubbing her temples in hopes of sparking some recognition, but nothing came to mind.

Her eyes filled with tears, as she suddenly felt all alone. Why hadn't she let Rip drive her to the door? She missed him already. She'd come to depend on him. She stared at the eight wide steps that led to a life, which supposedly belonged to her If only she could remember. The unknown gripped her soul and she turned to flee, to run, she didn't know where, but somewhere. She'd taken a few steps when she heard a voice. "Miss Cynthia, is that you?" The soft voice seemed excited.

Cindy turned to see a short, plump, elderly woman smiling as she descended the steps. The woman wore a black dress with a white apron draped over her full middle. She seemed friendly enough. The woman stopped at the bottom step and stood looking at her. "You've had us all worried," the woman said.

Cindy walked to within a few feet of the steps. Her whole body prickled with anticipation. Then the woman reached out to her. Cindy dropped her bag as the woman embraced her, saying, "Miss Cynthia, it's so good to have you home." She continued to hold her. Cindy didn't know why, but she felt safe in this woman's arms. The woman released her and stood gazing at her from head to foot.

"Mr. Osgood called to say you would be coming home today. Just look at you. You've lost weight, but after the ordeal you've been through, it's no wonder. Don't you worry, with some of Martha's cooking; you'll get some meat back on those bones. We waited for a call from you to send a car."

Cindy didn't know what to say, so she said the only thing that came to mind. "I had a ride and was dropped off at the gate. It is such a beautiful day I thought the walk and fresh air would do me good." She also wondered what else Mark had told them, if anything. She wondered where he was. He'd said he'd be here. Not that she minded that he wasn't.

"Well, never mind, you're home," the woman said. "Your father called a few hours ago and left a message that he'd be home in a few days, but right now, I'm sure you'd like to freshen up and take a little nap after your trip. Mary's got your room ready. She's put a fresh bouquet of flowers in the room just as you like. I can't tell you how sorry we all were to hear about your ordeal, but don't you worry. It'll all come back to you in time and when the good

Lord sees fit. You just wait and see." She gave Cindy's hand a light squeeze. "I'll give you a call when Doctor Emerson arrives, but you'll have time for a bath and rest."

"A doctor?"

"When Mr. Bradford called, he asked that I call the doctor. He wants the doctor to see to your general health. Don't worry; Doctor Emerson has known you since you were a little thing."

"I don't need a doctor. I'm fine," Cindy said. She didn't want some stranger pawing at her. She didn't care if she knew him before or not, she wouldn't see him. Oh, why had she come here? Rip had said that maybe being in the place of her birth might cause her memory to return. Well it hadn't. She smiled at the woman, who was only being kind. "I think I'll go to my room now." She started up the stairs and then remembered she didn't know where her room was. "Ma'am, I don't mean to sound stupid, but could you tell me where my room is?"

"Of course, Miss Cynthia, your room is at the end of the hallway on your left. I'll show you."

Cindy followed her up the stairs. She noticed a large crystal chandelier hanging from the ceiling, a beautiful focal point for the large vestibule. The staircase in the center of the room veered off at the top to the left and right. She noticed that the vestibule had many doors leading to other rooms and parts of the house. There would be time to explore later; right now, she needed to be alone to sort things out in her mind. As she followed the woman upstairs, she again rubbed at her temples in hopes that something would jar her memory, but she remembered nothing.

Cindy almost ran into the woman, as she stopped in front of a set of white double doors. Behind these doors, she hoped to find something, anything, which would help her regain her memory.

"Here we are," the woman said as she opened both doors and stepped aside, "your room, Miss Cynthia."

Cindy started to thank the woman when it dawned on her she didn't know the woman's name. "You've been most kind, and I want to thank you, but I don't know your name." Cindy felt foolish asking, but like Rip said, if she wanted to know something she would have to learn to ask.

"I'm sorry. Mr. Osgood told the staff that you had a memory lapse. We were sorry to hear about your accident. Now to your question, my name is Grace. I manage the household for your father and you. Now you get some rest and don't worry about a thing. Your memory will come back. Mr. Osgood said he would be stopping by later."

"Thank you, Grace. Did Mr. Osgood, I mean Mark, did he happen to mention what time he'd be coming by?" She really didn't care to meet with him. Yet she was engaged to him; anyway, that's what he said.

"I'm sorry Miss Cynthia, but when Mr. Osgood called he only said he'd stop by later."

Cindy entered the room and quickly excited, closing the doors behind her and leaned against them. Her pulse raced as her body chilled. She wrapped her arms around her waist and slid down the door to a squat, on the carpeted hallway. With her eyes closed, she pictured the room of the nightmarish dream. The room behind these doors and the dream were the same. How could that be? This was her room, her home. One's bedroom is supposed to be a place of refuge, not fear. She stood, and with more strength than she possessed, opened the doors again.

Yes, it definitely was the room in the dream, but as she looked around, a warm, comforting feeling washed over her and the chill left.

"I've come to run your bath," Grace said.

Cindy jumped and turned to see Grace standing in the doorway. Run her bath. Now why would she do that? She was capable of running her own bath water. Grace handed her some towels.

"I know Mary usually runs your bath, but since she's not here, I'll do it for you."

"Grace, I'm not that sick. I can run my own bath. Besides, I'm sure you have other matters to attend to." Cindy noted a dejected look cross Grace's face. One second it was there and the next gone. If the woman wanted to run her bath, what could it hurt? "Grace, if that's what you'd like to do, run my bath, please."

"Thank you, Miss Cynthia. I'll make it just like you like it, not too hot or cold."

Cindy opened the double glass French doors leading to a balcony that ran the length of her room. She leaned against the balcony's concrete side and took a deep breath of fresh air. She had a beautiful view of Chicago and the river that cut through the city. A spectacular view, she thought, as another view came to mind, Rip's home with its panoramic view. The view before her showed the business section with everyone bustling here and there, whereas Rip's place showed, the simpler side of life, a serene and quiet scene. Peaceful, Cindy thought. "Your bath is ready, Miss Cynthia," Grace called, interrupting her thoughts.

"Thanks Grace, I'll be there in a minute. You needn't wait." A few seconds later, she heard her bedroom doors close. She stepped back into the room and stood amazed at its size and furnishings. A king-size provincial bed, with matching chest of drawers and dressing table sat at one end of the room. The bed coverings were of white and pink satin, as were the curtains. At the other end, a small couch and chair of pink and white stripes faced a gas fireplace with bookcases on either side, which reached the ceiling. A small home in itself, she thought, as she moved into the adjoining bathroom. A heart-shaped pink, combination tub/Jacuzzi surrounded with marble sides, sat in the middle of the room. Grace had lit the numerous candles of pink and white that lined the sides. Another room to the left held the shower and toilet. To the right was a walk-in closet, which held so many clothes, Cindy thought she stood in a store. How could one person want or need so many outfits, she wondered, as she looked at the simple slacks and shirt she wore. They were drab in comparison to the clothes in the closet. She liked the outfit she wore; Rip had bought it for her.

Cindy lowered herself into the bathtub. As she moved about, the water began to bubble. Grace must have added some bubble bath. A floral scent filled the room as Cindy found herself relaxing deeper into the tub. She leaned her head against a towel on the edge and let the water calm her senses. She must have dozed for a few minutes when she heard Grace calling her name. Then she saw it, an intercom on the wall. "Miss Cynthia, Mr. Osgood is here to see you. I told him you were bathing."

Great, she thought, she had hoped he'd change his mind and wouldn't come, but why would he? Because she--oh she didn't know what she felt anymore. Besides, she couldn't keep running from the man. "Tell Mr. Osgood I'll be down shortly."

She pictured Mark, with his tall lanky frame, almost too skinny, she thought. She couldn't help comparing his body to Rip's tall muscular one. Mark's fair complexion to Rip's dark, outdoorsy, weathered look. Mark seemed weak compared to Rip's strength. She wasn't being fair. She really didn't know Mark, not like she'd gotten to know Rip in the past few weeks. In fact, she didn't know anyone but Rip and how she longed to be with him and Bandon! She wondered how they both were doing.

Chapter 23

Rip had driven less than three blocks when he pulled the truck over to the curb. I'm an ass, he thought. I should never have let her go to that house alone no matter how much she insisted. He'd been a fool. It wasn't like him to give in so easily. Then why had he? Well, it was too late now, she was probably already in the house. He pulled the truck back onto the highway, knowing she'd be calling him tomorrow.

He drove the truck up to the police station. A familiar place, it had been his second home for twenty years. He'd called Sarah and told her he would be stopping by. She suggested lunch, a quiet place to talk. He hadn't waited long when he saw her emerging from the building, a heavyset woman in her late fifties. Rip wondered why she continued to work when she had enough years to retire. When he asked her, she always said the department was her family. Everyone in the department loved her. Besides, she happened to be the best research analyst in the Chicago area. "Hi," he said as she climbed into the truck. "Long time no see and you're looking as lovely as ever."

"Rip, you are one hell of a liar. I look like shit, but thanks anyway for the compliment," Sarah laughed.

"How's the little lady?"

"She seemed a little nervous, no, more like frightened when I dropped her off. I don't like any of this. It all sounds--well the whole thing smells. Now tell me what you've found out so far?"

"Sure, but let's wait until after we've ordered lunch, I'm starved. For now, tell me, besides Miss Bradford, what have you been up to; how's the house coming and that book you're supposed to be writing?"

Rip waited for the waiter to leave. He'd been patient and they'd talked about how the house and book were coming; how the book had taken a back burner since Cindy's arrival, but now he wanted to know what she'd found out. "Well?" He asked.

"Rip," she began. "You know I've always followed the Bradford family, especially Cynthia. She leads a life that most women including myself, only dream of; rich beyond rich, with a home that's more like a castle, traveling, boating on the Bradford's private yacht, expensive jewelry, and the best clothes money can buy. I met her once at a charity event given for the Police Department."

Rip knew the family to be wealthy, but he hadn't known that Sarah had actually met her. "What did you think of her?"

"She wasn't anything like you describe. The woman I met was chic, sophisticated and snobbish. She definitely wasn't quiet, reserved, and sweet. Anyway, not the day I met her."

Rip leaned back in his chair. How could the woman he'd spent the last few weeks with be the woman Sarah just described? Yet--"Sarah, you did say in our last phone conversation that the woman at my place definitely was Miss Bradford? The picture, fingerprints and birthmark all checked out, right?"

"Yes, and that's what's got me baffled. That bump on her head must have caused a drastic change in her. I don't want you to get hurt, Rip, because you seem to care for her deeply. I mean, this woman I met isn't someone I could picture you with."

Rip couldn't believe that the Cindy he knew and the one Sarah described could be one in the same, yet they must be. "Sarah tell me, when was that benefit?"

"Let me see, I can't remember the exact date. No, wait a minute; I have my calendar in my purse. I always write important dates and events in it. Not that I have such a demanding social life, it's just a habit. Police training, I guess."

He knew Sarah to be a good judge of character, but the woman she described and the one he knew were as different as day and night.

"Found it, it was held on April first. It being April Fools Day, I sure was fooled, because I'd always heard Miss Bradford to be a kind, friendly, and a generous person like her father. Boy, what a surprise I got when I met her. She brushed her hand on her evening gown after we shook hands like the dark color of my skin had rubbed off on her."

Rip knew that being African American never bothered Sarah, or him either. She'd always been Sarah; the color of her skin never entered his mind. He shook his head as he couldn't picture Cindy ever doing anything so demeaning. "I'm sorry, Sarah." He couldn't think of anything else to say.

"It didn't bother me, but I sure got a good picture of her. If money makes people like that, they can have it, but listen; we're not here to talk about me. I found out some interesting things about this Mark Osgood you asked me to check out."

The waiter arrived with their food. They'd both ordered the shrimp salad and began eating as Sarah continued.

"It seems that before this Mr. Osgood came to work for Mr. Bradford, he hadn't held a job for more than a few months. When I contacted his other places of employment they were evasive and would only tell me that he'd been asked to leave. That in itself is suspicious."

"Then how come he's working for Mr. Bradford? It's been well over a year. I'm sure being the businessman that Mr. Bradford is; he would have had him checked out?" Rip couldn't picture any man owning a company as prestigious and large as Bradford Enterprises, who wouldn't check a prospective employee out.

"I think Miss Bradford had something to do with that. I did find out that Mr. Osgood and Mr. Bradford aren't on the friendliest of terms."

"Why is that? I mean, if Mr. Bradford doesn't like him, why keep him?" This thing was getting more interesting as the lunch went on, Rip thought.

"Miss Bradford is Mr. Bradford's world. When she became engaged to Mark Osgood, everyone knew he didn't like the match, but if that's what she wanted he wouldn't stand in her way. In fact, Mark Osgood got a promotion soon after the engagement. He now holds the title of vice-president of the Chicago branch office. A step-up for a man who'd only held the job of manager in any of his other jobs."

"Did you find out how the two of them met, Cindy and Mark?"

"Sure, they met at the park."

"Park, are you sure?" How could a man meet someone at a park and shortly thereafter become a vice-president of a wealthy company?

"You heard me right. It seems that Cindy likes to ride horses and she was out riding one day when something spooked her horse. It made for interesting reading in the paper. The headlines read, 'Cynthia Bradford on runaway horse saved by knight in shining armor.' The knight in shining armor was no other than Mark Osgood, who soon thereafter landed a job at Bradford Enterprises. It wasn't three months later that he and Miss Bradford became engaged."

"Any other findings about Mr. Osgood, like an arrest, tickets, anything?" The man had to have some background besides losing jobs, Rip thought.

"No, he's got a clean slate, not even a parking ticket, but I'll keep checking if you want. There are a few avenues that I haven't checked out yet."

"Sure, I want anything that you can find. There has to be something. When I met the man, I got the feeling that he wasn't to be trusted, a fake. He comes off too smooth and to me that can only mean he's hiding something. I want to find out what it is before—well, let's just leave it at that." He was about to say, before someone gets hurt, and by hurt he meant Cindy. There had to be more to this man. "Tell me Sarah, have you ever met this Mr. Osgood?"

"Yes and no, he was with Miss Bradford when we were introduced, but he stood talking to someone else. I will say this much, he sure was attentive to her."

Chapter 24

Cindy found a pair of cream slacks and matching top in the closet. She'd pulled her hair back and secured it with a hair clasp she'd found on the dressing table. Slipping into a pair of matching satin shoes, she was ready to meet Mark. She had to meet with him eventually. One thing was sure, she planned to break the engagement as soon as she found an opportune time. Memory or not, she didn't want to continue on with it. Maybe after her memory returned she'd feel differently, but for now she couldn't and wouldn't go through with the intended wedding.

She saw Mark at the bottom of the steps waiting for her. He wore a dark gray, pinstripe suit, a white shirt and gray tie. His blond hair, combed to perfection. A man of distinction, yet she felt this was all a façade. She'd have to handle this whole engagement thing carefully. Rip, now he was different. She sensed nothing but warmth and honesty when he was around. She made the last two steps and stopped in front of Mark. He reached for her hand. "I must say you are the most beautiful woman I've ever laid eyes on," he said, kissing the back of her hand.

What a bunch of bull, she wanted to say, but instead forced a smile. "I said I'd be down, and here I am."

"Yes, and I must say, I've never seen you look so radiant. The vacation and country air agreed with you. Maybe we should think of spending our honeymoon in the country instead of Paris. You know a quiet place in the country all to ourselves, while we rediscover each other. If you know what I mean?"

He'd winked at her. She knew what he meant, oh how she knew what he meant. The thought of him touching her made her ill. Had they--no, she didn't want to think that she could have....

"Grace has a small lunch ready for us if you're up to eating. I suggested we have it out on the verandah, your favorite place to dine." He saw a look of discomfort cross her face and knew that he'd have to handle her with kid gloves. The wedding was only a couple of months away and he didn't want anything to interrupt those plans. He'd worked too hard and come too far to mess it up now.

"The verandah is fine," Cindy said. Anything to keep them occupied. They sat across from each other as Grace served them a lunch of chicken salad on a bed of lettuce and a small bowl of mixed fruit. Cindy thanked Grace and began eating the salad. It had been a long time since Rip and she had eaten breakfast. Rip, she thought, and of the many meals, they had shared together, sitting at the small table in his kitchen with Bandon at their feet. Would she ever share another meal with him? "Cynthia, you haven't heard a word I've said," Mark said, breaking into her thoughts.

"I'm sorry, guess I was daydreaming." It wasn't about you. Why had she agreed to meet and have lunch with him? He was nothing but a stuffed shirt. Besides, what did they have to talk about anyway?

"Well, I hope you were dreaming about us, and the wedding. You know, it's not that far away and with you being gone for so long, we're behind on the wedding plans. We haven't decided on our guest list. We need to go over the list one last time. It's a wonderful, sunny day out. Why don't we sit in the garden after we've eaten and go over the list? I don't have any meetings this afternoon, but I do have a dinner engagement, so I won't be here for dinner. Will you be too disappointed, my dear? I mean, with you just arriving home."

"I won't mind at all. I'll have a light meal and turn in early. It has been a tiring day. Mark, about the wedding and list...."

"I understand, you're tired and need to rest. How inconsiderate of me. We don't have to do it today. You get your rest and we'll talk about it in a few days." He wouldn't let her postpone it any longer. He wanted to get this whole thing wrapped up before he made his next move.

"Mark, about the list, there is more to it than just the names. I still haven't regained my memory." He couldn't have forgotten that, she thought.

"I know, dear, but I know the names and I'll be able to help. The list may even help jog your memory." He really wanted to keep her in the dark until after her father got home, and then left again. This time he wouldn't return until a few days before the wedding. He had it all worked out. Everything was going as smoothly as clockwork. Her getting amnesia had turned out to be a blessing. Soon this would all be his, his empire.

"But Mark I don't...."

"No buts, you get some rest today and I'll come by tomorrow evening and we can talk."

Cindy sighed, as she watched him stroll back to his car. When he had leaned over to kiss her on the lips she'd pretended to be chewing and he kissed her cheek. His lips were soft and wet, causing her stomach to churn. How could she ever have liked him?

She was still sitting there a few minutes after Mark left, when Grace came to say that Doctor Emerson had arrived and was waiting in the living room. "Grace, could you direct me?"

When she entered the living room, a small, elderly man stood looking out the window at the back gardens. He couldn't be more than five foot, five inches in height, a thin man with thinning gray hair. "Good afternoon, Doctor Emerson," she greeted him. When he turned, Cindy saw nothing but kindness generating from this man. He had light blue eyes that blended with the navy blue suit he wore.

"Cynthia, how good to see you; and what is this, calling me Doctor Emerson. Is Doc not good enough anymore?"

"I'm sorry...."

"No need, Grace told me that you've had a bang on the head. Why don't you have a seat, so I can have a look?"

Cindy sat while he removed his stethoscope and listened to her heart and lungs. He examined the cut on her head that had all but healed. Then he patted her hand and wrote a few things on a tablet before coming to sit beside her. She had warmed to this man called Doc. She felt he was a man she could trust, but she still wasn't ready to trust anyone but Rip. Doc took her hand and gently patted it for the second time as he spoke.

"Well, you seem okay and the cut is healing nicely. I don't think you will have a scar. Whoever tended to you did a good job. Are there any other cuts or bruises that I should look at?"

"I've a few bruises, but they've mostly healed, nothing life threatening."

"Your memory, have you any re-call.?"

"Nothing, I wonder if I'll ever get it back."

"Well there are a few tests that I can run; to make sure you don't have any blood clots or vessel damage to the head. I want you to come to the hospital tomorrow. It will only take a few hours. If everything turns out fine, then we'll just have to wait. Amnesia is a funny thing; it has a mind of its own. It can't be rushed, but don't worry, it will come back when it is ready. I'll set up the request for the tests, you just show up at the hospital. I'll stop by a few days from now with the results, but for now I want you to rest. It's the best thing for amnesia. I can't have my favorite girl being sick on me."

Cindy sat in the back garden after Doctor Emerson left. She'd promised to go have the tests. She'd do anything to get her memory back, but right now she wanted to enjoy the afternoon sun. There weren't many days like this in Chicago in mid spring. Now how did she remember that? She wanted to remember the important things; her identity, this house, and if she had take drugs. She needed to know everything about herself. She wanted to get on with her life, and it didn't include Mark. Rip, that's who kept entering her mind. She hoped he'd call this evening. She needed to talk to him, to hear his voice. He was the only person she felt an attachment to: him, Bandon and his cabin. It felt more like home to her than this enormous place, she couldn't forget Matt with his burly face, and of course Martha and Frank, no she couldn't forget them. She liked Martha and wondered if she'd had her baby yet.

Cindy pulled her sweater about her, thankful that she remembered to grab it before coming outside. Dark clouds had developed and it looked like rain. She should return to the house, she thought, but what would she do in there; she wasn't familiar with the place. That's it, she thought, I'll explore.

She decided to begin with the lower level and work her way upward. She was about to enter the living room, since she knew

where that was, when Grace called her name. She turned to see
the plump woman smiling at her.

"I've put your mail on the desk in the library. I thought
you might want to go through it, since you've been gone awhile,"
she said. "The library is to the right of the stairs."

"Thank you." She would go over the mail first and then
explore the rest of the house. She walked to the tall wide heavy
door and stepped into the library. The aroma of old books hit her.
One side of the room held nothing but bookshelves that reached
to the twelve-foot ceiling. At the far end were French doors
leading to yet another verandah. In front of that, a large mahogany
desk, shined to perfection, faced the entrance door. A small desk
lamp sat on the top and a pile of mail lay in the center. Two
burgundy, leather bound chairs faced the desk. A matching leather
couch sat facing a gas fireplace. A portrait of a young girl on a
horse hung above the fireplace. The girl wore an English riding
outfit, with her dark reddish hair flowing from the hat. She
couldn't have been more than thirteen when the picture was taken.
Cindy got closer. She stared at the picture. She didn't know why,
but the girl reminded her of someone. Then it dawned on her, it
could be her as a child.

"You were as beautiful a child, as you are a woman."

Cindy turned to see Grace with a tray of refreshments and
cookies.

"I thought you'd like a snack while you went through the
mail," Grace said. "You always did and I thought…."

"Grace, that was thoughtful of you. Put it on the desk."
Cindy waited for Grace to set down the heavy tray. "Grace, you
seemed to imply that the picture above the fireplace is of me. Is
that true?"

"Yes, Miss Cynthia. Your father cherishes that painting.
Your father had it done on your thirteenth birthday. Why do you
ask?"

"I thought as much, just checking. Tell me, if it isn't too
much trouble, do I have a mother?" Grace who'd been smiling
seconds before suddenly dropped her head and Cindy saw tears in
her eyes. She started to say something, but Grace lifted her face
and the tears were gone. Cindy could've sworn she saw tears.

"Yes, she was a beautiful woman, your mother, in body
and heart. When she died, your father was devastated; he didn't
want to go on living. He had you, and if it wasn't for you, I don't

know what would have happened to him. He loves you very much; nothing is too good for you. He cherishes you. When he found out what had happened to you, he wanted to rush right home, but Mark told him that you're fine. He knows about the lapse in your memory and thought it best that you reacquaint yourself with the house before he returns."

"What did my mother die of?"

"She had a weak heart, always had, and one day it just couldn't go anymore. You were only ten when she passed away. Now if you'll excuse me, I've got to see what the cook has planned for your supper."

"Before you go, please tell me, how long have you been with the family?" This woman she felt sure could be of tremendous help with her regaining knowledge of this place. She'd have to spend more time with her.

"Since I was a child, my parents ran the household for your father's father and after my parents passed on, I assumed the responsibility."

"Then that makes you part of the family," Cindy smiled. She knew if anyone knew anything about the Bradford's it would be this woman.

"Now I must get back to the bread I have in the oven. If you need something, a phone is in every room. It also serves as an intercom, all you need to do is press the star key, and one of the household staff will answer."

After she left, Cindy scanned the books on the shelves, a collection of biographies dating back to Christ, reference books on almost any topic, and an array of fiction novels: science fiction, mystery, suspense, westerns, epic, and romance. One bottom shelf consisted of magazines. She picked one out and saw the headline, 'Harry Bradford III donates new maternity wing to local hospital.' It seemed her father was a generous man, she thought. She picked up another magazine that had her looking at herself with Mark. Mark had his arm around her while they posed for the camera. The caption read, 'Cynthia Bradford becomes engaged,' underneath the picture she read, 'sorry guys, seems she's found her man.'

Cindy quickly put the magazine back. Engaged indeed, well not for long, she thought, as she left the library to explore more of the rooms; the mail could wait. An hour later, she sat in her room. The house had overwhelmed her with its many rooms: an indoor and outdoor pool, game room with a billiard table and bar, an exercise room equipped with the latest machinery. Cindy noticed a small white cottage out back. The place appeared not to have been touched in years. She made a mental note to ask Grace about the little building. There was one room she hadn't checked, her father's. Why hadn't she? Because he was the master of the house, but that's foolish, she thought. He was her father, and if she wanted to know anything about him, that would be the place to look.

Cindy stood in front of his door. What was she afraid of? A man's room is his private domain, she thought. She started to turn away, but the next second found herself inside, leaning against the closed door. A spacious room had the aroma of the cologne he used, Old Spice. A man's room with large, bulky furniture and private bath filled with men's toiletries. He too had a private balcony. What caught Cindy's eyes was an eight-by-ten gold framed photo on the nightstand, a picture of a man, woman and little girl about nine or ten years old. She held the picture in her hand as she stared at what must be her parents and her.

Cindy felt dizzy and sat on the edge of the bed. A fuzzy picture came into view of the woman in the photo lying in a bed, holding Cindy's hand. The woman was smiling and saying something, which Cindy couldn't make out. Then it was gone just as quickly as it had arrived. Cindy felt shaken as her body trembled from head to foot. She felt something, not much, but enough to know that the woman in the photograph had to be her mother. She began to cry at the realization that the one person she remembered happened to be dead. She hugged the picture to her heart and prayed, please Mother, help me. She continued to stare at the picture through tears as her gaze went from the man to the woman and then to the child. She didn't look like either one of them. If not, then who did she resemble, a grandparent possibly. Her parents both had blond hair with light blue eyes and were very fair skinned. She couldn't tell their height, but no matter, she certainly didn't favor either one.

Cindy sat in her room long after supper staring at the phone and wishing it would ring. She'd called, but he wasn't home. She'd told him she'd call, but she couldn't expect him to sit home waiting for her call, he did have a life. He had safely dropped her off at home. He'd done his duty and that was that. Oh, he had acted as if he hadn't wanted her to leave, but had he really? She carried this thought with her until she went to bed and found sleep.

The next morning she woke up with a start at her new surroundings and then it came to her, this is home now. Home, yet it didn't feel like home. She missed the small room at Rip's place where when she awoke, she could smell the aroma of coffee, bacon, and eggs, and yes, see Rip's familiar face. Life is so unfair, she thought, and lay back against the pillows, staring at the ceiling. Life, what life did she have until her memory returned? A life without a past, that's what she had.

After a quick shower, she dressed in a pair of jeans and a light blue sweater. She sat brushing her hair when the phone rang. Rip, she thought, grabbing the phone and saying, "Rip?"

"No, Miss Cynthia, it is Mary. I wanted to see if you wanted breakfast in bed or if you would be coming down."

Cindy couldn't remember ever having breakfast in bed, but then there was a lot she didn't remember. "Thanks, but I think I'll come downstairs. When will it be ready?" She told Mary not to hurry, that breakfast would wait for her.

An hour later she sat drinking her second cup of coffee and thought of the times Rip and she enjoyed their second cup of coffee each morning. They would discuss their plans for the day. Plans, she had none. Oh how she missed Rip. The sun had come up and she knew it would be another wonderful day outside. Maybe she'd take a stroll in the garden. Yes, that's what she'd do, she thought as Grace came in to tell her she had a caller. She told Grace to send the person in and wondered who knew she was back.

"How's my partner?"

Cindy almost knocked the chair down getting up, as she ran to him. "Rip, how, why? Oh, I don't care, I'm so glad to see you." She reached him, almost tripping on her own feet and gave him a big hug. To which he picked her up, swung her around, and then set her back on her feet. "Come, have coffee with me," she said, all but pulling him to the table. Cindy turned to see Grace watching them.

"Would you bring another cup for Mr. Walker, Grace?"

After Grace left to get the coffee, Cindy took Rip's hands and held them tight. Gosh, he looked great. Had it only been a day since he'd dropped her off at the house? It seemed like weeks, or even months.

"How's it going so far?" Rip asked. "You look good. Has the house brought any memories back?" Rip gazed about the room. It reeked of money, from the Victorian table and gold plated silverware to the pictures on the wall. However, nothing looked as elegant as the woman sitting across the table from him did.

"It's going." She went on to tell him the things she'd done since arriving and the enormity of the house. She also told him of the little incident in her father's room about remembering her mother in bed. She told him about Doctor Emerson, and having some tests, which he was glad to hear. She didn't mention Mark intentionally. She didn't want to think about Mark. Rip was here and that was all that mattered. Then it dawned on her. He couldn't have gone back home and be here this morning, not unless he hadn't slept at all. "Rip, you didn't go home, did you?"

"It was late after I met with Sarah, so I just stayed at a hotel. When I got up this morning, I thought, why not come see you. You don't mind, do you?"

"Mind, you're a welcome treat. This place is beautiful and big, but there is nothing to do here. The house seems to run itself. I don't have a thing to worry about. Thanks to Grace, she is a gem. I like her. I haven't met all of the staff yet. Now, at your place, there was a lot to do."

"So now I'm a slave driver." Then she started to laugh. "What's so funny?"

"You are! I did what I did because I enjoyed it. I was only comparing that to how boring it is here. A person can only walk the gardens so many times. Besides, I had to earn my keep."

"Cindy?"

"Only kidding, now how about a walk in the garden? It's a beautiful morning and it's private." She trusted Grace, but what she wanted to talk about was for Rip to hear and Rip alone.

A half-hour later, they sat on one of the benches that lined the garden paths. Neither said anything at first as they enjoyed just being together. Then Cindy broke the silence. "You know, Rip, some of these specimens would look wonderful around your place. I'll talk to the gardener about getting you some starters if you'd like." He reached for her hands as they rested on her lap. The touch of his hands sent a warm sensation through her body, yet she shivered.

"Are you cold? It is a little nippy with the northeast wind. Maybe we should go in?"

"No, I'm fine, really I am, but what do you say, should I ask the gardener?"

"Of course, I'll have Matt plant them. He's good at gardening."

"Matt?" She wanted to plant them. "I thought that—well, you're probably right. Matt will do a good job."

Rip noted a change in her, as she suddenly pulled her hands away and sat up, stiffly. "Cindy, what's wrong? Did I say something wrong?" For the life of him, he couldn't figure out the sudden chill.

She decided to say it, and if he didn't want her at his place he would have to say so. "I thought I'd try my hand at planting them. I'm sure the gardener will give me some helpful hints. Besides, I miss the place. I miss Bandon, Matt, Martha, and Frank. Have they had the baby yet?"

"Not yet, but then we just left yesterday. I'll call you when they do. Now I've a few questions I want to ask. First off, have you talked to your father? Have you had any desire to take drugs? Is your body craving them now that you're back in these surroundings?"

"I missed Father's call. Grace said he'd be home in a few days that he had to stay longer than anticipated. Let's see, today is Friday; he should be coming in on Monday. As for drugs, the answer is no. I don't have even the teensiest craving." That isn't quite true, she thought. She craved him, having him around. She enjoyed his company. He made her laugh. When she returned to the moment, she noticed he seemed to be deep in thought, with his brow creased. "What are you thinking so hard about?"

"What you just said about the drugs? I don't like to discredit you fiancé, but I don't believe a word about you ever being on drugs. Why he cooked up that story is beyond me? But—well, let's just leave it at that for now."

"I too have trouble with that, and as for him being my fiancé, well, he may be engaged to the old Cynthia Bradford, but the new one, let's just say I plan to call it off." She saw a look of relief wash over him, or maybe she'd imagined it.

Rip was elated that she wanted to call it off. Would he have a chance? They were from two different worlds, hers glamorous and exciting, that of a woman of the world. He led a simple life, quiet and subdued. He knew her to be grateful for all he'd done. Perhaps that was all it could be, he thought.

Rip left shortly afterwards and Cindy felt empty. As she drifted through the house, she noticed from a window, a stable about five hundred yards from the back of the house. She decided to check it out. At the stable door, a tall, thin, elderly man in bib overalls greeted her. He had on a western straw hat. She could see sprouts of white hair sticking out from underneath it. As she approached, she noticed his big wide grin. "Hi, Miss Cindy, have you come to ride?"

Cindy liked this man right away and he had called her Cindy. She sensed him to be warm and kind, like Grace. She returned the smile and said, "I don't know. Do I ride?"

"The best rider in these here parts. You've won the last three state fair showings. Snickers has really missed you, but I've been giving him a good workout in your absence. Miss Cindy, it is good to have you home. Now would you like me to saddle up Snickers for you?"

This is all too much, she thought. She rode horses at the state fair. She sure had a lot to learn. "I don't think so, not today, but I will look in on Snickers." She began poking her head into the different stalls when the man said, "Last one on the right."

Cindy noticed that each stall had a plaque with the name of the horse. As she approached the last stall, the horse stuck its chestnut brown head over the top of the double door. He began whinnying and stamping his hooves. She reached out her hand and just as she did, her mind began to spin, as pictures of herself astride this animal came into view. In the next second, it all disappeared. She reached out and gave Snickers a big hug around the neck. A comforting, secure feeling enfolded her. In the back of her mind, she knew this animal. She pressed her thumbs against her temples in hopes of retrieving more memories, but none came. She gazed into the dark, almost black eyes of Snickers. "I'll be back soon." She gave him another embrace.

As she left the stable, a thought came to mind. One never forgets, like riding a bike. Once you get on, it will all come back to you. "Are you sure you don't want to ride, Miss Cindy?"

She looked at the man who had twice now called her Cindy, not Cynthia, as everyone else did around here. She asked him, "How long have you been calling me Cindy?"

"Why, ever since you came into this world. Old Jacob here always had a problem with saying your name. You never seemed to mind. Is that a problem now?"

Jacob, so that was his name. She walked up to him and put her arms around him. When she stepped back, she noticed his face had turned a shade of red. "Jacob, you keep right on calling me Cindy, and I'll be back soon to ride Snickers." She'd gone about ten feet when he called out. "Would you remind the Mrs. that I'm going into town to see the fellows tonight? It's card night, in case she might have forgotten."

"Yes, and enjoy your game."

"Grace," Cindy said as she entered the kitchen. "Jacob said," then she stopped, seeing her sitting at the table in tears. "Grace, what's wrong?"

"Oh, Miss Cynthia, I don't know how to tell you."

"Tell me what? What did you do, break something? Well, all things can be replaced."

"No, Miss, It's your father. It seems he decided to come home today and his plane--oh, Miss, it is awful, just awful."

"Grace, please tell me. What has happened?"

"His plane went down. Oh blessed be God, they all have perished. I'm so sorry, Miss. Your father was such a good man. He couldn't wait to get home to see you. Praise be-- what are we-- you going to do?"

Chapter 25

Cindy sat at the funeral services with Mark on her right and Rip, wonderful Rip, to her left. What would she have done without him these past few days? Had it only been a few days? It seemed like a lifetime. She'd gone through the motions, and Mark had seen to the arrangements, something she'd been grateful for. She hadn't known what else to do.

The preacher stood, saying what a wonderful man her father had been, a pillar of the community. How, he would be missed by all; especially by his daughter whom he loved deeply. Dust to dust, ashes to ashes, he continued, but Cindy wasn't hearing him anymore. She kept picturing the man lying in the casket before her. When she'd first seen him lying there, she'd hoped and prayed she'd have some recollection. It had been like looking at a stranger. She'd cried and everyone thought it was because she missed him. The tears were for not having had a chance to know him. Rip gave her hand a light squeeze. "Cindy, it's time to go." She saw that people were leaving. After the last of the many friends had gone, Cindy placed the flowers Mark had given her on the casket and said, "In time, Father, I'll remember." "Time will heal all, my love," Mark said, taking hold of her hand. Rip held her other hand.

That was two days ago. She now sat in a lawyer's office, for the reading of her Father's Last Will and Testament. She'd wanted to come alone, but Mark had insisted, saying that he'd soon be her husband. She looked over at the man behind his desk. She'd been told he'd known her father for years that they'd gone to college together. He smiled at her.

"Cynthia," he began. "I'll skip all the preliminary stuff and get right to the point. Your father has left you everything. You are now in charge of the whole estate, including his banking empire. I'm to oversee you until you feel comfortable with the running of said estate."

Cindy sat there numb. What did she know about running a banking business? The house yes, but banking, that was something else. Thank goodness, her father had the foresight to have the lawyer oversee things. She didn't know what to say, but stared at the man who had known her father and said only, "Thank you."

She stood up to leave and Mark put his hand on her elbow as they left the room. "Mark, if you don't mind I'd like to go back to the house alone." She saw the dejection on his face.

"Cindy, I thought we'd have a nice lunch and go over some business. There are decisions that need to be made. I want to make everything as easy as possible for you. Since we are soon to be married, I can now take some of the burden off your shoulders. I thought it would be a good idea if I sort of stepped in until you regained your memory."

Non Mark, you are wrong. You are not going to be my husband. That is what she wanted to say, but not here, not today. Instead, she said, "I'm not in the mood today. I need a few days to sort through things. Now, if you don't mind I think I'll have my driver take me home." With that said, she turned and walked out of the building, alone.

Her father's driver, who'd been with her father for years, gave her a kindly look. It seemed that way with everyone she met. They'd all known her father for years.

"Would you like to go home, Miss Bradford?" The driver asked.

"Yes Edgar, the faster the better."

Cindy enjoyed the ride back to the house. She watched the now familiar countryside go by, recognizing it from having made numerous trips to town, with the funeral and all. Everything had happened so fast. She hadn't had time to get used to being Cynthia Bradford, when suddenly she was in charge of a banking empire. How would she cope? Well, one thing she knew for sure, Mark wasn't going to run it. Her father, even though she had no recollection of him, had put her in charge. He wouldn't have left it to her if he hadn't thought her capable, and where Mark was concerned, well, she'd just have to deal with him.

She leaned back and remembered how the other day Mark had been offended when he tried to embrace her. She'd all but pushed him away, and he'd said, "I've given you plenty of time to adjust and yet you still act like I've got the plague or something." Or something is right, she thought, but that something she couldn't put her finger on. When he touched her, she wanted to be sick.

Mark leaned back in his chair, as he had a terrific headache. That damn woman is causing me nothing but trouble, he thought. He was elated when he heard that old man Bradford's plane had crashed and there were no survivors. Now he didn't have to worry about him. He knew the man didn't like him, but Cynthia had. The old man always gave her what she wanted.

It had been so easy. All he needed was one date. After that, it had been simple. He wined and dined her, giving into whatever she wanted. He was perfect, and she had fallen head over heels for him. Then her father started pumping her with all that nonsense that he wasn't good enough for her. He had to fight harder to make her see that her father was afraid of losing his little girl. Her father became a big problem. He'd started snooping into Marks' background. It wouldn't have been long before he found out the truth. Cynthia had started having doubts. He couldn't take any chances. That's when he'd come up with the plan to drug her. Get her out of the way, sooner than he had originally planned, but the wedding had to take place. A month, that's all he had to wait. Then he'd see to miss high and mighty, memory or no memory; she'd be history. He picked up the phone and dialed the number he knew by heart. "Hello, how about celebrating? Soon you will be Miss Cynthia Bradford. Then it will be Mrs. Mark Osgood. How does that sound?" He heard her giggle. "Just hang on, baby. I told you I would take care of everything. I'll be there soon with the champagne. You provide the loving." That's what he needed, a good night of sex to relieve the headache that the bitch has caused.

* * *

"Rip, I'm so glad you called," Cindy said the next morning as she sat drinking her second cup of coffee. "I wish you could have stayed after the funeral. How is everyone? Is Bandon getting big? Does he miss me? How's Matt doing with his arthritis? Has Martha had the baby?" She had so many questions.

"Whoa, hold on a minute. Everyone misses you; Matt is fine and says hi. Yes, they've had the baby. In fact, little Robert is only two hours old. They've named him after me, and have asked me to be his Godfather. Of course, I accepted, happily. I just left the proud parents, but more importantly, how are you? How'd it go today? I imagine it was pretty tough."

"Fine, I've got a house to run and a banking empire of which I know nothing, but other than that I'm fine."

Rip noted a double meaning to her last statement. From all he'd read about the Bradford family, father and daughter were very close. Bradford had been prepping her for the takeover. If only she'd recall everything. Then he remembered the real reason he called. "Cindy, I was wondering if you'd like to see Bandon. The darn little thing has been moping for you. I mean, your place is big and I thought...."

"Think no more, partner. When can you come?"

"Is tomorrow too soon?"

"Too soon, no, in fact I wish you were here right now." Had she really said that? What must he think of her? Then he said, "me too."

He'd be here tomorrow. She could hardly wait, and Bandon would love the place, but most significant was what Rip had said, "me too." He missed her. Did that mean that he maybe, just maybe had some feelings of the heart for her? Tomorrow couldn't come soon enough. Now if she could only get her memory back. Cindy sat at the table long after Rip's call and thought of her life. To her it was short, only remembering waking up in Rip's house. It was as if she lived two lives, one she knew and one she didn't; if only the two of them would meet. First thing in the morning she had some errands to attend to.

"Mark, can't you get the wedding moved up? A lot can happen in a month. I don't want to take any chances. I won't rest till that woman is dead."

Mark looked over at the woman he had slept with last night. She looked so like Cynthia that it frightened him, but he needed them both for now. One gave him heavy heated sex. The other would give him the riches. He grinned at the woman next to him. "Patience, my dear, have patience. Soon it'll all be ours and no one will be the wiser. It won't be long now. Right now, I need some more of your love."

"Mark you haven't--I mean…."

"No, damn it woman, I haven't. Besides, she'd probably be cold. I need a woman that's hot and right now, you are hot."

"The phone, Mark, get your cell phone and hurry, I'm about ready to come."

"Yes, what is it?" Mark all but yelled into the phone.

"I'm sorry, Mr. Osgood."

"You should be. I've told you never to call me unless it is an emergency."

"I know Mr. Osgood," said his secretary. "But, Miss Bradford is sitting in your office."

What the hell is she doing in my office? He thought. He pulled away from the woman in the bed with him. He watched her stomp off toward the bathroom. Women, they're nothing but a nuisance, but he needed them, for now anyway. He said into the phone, "Did she say what she wants?"

"No sir, only that she needed to see you, something about calling a meeting," his secretary said. "She seemed upset that you weren't here."

Damn her, what did she think he did, sit at his desk all day? "Tell her that I had some business to attend to and will be along shortly." He hung up the phone as the bathroom door opened.

"I'm sorry honey," Mark said as graciously as he could. "I've got to go. I promise to be back tonight and then we can continue where we left off."

"It's that Bradford woman isn't it? I tell you, we've got to move on this now."

Mark didn't answer her, but knew she was right right. He entered the office building wondering what his secretary had meant about Cynthia wanting to hold a meeting. A meeting, about what, she didn't know a thing about the business, unless---her memory had come back.

Cindy sat in front of Mark's desk and took it all in. It was a typical office, neither big nor small, with an oak desk, and a big map of the world with red dots in different areas. A small liquor cabinet, a small bookcase, and the two chairs in front of the desk were all the furnishings. His desk faced the door and behind the

desk, a window looked out onto the streets below. She noticed a
picture of the two of them on his desk. She picked it up and stared
at herself. Mark had his arm around her and they were smiling as
they were in all the pictures she'd seen of them. She recognized
the setting. It was in the back garden at the house by the oak tree.
She looked happy in the picture. What had happened to change all
that? Mark she had to admit had been kind and cooperative, and
some women would find him attractive. Then why did she have a
feeling that he wasn't as he seemed. "Miss Bradford?" Cindy
turned as the secretary entered. "Mr. Osgood is on his way." She
started to leave when Cindy asked, "Would you be so kind and
show me my father's office?"

"Maybe you should wait for Mr. Osgood?"

Cindy wondered why she should wait for Mark. She
owned the place. Didn't this woman realize that? "Miss, I would
like to see my father's office, now."

The secretary's hands shook as she unlocked the door.
Was she afraid of Mark? Why had the door been locked? Who
had given the authority? "Thanks," Cindy said to the suddenly pale
secretary. She shut the door behind her.

Cindy felt warmth as she stood in the middle of the room,
amazed at the comfort it projected. She knew instantly that her
father had been a warm and kind person. The mahogany desk and
matching furniture showed signs of wear. She looked over at the
leather couch and knew that many a person had sat there.
Numerous fresh flower arrangements adorned the room, showing
that someone had seen to it everyday. There were pictures of her
on every wall; some by a tree or in the flower garden, but the
biggest picture above the fireplace had her beaming at the camera
as she sat on her horse. Tears welled at the thought that she'd
never get to meet the man called her father.

She went behind the desk to the big picture window that
overlooked the front of the office building. She could see a view
of a park, not far, to her left. A picture of her walking in that park
flashed before her eyes. She was a little girl skipping along the
path. A man and woman were telling her to not go far. She
couldn't see their faces, but their voices were soft and caring.
Then it vanished just as fast as it had come. She turned back to the
desk and saw a portrait of a man, woman, and herself. She leaned
over for a closer look and stared at it long and hard. Just like in
the other photo, she didn't resemble either of them. This

recollection had come to her before at the house, when looking at the family picture. She shook her head and thought, this is silly, and everyone said that they were her parents. She had to look like one of her grandparents. She took a seat at the desk. The lawyer had said it all belonged to her. Mine, she thought, and she didn't have a clue as to what to do. That is why she wanted to call a meeting. It would at least be a starting point.

She leaned back in the chair as the aroma of English leather reached her senses. She closed her eyes and whispered, "Father help me," but the voice came out as that of a little girl, and a picture of her sitting on her father's lap asking him to help her learn to ride a horse came to mind. She opened her eyes and gazed at the picture, and said aloud, "This is a lot harder than riding a horse, but I need your help." She closed her eyes again and thought. Now, I'm getting nutty, talking to a picture.

She tried to open the center drawer, but found it locked. She was about to use the intercom to call the secretary to find out if she knew where the key was, when she saw a flash of her father standing by the fireplace. The picture, she remembered, and then as if in a trance she walked over to the fireplace and pulled on the picture frame of her on the horse. The whole picture opened to the left. Cindy found herself staring at a gray safe. She reached out and punched in the numbers two-ten-seventy-two, and turned the handle. The door opened. Now, how had she remembered those numbers? Suddenly she felt a draft on the back of her neck; then a hand brushed across her hair. She turned but no one was there. She spotted a small leather bound case and on top of it, a small set of keys. There were also a few thousand dollars in the safe, but nothing else. She removed the case and keys, leaving the money, and shut the door. It was as if she moved in a daze and was outside her body. Then the door opened. She looked up to see the secretary. "Mr. Osgood is in the building and will be with you shortly," she said.

"Thank you."

"Will you be meeting him in here or his office?"

Cindy pondered that question for a moment then said, "Tell Mark, I mean, Mr. Osgood to come in here." She wanted to let him know that she intended to do as her father had requested, be in charge. She put the case back in the safe. She'd sort through it later.

"Cindy, what a pleasant surprise," Mark said. "I wish I'd known you were coming, I'd have been here."

He approached her and leaned over to give her a kiss, to which she turned her right cheek. The aroma of a woman's perfume filled her senses and it wasn't hers. She smiled at Mark. "So you were at a meeting this morning?"

"Yes, a local bank needed some clarification on a few things."

More lies, Cindy thought. She wondered how many he'd already told. If he'd been at a meeting, why was his shirt buttoned wrong. Besides, he reeked of that perfume. She didn't let on and instead said, "Well, you're here now and I thought we'd go over a few things. I feel I need to abide by my father's wishes."

"Really, I wondered, when my secretary said you wanted to have a meeting. Surely, you can't mean to run the business. Don't get me wrong, I'm sure you're capable, but since you've lost your memory, I don't think it is a good idea. This isn't some small organization; it's national and requires a lot of hours."

"Hours, I'm willing to put in and maybe it will jar my memory. First, I need to have a meeting with all the top executives to get a feel for what is going on. I know I've a lot to learn, but there is no time like the present."

Mark seemed taken back by her statement. She noticed beads of sweat developing on his forehead and it wasn't warm in the room at all, in fact it was chilly. "Cindy, you've got to be reasonable," he said reaching for her, but she eluded him and sat behind the desk. She put on her best smile as he sat in one of the chairs in front of the desk.

She sat staring at him. He's upset, she thought, as his jaw tightened, showing more of the bony structure of his face. "Mark, I'm doing what my father wanted. He gave me complete charge. He must have had confidence in me, which is more than you seem to have."

"Cynthia, I mean Cindy; you've been through a lot lately, and in case you've forgotten, you're not the Cynthia Bradford he left in charge. I think until you get your memory back, you should leave the running of the company to me." He was thankful that her memory hadn't returned. This nonsense about her running the business, well he wouldn't let it happen. He put on a big smile. "Besides, after we're married, I'll run everything. I don't want my wife working. I want to start a family right away. Not that you won't have any say. I'll keep you informed of everything."

Cindy wanted to be sick again. A family with Mark, no way, as there wasn't going to be a marriage. However, she had to admit Mark had a point, at least about the business, for now anyway. "Mark, I don't know, let me think about it for a few days. When is the next board meeting?"

"In two weeks. It's always the last Wednesday of the month."

"Good, I'll be there and for now, I want everyone to continue doing as they have been. At the board meeting I'll decide what part I want to play in all this." At her statement, he seemed relieved. His jaw had relaxed and he didn't seem so tense.

"It's near lunch," Mark said. "Why don't the two of us have a nice lunch at El Rico's and then maybe take a stroll in the park?"

Lunch with him was the last thing she wanted to do. In two weeks, she planned to make her decision about the company. She also planned to tell him that the wedding was off. She put on her best face, as she didn't want to offend him; besides, she needed him to help with the company. "Oh Mark, I'm sorry, but I'm really not hungry, I had a large breakfast, but maybe next time." She got up, walked around the desk and even though she didn't want to, slipped her arm under his and guided him to the door. "I think I'll stay here and go through some of Father's things. Maybe there's something here that will jog my memory." She didn't give him time to respond and quickly shut the door.

She locked the door after him. She didn't want any interruptions. She opened the safe without any difficulty. She sat behind the desk with the leather case and keys. She gazed at them for the longest time. These things had belonged to her father. She hoped they held the key to her memory. Memory, she thought, as the headache she'd developed pounded harder. Aspirin, she needed an aspirin. She reached into her purse and opening the bottle, took two. She swallowed them, not needing any water. She seemed to be getting headaches a lot lately, especially when she'd been around Mark.

After a few minutes, the headache started to subside. She hoped the keys opened the desk, which they did. She didn't know what to expect, but it certainly wasn't the gun that stared her in the face. A small shiny silver pistol lay before her. She quickly shut the drawer. She sat gazing at the closed drawer. Why did her father have a gun? Was there someone he didn't trust? If so, who was it? She looked at her watch; Rip would be getting to her house soon. She pushed the intercom and the secretary's voice asked, "May I help you, Miss Bradford?"

"Yes, I'd like all the financial reports for the past year, please, and I'd like them right away." There wasn't a better place to start than to see what the company's financial status was. When she went to the board meeting in two weeks, she would at least have some knowledge of the company, and its operation. "Is something wrong?" She asked, when the secretary didn't answer.

"No, I mean, has Mr. Osgood approved...."

Cindy cut her off. "Miss," then remembered she didn't know her name, when the secretary said, "Anderson, my name is Beth Anderson."

"Well, Beth Anderson, as I said before, Mr. Osgood doesn't run the company, not yet anyway. Now I want those reports as soon as possible."

"Yes, Miss Bradford, I'll get right on it," she replied sweetly, over the intercom. Cindy leaned back in the chair and smiled. She felt concern over the fact that the secretary thought she had to okay everything through Mark. She was supposed to be her father's private secretary, not Marks. The intercom went off. She picked it up ready for another argument from her. "Yes," she said.

"There is a gentleman on the line by the name of Rip. Do you wish to speak to him?"

Chapter 26

"Rip, is anything wrong?" Her voice dropped a few notes in fear that he'd changed his mind and couldn't come today. She so longed to see him.

"No, nothing's wrong, unless you'd be upset that I arrived earlier than I expected."

He was here! She was excited to hear his voice. He's here in the city. Her body tingled in anticipation of seeing him. "You're here?" She asked in hopes she'd heard him right.

"Yes, I'm parked out front."

Cindy all but ran to the window, and spotted his truck parked directly below. She unconsciously touched her chignon, making sure every hair was still in place. She'd worn it in a twist, thinking it appropriate for the office, along with a navy blue suit and matching heels. She leaned her forehead against the window to cool her heated body. "I can see you. Look up to the top window." She watched him get out of the truck and her heart all but stopped at the sight of him. He had on a pair of cream slacks and a yellow polo shirt that enhanced his dark complexion. God is he ever handsome. He stood waving as he shaded his eyes against the afternoon sun. He gestured with his hands that he was coming up.

"No," she shook her head, motioning that she was coming down. She locked the desk and grabbed the leather case and her purse. It's a beautiful day, she thought as she stepped from the

office. She stopped long enough to   tell Miss Anderson that she'd
be back later for the papers.

The elevator seemed to be working at a snail's pace as it
descended. Couldn't it move any faster? She pushed the first floor
button impatiently. The others in the elevator gave her a strange
look, which she ignored. Let them think what they wanted; she
had the most wonderful man in the world waiting for her. When
the elevator came to a stop on the first floor, and the door opened,
Rip stood there with the biggest lopsided grin. "Hi," she said,
suddenly shy.

"Hi yourself," Rip replied.

They stood there staring at one another, their eyes locked,
oblivious to the others who had to step around them. It was as if
they were the only two people in the world. Rip broke the trance.

"You look beautiful, very professional." Indeed she did, he
thought. He wanted to take her in his arms and crush her against
his chest and smother her with kisses, and never let her out of his
arms, but he didn't. Instead, he reached for her arm and linked it
with his as he guided her out the door, and to his truck.

"I wanted to look the part my first day on the job," Cindy
said.

"Well, working lady, have you had lunch yet?" Rip asked as
they reached the truck. Lunch, he knew what he'd rather do. He'd
like to take her someplace private and feed her nothing but healthy
sex until they were fulfilled. He didn't think he could ever get
enough of her. If only she felt the same way about him. He had to
remember that she was engaged to Mark, a skinny specimen of a
man that claimed to have rights to her. He wondered what Cindy
had ever seen in him. Oh, he seemed kind enough, yet why did he
get this feeling every time he thought of the man whose persona
just didn't ring true?

"Lunch would be wonderful, I'm starved," Cindy said as he
helped her into the truck, which wasn't an easy task with her in a
skirt and heels. The touch of his hands sent a warm shiver through
her body. She felt on fire, a fire that only heightened as she sat
next to him. She wanted Rip, wanted him in her life, but knew that
she had to find herself first.

"Where would you like to go?" He asked.

"You choose," she replied nervously. Why was she
nervous? It's not as if she didn't know Rip. She'd lived with him
in his house. His house, she thought. She missed it with its birds,

rabbits, and squirrels; and Bandon, she missed playing with him out in the yard. She drank in Rip's profile, his striking appearance having always amazed her. She knew him to be older, but not that much older than herself. Rip turned to her as they stopped at a red light. "I hope I haven't interrupted anything important by coming early?"

"No." She wondered if he missed her as much as she missed him. Was that why he came early? Then she got her answer.

"I had a call after talking to you. It was from my agent. He wants to see what I've finished. He has a publishing house that may be interested, and a possible advance on writing the book."

So, it hadn't been because he couldn't wait to see her. He'd come earlier to see his agent. Happy for him, she said, "Oh, how wonderful Rip." She knew how much the book meant to him. If anyone deserved a break, he did. Life had dealt him a real blow, with his wife's death. She knew he'd loved her dearly for he'd said as much. She wondered and yes hoped that he would feel the need to love again.

"I could've sent it express. Then thought, since I'd planned on coming here anyway, why not come early and drop it off. So here we are, Bandon and me."

In her excitement at seeing Rip, she'd forgotten about Bandon. Cindy turned to the cage in the truck. "Rip, Bandon is gone, he's not back there." Fear gripped her that he'd somehow gotten out and had been hit or worse yet, killed by another vehicle.

Rip saw the worry etched into her beautiful face as he pulled into the restaurant's parking lot. He reached over and touched her arm. "Cindy, Bandon is fine. He's at your place. I went there first. Grace told me that you'd gone to your father's office. I didn't think Bandon could stand being cooped up any longer, the trip was long enough. Grace didn't mind. In fact, the two of them were getting along fine when I left."

"Grace is a good person. I like her, and she's been a big help with my adjustment to all of this."

"I liked her right away, also. Now, how about some food, I'm hungry? This restaurant is one of my favorites. You'll like the food; that is, if you like Mexican," Rip said as he pulled up in front of the restaurant.

"I don't know, but I'm willing to try." There was a lot she didn't know, and her favorite foods were one of them. El Rico's, the finest in Mexican cuisine, she'd read, forgetting that Mark had asked her to lunch there.

Cindy ordered the small sampler plate. Rip ordered a meat dish that the server set on fire before them. Rip also ordered them each a glass of wine, Chamborney. After the wine arrived, Rip asked if she'd had any more flashbacks.

"Rip, I don't know if I'll ever get my memory to return. I've been here for awhile now and nothing has changed. I've had some flashes of remembrance, but nothing significant."

"Anything that you remember is important. I've done a bit more reading in that book on amnesia. I read that no matter how small or insignificant one may think it is, each memory is meaningful. It's a sign that the mind is repairing itself. Soon Cindy, I believe it will all come rushing back to you." She seemed so innocent, yet worldly. Would she give him the time of day when she became Cynthia Bradford again? Would the Cindy he knew be gone? Then she put a finger across her lips, indicating for him to be silent. Her face, which had been glowing now, looked a pale gray.

"Cindy, what is it?" He asked in a hushed voice. Whatever it was had her shaking. He reached over for her hands in hopes of calming her, but she pulled them away and nervously began playing with her napkin. She motioned with a nod. He looked behind her only to look into the divider with a planter that had green ivy of some sort sprouting. Then he heard a familiar voice. He leaned a little to his left and quickly moved back. Mark sat at a table not ten feet away, facing them. A woman with dark hair sat across from him. He couldn't see her face, but one thing was certain--they knew each other. They were holding hands. Now he knew the reason for Cindy's state of shock. Here she was engaged to the man and he was having lunch with another woman. He reached for her hands and this time she didn't pull away. "Cindy, I'm sure there is a good explanation for this. She is probably a client."

"Please Rip, I want to leave. I don't want him to see us."

Rip left a few bills on the table, enough to cover the meal they hadn't eaten. They walked out with their backs to the planter and Mark, and the woman, whoever she was.

Outside where she could finally breathe, she leaned into Rip for strength. "How could he? One minute he is professing his love for me and the next--never mind, it isn't your problem and I'm sorry for spoiling your lunch."

"You didn't spoil a thing, besides, I really wasn't that hungry." A lie, but he could see how upset she was. "Cindy, please don't let what you saw upset you. I'm sure it isn't anything." Her coloring had returned. He reached for her as they walked to the parking lot and the truck. He couldn't help wondering why she'd been so upset. She said she wanted nothing to do with the man. Had she changed her mind about Mark?

He drove her back to the office building and waited while she got her car. Following her home, he thought of the woman who'd been sitting across the table from Mark. He didn't know what Cindy had seen, but he knew a business lunch from a date, and this hadn't been about business.

On the drive home with Rip close behind, she thought of Mark and the woman he'd sat with at the table. She gripped the steering wheel as her body began to shake, and her throat got tight, making it hard to breathe. She slowed down and pulled off to the side of the road. She had to get air and fumbled with the door handle, as it swung open. She stepped from the car as another one went flying by, blowing its horn. Then she felt arms as they enfolded her. She recognized those arms and suddenly felt safe again. "Cindy, are you all right?" She could hear the voice that gave her comfort. Then there was nothing but blackness.

"She's just fainted and needs rest," Rip said to Grace as he carried Cindy into the house. "Where is her room? Also, get a washcloth with water, please?"

"Sir, I don't think...."

"Grace, please, now is not the time." She must have seen the concern on his face for she finally said, "Up the stairs, last room on the left."

"Thanks," he'd called back.

Rip gently laid Cindy on the bed as she moaned. "Cindy, wake up," he said as he moved the hair away from her forehead. She felt clammy and damp. He reached for her hand just as the Grace returned with a bowl of water and washcloth. She set them on the nightstand and stood watching as Rip placed the damp rag on Cindy's forehead. Cindy moaned again and then slowly opened her eyes.

"What happened?" Cindy asked. She felt confused. Then she remembered she'd been driving. "Have I been in an accident?

Is anyone hurt?" She looked from Rip to Grace, who seemed frightened.

"No, you didn't hit anyone. For some reason you pulled off the road. When you got out of the car, you fainted. I caught you or you would have fallen into the road."

"I don't know what happened out there. I was driving and I couldn't catch my breath. I needed air. Then I felt your arms around me and knew I'd be all right." Cindy attempted to sit up, but fell back again, as her head felt like it weighed a ton. "I think I'll take a little nap." She said to Grace, "Put Mr. Walker in one of the guest rooms." She smiled at Rip. "I'll see you in a few hours, but don't let me sleep too long."

"Cindy, I can't stay here. I'll get a room at the hotel in town."

"Rip, don't be foolish. Tell him, Grace, not to be foolish." Cindy relaxed as Grace took hold of Rip's arm and all but pulled him from the room.

Cindy didn't even remove her clothes; it would take too much energy, something she lacked at the moment. She slipped under the comforter and closed her eyes, as pictures of her with her father floated before her, filling her thoughts.

She rode like the wind and sped across the fields, her long hair shining in the sun. She rounded the tree and came to a halt. He came alongside her. "You've won again. I remember a time when you couldn't beat me."

She laughed with joy with the man who sat proudly on his horse. A handsome man, her father was, with his striking white hair, and well built for his age. She'd asked him why he'd never married again after her mother died. He only said she'd been the best wife a man could ask for. Then sorrow filled his eyes, and he began yelling at someone. A man, only she couldn't see who it was, his face was fuzzy. She couldn't tell what her father was saying, but it wasn't pleasant and then this man was pulling her away. NO! NO! She heard her father calling.

Cindy quickly sat up in bed, her body soaked with perspiration. She realized it had been a dream, but it had seemed so real. Then she remembered what had happened earlier, before she'd fallen asleep. She'd seen Mark kissing another woman. She wasn't jealous, but they were supposed to be engaged. Well, not for long, that was for sure. She looked at her watch. She'd only been sleeping for a little over an hour. Rip, good dependable Rip,

she'd left him alone in a strange house. She quickly got up and
went to shower. She couldn't wait to see him.

Rip followed Grace out into the hallway. He hadn't had a
choice as she practically pulled him out the door. He'd followed
her to another wing of the house where she showed him to a
room. She'd said, "Mr. Walker, I don't know much about you, but
if Cindy likes you, then you are okay in my book." With that said,
she left, closing the door behind her.

Rip stood out on the small balcony connected to the room.
He faced the stables, which had the letter 'B' in black iron in the
center by the roof, the same lettering that marked the gate upon
entry to the estate. He saw Bandon tied to a small post by the
barn. Then it dawned on him, he'd forgotten to have someone go
and get Cindy's car. He'd left it alongside the road. He'd tell
Grace; she'd have someone drive it home. The room he'd been
given was spacious, with a king-size bed, dressers, and a private
bath. He had to admit, what he'd seen of the house so far was
impressive. It reeked of old money, but if he had to pick, he
preferred his place with its cozy ambiance. Cindy had seemed
happier there, not troubled and uptight as she was here. Yet he
knew she belonged here, and he didn't. He should go, but first he
had to see about getting her car home.

Rip found the kitchen, without much trouble, as the aroma
of baked apple pie couldn't be missed. As he approached, he
heard two women talking, Grace and another. When he heard his
name mentioned he paused. Not wanting to eavesdrop, the cop in
him--well, he stopped just shy of the door and listened.

"I tell you, I heard her say it with my own ears." That was
Grace speaking, he knew that much. Then the other replied, "But
how did he save her, and from what?"

"One thing is for sure," Grace said. "He is one handsome
fellow, and I could see a bond between the two of them." To
which the other said, "But she is engaged to Mr. Osgood."

"Him," Grace said. "That man I don't trust and you know,
before Mr. Bradford left, I heard him on the phone to some fellow,
saying he wasn't happy about the engagement. Ever since you met
Osgood, you hadn't been yourself. He said he had some more
checking to do, and that the wedding wouldn't take place. That,
he'd be dead first."

Then the other woman said, "Yes, and dead he is. Who is going to help her now? Especially with her having amnesia. Maybe this new fellow will help. She does seem to care for him. Maybe Miss Cynthia will give Mr. Osgood the boot."

Rip had heard enough. So Mr. Bradford had been checking on Mark. If only he knew what Cindy's father had found. The women had stopped talking so he opened the door to the kitchen.

"Oh, Mr. Walker, how nice to see you," Grace said warmly. "Is everything all right with your room?"

"The room is fine, but I won't be staying. I've rented a room. I came to ask you, if there was someone here who could follow me to Cindy's car and back. We left it along the road." He eyed the three pies cooling on a wire rack.

"Don't worry about the car I'll send someone to bring it back. Would you like a piece of hot apple pie? Grace asked. Ann makes the best pies," The other woman, Ann, smiled proudly.

"Thank you, but I'll wait for Cindy. He was about to leave when Grace offered, "I've a ham bone that I think your dog might like."

Rip reached for the bag she handed him. "Thanks, Bandon will love it. He's not a dog, but a wolf." He saw the surprise on their faces. "Don't worry; he's just a pup, and friendly, too." Rip chuckled as he headed outside.

"Here you go boy," he said to Bandon, who jumped at the offering and began chewing with delight. "Cindy will be out soon to see you." At the sound of her name, his ears perked up. Rip patted his head and then decided to look around the stables.

He didn't see anyone when he entered the building, but then a man in bib overalls stepped out from the far stall. "Can I help you, sir?" The elderly man inquired with a wide grin. His gray hair sprouted from the straw hat he wore. The man pulled his work glove from his right hand and reached out his hand. "I'm Jacob. I run the outside of this place. My wife Grace takes care of running the house." Rip shook his hand. He had a firm grip and soft kind eyes. Rip liked him on the spot. "I'm Rip, Rip Walker, a friend of Cindy's." He saw his face light up at the sound of her name.

"Glad to meet you, Mr. Walker."

"Please call me Rip. Mr. Walker sounds so old."

"Well, Rip, have you come out to go for a ride? I just finished brushing Miss Bradford's horse in case she wanted to ride today. She never used to miss a day of riding. Loves horses, that girl, she does. She's loved them since she was nothing but a wee thing. She and her daddy, the late Mr. Bradford, they were more like friends than father and daughter. Yes sir, them two surely loved one another. It's too bad about that plane crash. I still have a hard time believing that he won't be around anymore."

"Maybe Cindy will want to ride when she wakes up. It's been awhile since I've been on a horse, so…."

"Don't you worry; Jacob here will take care of you. I've a nice and gentle one to get you started. Just let me know when you're ready."

Rip stepped out into a cold blast of air. The skies promised a storm, and he knew it would be raining shortly. Well, they wouldn't be riding today. He reached down and unhooked the chain that held Bandon to the post. "Hey, little fellow, let's you and I take a walk."

Cindy stepped out from the warm shower. She felt much better, but she still couldn't figure out what had made her pass out. She probably just needed rest. It had been a trying morning going into her father's office and attempting to take it all in. Maybe Mark was right, it was just too much, and she should let him handle things, for now anyway. Besides, her father had trusted him. Rip was here and waiting. She pulled on a pair of jeans, a cream, lightweight sweater. After putting on a pair of tennis shoes, she looked in the mirror and saw the dark circles under her eyes. She applied some cover-up and little blush, then brushed her hair and pulled it back into a ponytail. With another glance in the mirror, thinking it would have to do, she headed out the door.

Cindy first went to the room that she knew Grace would have given Rip, but he wasn't there. In fact, it didn't look like he'd been there at all. No, she thought, he couldn't have left. She hurried to the kitchen to find Ann washing up from baking the pies. "Ann, where is Grace? I need to speak to her."

"I'm sorry; Miss Cynthia, but Grace and Jacob have gone to fetch your car. Is there something I can help you with?"

"No. How soon do you expect them back?"

"Well, I don't know. Jacob was going on into town for something. I think Grace was going with him and then they were going to pick up the car on the way back, but I can't say for sure."

Disappointed, Cindy headed outside. A walk in the garden was what she needed. She still couldn't believe Rip would leave. She didn't see Bandon, a sure sign he'd left. Maybe he decided not to stay and checked into a hotel. That's it, she thought as she rounded the corner of the house and headed toward the back gardens. Then she heard a howl. Bandon, she thought. She picked up her pace and hurried toward the sound. It came from the gardens ahead. Then she saw the two of them, and relief washed over her; they hadn't left. Bandon spotted her and came charging. She knelt down as he reached her and he began licking her face, as she ruffled his ears. She hugged him to her heart. Oh how she'd missed him. They rolled on the ground and she laughed while Bandon barked in delight.

"Now isn't this a sight!" Rip stood looking down at her and couldn't help but chuckle. He reached for her hand to help her up. "I guess I don't have to tell you how much Bandon's missed you."

"What about you?"

For an answer, he pulled her to him. She leaned into him as her heart beat wildly and they embraced. He started to pull away, but she wrapped her arms tight about his waist. He was her strength and she needed him now more than ever. With him she could breathe, not suffocate as she did around Mark. She gazed up into his eyes, which sparkled like the ocean on a warm sunny day. She wanted to dive into them and lose herself in their depth. Their lips were a breath apart, their gaze locked and held. It seemed only natural their lips do the same. His lips closed over hers, soft and wonderful. She responded and could feel his arousal against her stomach, sending thrills up and down her spine. She too felt the need as the area between her legs moistened and throbbed with want, and need of release. She heard a moan and realized it came from her throat as she deepened their kiss. She wanted Rip. Then he gently pulled them apart. She felt a cool breeze come between them. She gazed into his eyes and knew that he too wanted more.

"Cindy, I'm sorry, I shouldn't have...."

"Shush," she placed her fingers over his lips, which seconds ago had given her so much pleasure, beyond anything she'd ever experienced. "Rip, don't apologize." She reached over and touched his chest where his heart lay. "You've touched my heart, Rip Walker." She reached up and gave his lips a light brush with hers.

Rip considered the woman who had stolen his heart, his life, something he thought would never happen again after the death of his wife. "Okay, I won't say I'm sorry, but I shouldn't have. I've taken advantage of you again when I said I wouldn't. Not until you regained your memory. Besides, we're partners. I'm here to help you."

So, that's what it was to him, a job. The kiss had been in the heat of the moment. She pulled away and attempted to regain her composure. A few raindrops signaled the storm as the rain started to come down harder. They ran for the house under the almost black skies with Bandon at their heels.

They'd just stepped inside the kitchen door when the dark skies really let loose with thunder and lightning. "That was close," Rip laughed as he shook the water from his hair. Bandon stood shaking his fur. Cindy couldn't help laughing too, for they sure were a sight, man and beast shaking their heads.

Rip pointed to her, and she began swishing her ponytail back and forth, as together they were caught up in the joy of the moment.

Rip suddenly got quiet and stood staring at her. Cindy glanced at herself and saw she looked a sight. Her bra was visible, for her blouse was saturated. She noticed his eyes as they moved over her and lingered on her breasts; her nipples had hardened from the dampness. "I think we need to change, get out of these wet clothes and into something warm. Then we'll have some hot coffee and a piece of Ann's apple pie."

"Sounds good," he said, trying to keep his voice calm. The sight of her all wet, and those nipples, not to mention the way her tongue had moistened her lips, had him starting to harden again. He wanted to grab her, take her right there and then on the kitchen floor. What he needed was a cold shower, as his body was on fire with its need of her.

"See you in about a half hour," Cindy said as she hurried from the kitchen and up the stairs to her room. She had to get away, for she couldn't trust herself alone with him now. She didn't want to make a fool of herself when Rip had all but told her that he thought of her as a partner.

Chapter 27

"I haven't tasted apple pie this good in a long time," Rip exclaimed as he finished off the last bite and leaned back in the chair, and rubbed his stomach, "mighty good."

Cindy smiled. She liked to see a man enjoy his food. Now where did that come from? Then a picture of the man who everyone said was her father came before her eyes. He sat across from her praising the meal she'd made. The meal consisted of meat loaf and mashed potatoes made with real potatoes. He too had sat back and patted his belly. "You reminded me of my father just now," she said as she got up to refill their coffee mugs.

"Do you know what you've just said, Cindy?" Rip asked as he watched her move about the kitchen. His eyes focused on the way her jeans fit snug across her bottom. She'd let her hair down around her shoulders, the way he preferred. He pictured her body that day when she'd lain unconscious. It had been smooth and firm. That seemed like ages ago, but in fact, only a month had passed. She kept getting flashbacks, and they were coming more frequently. He knew it wouldn't be long and she'd have her memory back. Something he wanted and yet dreaded.

"What?" She asked of his question.

"You are starting to remember. Like now, saying I remind you of your father. It's a start in the right direction; soon you'll have total recall."

"I hope so," she said as she set their mugs on the table. "Leading two different lives is unnerving."

Mark had let himself in through the front door and hearing voices, headed toward the kitchen. He stopped short when he heard the mention of total recall. Had she gotten her memory back? If so, he was dead. It was entirely Walker's fault. He'd had him checked out and found out Rip had been one hell of a detective. The man was a threat. He'd hoped that once he knew Cynthia to be with family, Walker would leave them alone. He might have to do away with them both. He'd have to come up with a plan. They couldn't be together, because Cynthia's body could never be found, not if he wanted the plan to work. He braced himself and stepped into the kitchen. "Did I hear someone say perfect recall?"

"Mark!" Cindy said. "Yes, you heard right, but only in hopes of it returning. What brings you out on a stormy evening?" She wasn't glad to see him, especially after what she'd witnessed this afternoon. She set her coffee mug down and didn't attempt to get up.

"How can you ask such a silly question?" he asked as he approached her chair and reached down to kiss her. She turned her head and he kissed her cheek. She wanted to wipe away his wet kiss, but she clamped her teeth together for strength. She couldn't wait to end this farce of an engagement, and the sooner the better, but now wasn't the time. It seemed like there never was a good time. Maybe her subconscious didn't want her to call the wedding off. No, she just couldn't marry this man. Then Bandon growled as Mark attempted to pet him. Mark jumped.

"Bandon, stop that," Rip said, picking Bandon up as he continued to growl. He didn't like Mark for some reason. Rip hadn't liked him from day one. Bandon was friendly with everyone but Mark. "It's okay, boy," he said and patted Bandon on the head. Bandon quieted down, but kept a close eye on Mark's every move.

"That's one mean dog," Mark said. "Animals don't take a liking to me, never have." He gave Cindy's shoulders a light squeeze, to which Bandon growled. Ignoring the mutt, he pulled out a chair and sat at the table.

"Bandon," Cindy said. "You be quiet now. I've never seen him act that way before. He's mine, Mark, and he's not a dog, he is a wolf."

"You can't be serious, Cynthia?"

"I'm very serious. He lost his mother in a snowstorm and I'm Bandon's mother now." She saw Bandon's ears perk up. Then she remembered her manners. "Would you like some coffee and a piece of apple pie?"

"Thanks, I'll have a cup of coffee. As far as the pie, you remember, no, I guess you wouldn't, I'm a diabetic." A look of surprise crossed her face; good, he thought, her memory hadn't returned. He still had time.

"You can't be serious, Cynthia, I mean, it's a wolf, not a dog."

This angered her, and she felt the blood rush to her face. "For starters," she said trying to calm her nerves. "His name is Bandon, and yes I know he's a wolf, and yes I plan to keep him. There's plenty of room around here for him to roam." She got up to get Mark a mug of coffee. "He's mine and that's it." She set his mug in front of him roughly, causing the hot liquid to spill.

Rip had to steel himself not to react to the humor he saw in what had just transpired. She's so damn beautiful when she gets her dander up. He said, "Cindy if there's a problem with Bandon staying here he can stay at my place. You can visit him as often as you like."

Rip, she thought, how kind of him. "That won't be necessary. Bandon is mine and he's staying here." She'd made up her mind and this was her place. Anyway, that's what everyone told her. She'd decide who stayed and who went and right now she wished Mark would leave. She started to ask why Mark happened to come by when he answered the question.

"I almost forgot what I came by for," Mark said. "I stopped by the office to see if you were still there and Miss Anderson said you'd asked for some reports."

That woman couldn't wait to tell him, she thought. Well, she'd deal with her later. She turned to Mark. "Yes, I asked for the financial statements for the past year." Darn, in her haste to get back here after seeing Mark and that woman, she'd completely forgotten the papers. "Is there a problem? A company our size surely wouldn't have any trouble coming up with such a statement." Mark sat thumbing the rim of his coffee mug nervously. "Well?" She asked again. She looked over at Rip who sat there quietly. He gave her a slight wink. Now why did he do that? Then Mark replied.

"No, Cynthia, there isn't a problem, but I can't for the life of me understand why you'd want to burden yourself with such matters at a time like this. Your father has just passed away, and the wedding isn't far off. You should be working on the invitations, not worrying about financial papers. We started a list a few months back. I'm sure it's in one of the drawers in the library." He reached for her hand, but she'd gotten up from the table and now stood leaning against the sink. It seemed every time he tried to get close, that she pushed him away. Why? Unless…he looked over to Rip who sat there so smug. Did it have something to do with him? He smiled at Rip and said, "Don't you agree, Rip, that she shouldn't concern herself at a time like this?"

Rip didn't answer right away. He looked to Cindy and then back to Mark. "Mark, I can't answer for Cindy, but if getting involved and seeing what her father did might help bring back her memory, then I'm all for it. Besides, what harm can come of her knowing? Isn't that what we all want?

"Of course, getting her memory back is first and foremost," Mark, answered.

Cindy didn't like doing it this way, but it had to be said. "Mark, I want to postpone the wedding." There, she said it. She saw a look of disbelief cross his face and then anger as he moved towards her. He stopped as Rip stood up in his way.

Mark backed away and leaned against the kitchen counter. He couldn't believe what she'd said. This couldn't be happening. "You can't be serious. I mean, it's so close. The invitations…." He had to regain control. He could lose everything. "Please, Mark, hear me out."

"For one, the invitations haven't gone out; and with Father's recent death, I don't think it's proper to have it so soon. There needs to be a period of mourning and respect for him. More importantly, I'd like to have my memory return before I take such an important step. I would think you'd want the same."

"Cynthia, you're upset over some silly papers. If that's what you want to do, I don't care. I've brought the papers with me. They're in the entranceway on the table, but as far as the wedding is concerned, we've made all the plans." He knew he was begging, but he couldn't have her calling it off. "It's what your father wanted, you and I together." She had to see, she just had to, but one look at her face and he knew. Then it came to him. He'd use another tack. "How about giving it just another two weeks?"

Two weeks, Cindy thought. She'd originally planned to tell him then. Maybe in that time her memory would return, and what if she did feel differently about him after that? She shivered at the thought. She considered Rip, whom she knew she cared about deeply as Cindy, but as Cynthia, she was engaged to Mark. She considered Mark, who pleaded with his eyes. He really must care for me, she thought, but what about that woman in the restaurant? "Mark, who was that woman I saw you with at lunch today?" She thought she saw a spark of surprise, but in the next instant, it disappeared.

"Cynthia, is that what all this is about? I ran into her when you so politely refused to dine with me. She's the sister of an old friend of mine. We used to date, but there is nothing between us now. You're the only one for me. She invited me to sit with her since she was alone." Quick thinking, he thought. "Is that the reason for this sudden change of heart? You know how much you mean to me. I did ask you first to have lunch with me."

"I know, but after Rip came, I changed my mind."

Rip was quiet; he didn't believe a word the man said. Old friend, my ass, he thought. He couldn't keep his hands off the woman. Cindy looked confused and he could understand. She'd been through so much lately that she didn't know which way to turn, but he wouldn't push her. It would be her decision and hers only. Then his heart fell.

"Okay Mark, I'll give it the two weeks. It's only right that I give myself time to heal, but I still may want to postpone the wedding because of Father."

Rip watched as Mark rushed to take her hands in his. This time she didn't pull away. Rip got up without saying a word, picked up Bandon and walked out the door, never glancing back. It had stopped raining and he needed some fresh air.

Cindy saw Rip leave and wanted to go after him, but Mark kept rambling on about how happy he was that she hadn't called off the wedding. He slobbered kisses on her hands, which made her stomach churn. Besides, two weeks wasn't forever. Then maybe, just maybe she'd have her own self back. Right now, she wanted him to leave. After convincing him that it had been a long day and she needed to sleep, he finally did.

She picked up the mugs and plates and placed them in the dishwasher. She wondered where Rip had gone off to. She grabbed the light sweater hanging on a hook by the door. It fit like a sack of potatoes; it must belong to Grace. Well, she didn't want to go all the way to her room to get hers and didn't think Grace would mind.

She stepped out into the chilly evening. The rain had stopped. The night was almost too dark for her to see, as there wasn't a star out. She wrapped the sweater tightly about her and followed the walkway around to the back, thinking that's probably where they'd gone. She called out but no one answered. Hearing and seeing nothing, she headed back to the house, and then heard someone call her name. She stopped dead in her tracks as fear engulfed her, since the voice wasn't Rip's. She had nowhere to run. The house stood over twenty yards away. A second later Jacob came around from the side of the house. "Miss Cynthia, you were calling?" Relief washed over her at the sight of him.

"Jacob, I'm sorry, yes I was. Have you seen Mr. Walker? He took Bandon out for a walk and I haven't seen him return." She pulled the sweater even tighter, if that were possible.

"Yes, a while ago," Jacob said. "He brought the wolf out to the barn. Said he was calling it a night, then drove off. But don't you worry; I got your pet all set up nice and comfy."

"Thank you, Jacob. By chance, Jacob, did Mr. Walker say where he was going?"

"Yes, said he was headed to the hotel. Miss Cynthia, you don't have to thank me for doing my job. I have always taken care of your animals since you were a babe. Your daddy trusted me, and he paid me well. You just ask old Jacob and it will get done."

That seemed to be true, for though she hadn't been there that long, the stables were always neat, clean and everything ran smoothly. "Good-night Jacob," she said, about to go inside. She'd only taken a few steps when she turned back around and said, "Jacob, you and Dad were more than employer and employee, you were friends, right?"

"Why, I like to think so, Miss. We had many a good night of Gin Rummy. I think I was up on him by two games," he laughed. Then his face saddened.

"I'm sorry, Jacob, but since I'm trying to remember everything, I've got to ask."

"Don't be sorry, I'm just a sentimental old man. I truly do miss your father. Please, feel free to ask me anything at anytime and I'll do my best," he patted her arm. "Now you get in there before you catch your death of cold."

"I will, but there is one more thing." He nodded so she asked, "Do you know why my father would own a small pistol? I know he has a few rifles. I've seen them in the library in a locked case."

"No, but I do know he'd been on edge the last few weeks before taking that trip overseas. Maybe it had something to do with that. It doesn't sound like Harry though. He didn't believe in violence of any kind. Always felt he could work things out calmly. That was Harry Bradford's way. Cindy, what is really bothering you? I mean all these questions?"

Not wanting to alarm him, she said, "I just was wondering since he had one at his office. Now I think I truly will turn in, and thanks again," she gave Jacob a hug and let herself into the house, but she saw his look of concern.

Disappointed that Rip had decided not to stay, she headed to her room.

Rip lay awake long after he'd gone to bed. He could not understand why Cindy had done what she did tonight. Why didn't she come right out and say the wedding is off. He'd left without saying goodnight because he'd been afraid of what he'd say. He was angry and hurt. He didn't want her marrying that man. He'd been elated when she'd wanted to postpone the wedding. He didn't trust Mark, but most of all he thought it gave him a chance, but then in the next breath, she'd backed down. Why? Did she have feelings towards him? She'd been upset at the restaurant when she saw Mark with that other woman. Had she been angry or jealous? Then he remembered the way she'd come on to him in the gardens. Had he only imagined it? No, he thought, as he pulled the covers back and got up to stand before the window. As he gazed out at the black sky, he thought of their kisses and knew she'd felt something. Why the sudden change? These and other questions played.

Cindy stopped on the way to her room and picked up the envelope that Mark had left. She'd go over the papers, since she wasn't tired. She slipped into a pair of lavender, silk pajamas and crawled into bed. She emptied the contents of the envelope. She gave it all a quick once-over and noted that everything seemed in order, but then math had never been her forte. Now how did she know that? A smile crossed her lips. There were many things popping into her thoughts lately, just as Rip had said would happen. At the thought of his name, she remembered their embrace and the kisses they'd shared earlier that day. They'd been having a wonderful day until she saw Mark at the restaurant and then later when he arrived unexpectedly. None of which had been her fault. It bothered her that Rip had left without a word. Had he been angry? Unless he regretted what had happened in the gardens. No, they'd been comfortable together when Mark interrupted them. Then why had Rip left so quickly?

Chapter 28

Cindy awoke to the birds chirping and the sun streaming through the windows. She stretched and ran her hand through her long tresses. She just knew it would be a beautiful day. As she arose, the papers that had lain about her bed fell to the floor. She began gathering them up, stacking them neatly back in the envelope. She'd go over them later with a fresher mind than she had last night. Now, the sun was shining and she couldn't wait to begin the day. A glance at the clock showed she'd overslept, nine o'clock.

After a quick shower, she put on the jeans from the night before and a blue denim shirt. She applied very little makeup and with her hair brushed, headed downstairs. In the kitchen, she found Grace and Ann going over a grocery list.

"Well good-morning, Miss Cynthia," Grace greeted her.

"Good-morning Grace and Ann," she returned and fixed herself a cup of coffee.

"Mr. Walker called earlier."

Cindy almost dropped her coffee. "Grace, why didn't you wake me?"

"I wanted to, but he insisted that I not. He said to tell you that he had some business to attend to this morning and that he'd stop by sometime this afternoon."

"He didn't give a time?"

"No. Now, what would you like for breakfast?"

"Toast, just toast and bring it out to the verandah, please."
With her coffee in hand, she left. What had started out to be a
beautiful day suddenly clouded at the thought of spending most of
her time alone. Business, he'd said. What kind of business took
most of the day? Then she remembered his book. That's it; he
went to meet his agent. Feeling better, she said to Ann as she
brought the toast, "Yes, I think I will have some breakfast after all;
a couple of scrambled eggs and a glass of orange juice, if it isn't too
much trouble. Then, I think I'll have Jacob saddle up Snickers for
me. It's such a gorgeous day for a ride."

"That's a fine idea, Miss Cynthia, and I'll have the eggs and
juice for you shortly."

Cindy heard Ann tell Grace, 'I think we've got the old Miss
Cynthia back.' If only that were true, she thought, but right now
she wanted to go for a ride.

"Be careful out riding, Miss Cynthia, with that rain last
night the hills will be muddy," Jacob advised as he handed her the
reins. "I suggest using the west-side of the property, its sandier
ground."

"Thanks, I'll do just that, and don't worry Jacob, I'll be
fine."

"I know you're a good rider Missy, but with that hit on the
head, well--I just don't want—just be careful."

"I will, I promise and don't worry. I feel like I belong
here," she said. She truly did as she reached down to pat Snickers
neck. "He'll take good care of me, won't you boy?" Snickers
made a nod. "See Jacob, nothing to worry about." She gave a
wave and started out only to hear Bandon yipping. "Not this time
Bandon, let me get used to this first, then you can go." She headed
to the trail leading to the west side of the property. Snickers
seemed to sense her apprehension, as he trotted at a slow pace, for
which Cindy was grateful. It gave her a chance to see the property.
She hadn't realized how enormous the Bradford lands were, all
handed down from the past three generations and now it hers. It
suddenly dawned on her what a large responsibility she'd inherited.
Her father had trusted her with this and she wouldn't let the
Bradford name down. She didn't have a brother and for the first
time, a woman held the title. "Now what do you think of that,
Snickers?" she asked, coming upon a small stream and stopping. A
good spot for a rest, she thought, and dismounted.

She sat leaning against a tree while Snickers enjoyed his drink. He then started nibbling at the plentiful green grass that grew along the stream's banks. She'd asked Ann to pack a small lunch and thought fondly of Ann and Grace as she pulled it out: a piece of fried chicken breast, a small container of potato salad, a bunch of grapes and a nice sized piece of Ann's apple pie. She had worked up an appetite and devoured her feast. When she finished, she got up and went to the stream to wash her hands. As she bent over the clear blue water, she saw a trout swimming. She gave a giggle and sat down as the fish continued on it way. As she continued to sit there, memories of another time by this stream came to mind. She'd been young. She sat with her mother, who had her arms around her. She could see her father over by the stream fishing. Then her mother was whispering something into her ear, 'I love you so much, Cynthia. I knew you were mine when I first saw you,' and then she'd hugged Cindy. All this she remembered as she lay back on the grass and stared up to the clear blue sky. "Mother, please help me. Help me remember," she called to the heavens.

Later as she approached the stables, she saw Rip's truck in the driveway by the barn. "Well, Snickers, you've been waiting for a good run, let's go," she said as he took off. She felt free, as Snickers sped towards the stables. She had never felt so elated and happy. It was as if she had born for the saddle.

Rip heard the pounding of horse's hooves and turned in the direction of the noise. He saw a woman and horse bounding towards him. Seeing it was Cindy, he thought, how beautiful she looked with her hair flying in all directions. His heart beat rapidly. He knew he cared for her, but he had to be realistic, she didn't know herself, and until she did, they didn't have a chance. He knew she wanted to call off the engagement to Mark. Would she still want to once she got her memory back? A true horsewoman, he thought, as Cindy and the horse came to a halt a few feet from him. "You ride like you know what you're doing," he said as he gave her a hand dismounting.

She smelled of fresh air as she leaned into him, almost losing her balance. He pulled her closer and her hair brushed against his face. His groin began to pulse and throb as he continued to hold her. She gazed into his eyes. He wanted to float into the depths of their wonder. He then took in her lips. They looked so soft, he couldn't resist as he found himself reaching toward them. He needed to taste her and he did. Their lips met and he thought he'd gone to heaven. They held on to one another trading kiss for kiss. He'd never believed he could feel this way again about anyone. Then they both pulled away suddenly at the sound of a vehicle. He stepped back and they turned to hear Mark's voice calling to them.

"Hi, you two," Mark said, coming towards them. "Going riding, I see? Well, if you wait, I'll have Jacob get one ready for me. I could use a good run." Then he noticed that Rip didn't have a horse.

"I've returned from a ride. Rip just got here."

"Well, another time then," Mark said. "I really need to be getting back to the office. I came by to have you sign some papers, Cindy."

"Papers, I don't know, Mark. I really wouldn't know what I would be signing at this point. Besides, can't they wait until I am more familiar with things? Give me a week or so, and then I'll have a better handle on things." She saw that he wasn't happy with her as he ran his fingers through his blond hair, something he did when he didn't like what she said or implied. "It can't be that important?"

"It's the monthly report. It needs the president's signature before it can go to the stockholders. It's just a formality, let me get the papers."

"I'll look at them this evening," she said, taking the folder he handed her. "You can pick them up around noon tomorrow." She placed the file under her arm. "Right now, I could go for a nice cool glass of iced lemonade. I'd just been about to ask Rip if he'd like one." She glanced to Rip. She smiled when he nodded. "Good. Since you've got to get back to the office, Mark, I'm sure you don't want a drink."

"Cindy, wait," Mark said, taking hold of her right arm. "I also wanted to know if we could have dinner tonight, alone." He looked at Rip. The man seemed to be everywhere. "We really do have a lot to discuss about the wedding. Let's have a nice cozy dinner, just the two of us? I thought maybe we'd go to your favorite place, Ricardo's. What do you say?"

Rip stood there watching the two of them. Cindy had been so warm and pleasant earlier, but with Mark here, she acted like a different person. Yet, they're engaged. If she were going to have dinner with Mark, he'd just forget the drink and be on his way. He needed to touch base with Sarah. See if she'd found out anything more about Mark. He'd also asked her to check on those two men he'd seen in Buford. Something about them still didn't ring true. In fact, this whole idea of Cindy and drugs stunk. He was about to bid his good-bye, when he heard Cindy say,

"Mark, I really can't make dinner. I had planned on a quiet evening reading a good book, besides; it looks like I'll have to replace the book with these papers." She held up the file folder that he'd given her. "I'll be up most of this evening reading them. You did say you needed them right away?"

"Yes, of course," Mark said. He looked over at Rip. "I guess you won't be staying long either, since Cindy is so busy."

"I--no, I had to come to town and thought I'd stop by and see how Cindy and Bandon were doing." Not true, but it was the best he could come up with, and he really had wondered how they were doing. "I see that they're both doing fine." The truth was that he missed Cindy. The time she'd spent at his place had opened him up to what he'd thought he'd never feel again. She brought meaning to his life. He'd felt stagnant, he had been going through the daily motions he once thought made him happy, but in reality he'd been in hiding. Oh, he had his book to write, but he realized now that it wasn't enough. Cindy gave him purpose in his life. He looked on as Mark gave her a kiss on the cheek, saying he'd see her tomorrow. Mark gave a not-so-nice glance towards him and said, "See you around, Mr. Walker." Rip watched Cindy brush at her cheek where Mark had planted a kiss.

Mark drove away angry as he looked into the rearview mirror. Cynthia and Walker were walking arm in arm toward the house. That man was becoming a damned nuisance, he thought, and banged his fist on the dashboard. He needed Cynthia to read and sign those papers, which she damned had well better do. She didn't know anything about the business. All she had to do was to take his word for it and sign things. Well, soon he wouldn't have to worry about any of this. He wouldn't need her signature. Refusing dinner, saying she wanted a quiet evening, that was bullshit; she wanted to spend the evening with Walker. Well, not for much longer, he thought. He'd have it all, the Bradford empire. He'd worked hard to get where he was and soon the only thing in his way would be eliminated. It had been a narrow escape when she saw him at lunch. Good thing she'd worn the wig. If not, it could have been a disaster. Thinking of the woman that waited to become Cynthia Bradford made his body warm. He needed some sex and headed his car toward the apartment building where he knew she'd be waiting. He had to keep her happy. The woman was so smitten with him; she didn't realize she could have it all. The Bradford estate could be all hers once Cynthia was out of the way.

Chapter 29

Cindy and Rip sat drinking their second glass of lemonade on the verandah. Bandon lay between them. They'd talked about Matt, Martha, Frank, and the new baby, all happy things. Cindy told him about her wonderful ride on Snickers, omitting the part about her mother. It felt too new and close to her heart. Rip in turn talked about his book. Both chatted about everything but what was truly on their minds, Cindy's memory, and their feelings for one another.

"Cindy, I'm still troubled about why you were running in the woods," he said, changing the subject. Her body stiffened at his statement. "I don't want to upset you, but we need to discuss the matter. I don't believe it happened the way Mark says it did." He reached across the table, gathered her shaking hands and placed them in his. "It just doesn't the cut ice with me. I bathed your body." Her face flushed and he squeezed her hands. "A beautiful body I must say." She smiled and lowered her eyes.

"Look at me, Cindy." Her head came up, their eyes met. "You've nothing to be ashamed of; you were a mess, bruised and scratched from head to foot, and yes, I still saw the beauty in you." She lowered her head. "No, look at me. I want you to understand." Again, their eyes met and held as he continued. "As I cleaned you and attended to you, I checked for anything that might need more attention than I could give." He took a deep breath, "I didn't notice any, not even one needle mark; and your body showed no withdrawal symptoms, even if you'd taken drugs orally." She started to say something. "No, hear me out please, and then you tell me what you think. I've been a detective a long time and memory loss or not, the body still needs a fix. I think there is more to you being in the woods than Mark is letting on, and I don't buy his story that you didn't want your father to know. From what I gather, the two of you were very close and I don't think you would have been able to keep something like that from him. I believe that you were drugged, but not that you were on drugs." He let go of her hands and sat back in his chair. He watched as he let what he'd just said sink in.

"Rip, I'm so glad to hear you say that. I too have been struggling with the idea that I had been hooked on drugs. I just know I couldn't have done that. Don't ask me how I know, I just do. I do know that I may have looked to the public like a spoiled rich person, but I truly can't picture myself as that either."

"What do you think you were like?"

"That's a good question, one that I've asked myself many times." She rubbed her temples, something she did a lot lately, but it seemed to help her concentrate. She knew she could trust Rip, that he wouldn't think her foolish or stupid.

"I know that being wealthy has its advantages. I could have anything I wanted, but that didn't make my life any easier. I think I always struggled with the thought that men wanted me for my money. The magazines I've read portray me as fickle, dating one man after another, never getting serious about anyone. All I ever wanted was a man to love me for me, not my money or status. I think most of those men were escorts. One in my position wouldn't attend a function alone. To be honest, I believe, I truly was a loner.

"I know my father worried about me. He always said I loved my horses more than any man did, which in retrospect could be true. I could have loved horses because they didn't expect to gain anything but my love and admiration. I know, I love children and hope someday to have them in my life. I've seen pictures of me, if that truly is me attending the orphanages for fundraisers." She kept her head low, staring into her hands clasped together on her lap. She turned her gazed to Rip. She didn't know what she expected, but it surely wasn't the compassion she saw. He truly did care what she thought. She continued. "I feel that I'm a quiet person, with concerns for the future of others as well as myself. I believe I'm gentle, and forgiving; a woman of integrity with a lot of fortitude."

"Caring, sincere, and yes loving," Rip said. He too thought those things of her; but one thing nagged at him. "Then tell me, how is it that you became engaged to Mark?" She began to rub her temples.

"That is one question I can't answer, because I don't know. Mark says I loved him. The newspapers and magazines say as much. Maybe I truly did at one time. I don't know." She looked at her left hand. She wasn't wearing a ring. "Mark said I had a ring. He says I must have lost it while running in the woods." Had she worn a ring that day? If not, what had happened to it? She began petting Bandon who'd jumped up on her lap wanting attention. She had more feelings for Bandon than she did Mark. She considered Rip and thought, I care more for you too, but she didn't say it. Instead, she said, "I don't want to be engaged to that man."

Rip felt confused. Just yesterday, she'd told Mark that she wanted to postpone it, that didn't sound like she wanted to call it off. He started to ask her when she continued.

"I know I sound mixed up, and I guess I am a little, but you've a right to know. Since I don't know my own self, I have to be fair with Mark." She saw the confused look cross Rip's face as his brows creased together. "As Cindy, I don't want to marry Mark, but Cynthia may think differently. By postponing the intended marriage, I have a chance to regain my memory, and only then will I know the true me." One thing she knew was that as Cindy, her heartbeat for Rip. As Cindy, she didn't want to go on without him. If only her father were alive.

Rip's cell phone began chiming. Sarah, he recognized the number. "Excuse me Cindy, this is a call I've been waiting for."

"Rip, I'm glad I caught you," Sarah said. "Are you still in town?"

"Yes."

"Good, I've got something interesting on those two guys, plus something else I think you'll be interested to know. Can you come by in about a half-hour? I get off work then and we could grab something to eat."

Rip watched Cindy who stood tossing a ball, trying to teach Bandon to fetch. "Yes, but make it closer to forty-five, I've a few things to wrap up." He snapped the phone shut. He'd hoped to spend the evening with Cindy. Maybe he could join her for a drink later, then he remembered her telling Mark she wanted a quiet evening.

"Cindy, I'm sorry, but something has come up and I've got to run into town. It will take awhile. I'll stay in town tonight and head back home in the morning. I'll give you a call when I get there."

She tried to hide her disappointment, but Rip saw it in her eyes as they'd begun to tear. She wiped at them, claiming something flew into her eye. Rip wanted to stay. He wanted nothing more than to spend the evening with her. A quiet night, just the two of them like they used to have at his place, but Sarah's call had sounded so urgent. He thought about telling Cindy about meeting Sarah. He didn't want her to worry. He had no illusions about her being Cynthia Bradford. He had a gut feeling, call it a cop's intuition that her life was still in danger. Not so much now, but once she got her memory back. He had to find out before that happened.

"Rip, can't you stay a little longer? I mean, do you have to go back to your place? I thought you could go to the office with me tomorrow." Cindy leaned in through the truck window. "Tomorrow is Friday and afterwards I could go with you. I'd like to see Martha and the baby. I miss the place. It really feels more like home than this place." She'd like to see Matt too; he'd saved her life and she hadn't had a chance to thank him properly.

"Cindy, I'd like that more than anything. I just don't think now is the time. We'll plan it soon though, I promise. Now I've go to go or I'll be late."

Cindy watched him drive away. She'd all but got on her knees and begged to go with him, and he'd said no. Tears welled in her eyes. What could be so important that it couldn't have waited till morning? Then it hit her, maybe he was meeting another woman. The thought that he could be meeting a woman hurt her. Cindy had been a nuisance for him and now he could finally get back to his previous life. Then she remembered how he'd held her and the feelings that transpired between them. She'd been a fool to think that they'd meant anything. Why would he want a woman who didn't even know herself, especially someone who had planned to marry another man? Marriage, the thought of it angered her. She couldn't marry Mark. In fact, she'd call him right now. She'd tell him it was a no go. The wedding was off. With that set in her mind she marched up to the house.

Rip hated lying to Cindy, but she'd understand later when he explained. He planned to spend the weekend in Chicago. He would've liked nothing more than for the two of them to spend a few days at his place. He knew Matt missed her and Martha had asked about her coming for a visit. Martha and Frank were so proud of the baby; they couldn't wait for her to see him. Another time, he thought, as he pulled into the restaurant's parking lot. A smile crossed his face as he spotted Sarah waiting in her car. He hoped she had good news. Time was running out.

Chapter 30

Mark stared at the phone and seeing it was Cynthia's number, picked it up. "Hi Cynthia, I hope you've called to change your mind. I really need those papers." He did, there wasn't anything in them, only the monthly reports. He hadn't changed a thing since Mr. Bradford had started looking at them more closely. Harry had questioned him on a few shortcuts he'd been using to hide money. A man had to live and the meager salary he was paid wasn't enough for the lifestyle he wanted, but that wouldn't be a problem for long. He just had a little matter to take care of first, and this time he wouldn't fail. A smile creased his face as he remembered how he'd fingered the accountant for miscalculation of the funds. He'd hurriedly put the money back and the old accountant had taken the blame. Of course, Harry hadn't fired his longtime friend. He told the old man to get his glassed checked. After that, Mark hadn't taken any chances. He'd felt Harry's eyes on him often in the past months. What luck when that plane went down! He heard Cynthia say something about dinner. He hadn't been listening, but then she said something that got his attention.

"I'll bring the papers. I should be there within the hour. Meet me at El Rico's restaurant."

A smiled played on Cindy's lips as she heard his intake of breath, and remembered the last time she'd been there. That was where she saw him with that woman. He'd explained it away, but something about the situation bothered her. The woman had seemed too friendly.

"Yes, sure, I'll have a table ready," Mark said as he hung up. He picked up the phone and dialed. "Hello," he said. "I won't be able to make dinner after all. The queen is coming and I have to meet her. I'll be by later and make it up to you. In the meantime, I want you to start practicing your walk and memorizing the list of household staff. You may look like her, but you also have to act like her."

Cindy felt relieved as she pulled away from the house. Would she ever feel that it truly was home like she did Rip's place? Bandon slept in the carrier on the back seat. He too was going home. She thought of the suitcase she'd put in the trunk, after quickly packing a few things. She packed in a hurry, but if she'd forgotten or needed anything she'd buy it in Buford. The mention of the town and its comforts soothed her, but first she had something to do. Grace hadn't been pleased, but understood when Cindy explained that she needed to get away, to think.

She leaned back in the car and thought of the conversation she had with Grace a few hours ago. She asked her about her mother. Grace had said that her mother was a quiet person and had never wanted anything more than to have children. When she brought you home that day, Grace said, with your wrinkled face and mop of dark hair, she said you were the most beautiful baby anyone could want. All mothers thought their babies were beautiful. Cindy asked Grace why she was an only child. "Because," she'd answered, "that's just the way it was. Your mother and father thought the world of you and yes they spoiled you, but loved you dearly." Now she couldn't wait to get this one thing over with. Cindy got the impression that Grace was holding something back but couldn't put her finger on it. Well, no need to worry about that now, she had other important matters.

Cindy spotted him at a far table. He pulled a chair out for her as she approached. "I hope this table is okay. I thought we'd have more privacy here."

"This is fine," Cindy said, taking the seat he offered.

"I've ordered the wine, your favorite, Chamborney. I hope you don't mind."

"Of course not." She doubted he'd want to celebrate after hearing what she had to say.

"I did a little, how would you say, bribery."

"You didn't have to do that, we could've gone elsewhere, but this place is nice."

"Now let me see, what do I want to eat?" Mark asked.

She glanced over the menu. "I think I'll just have a chef's salad. I'm not really that hungry," she laid the menu down. Mark ordered prime rib, saying he hadn't eaten all day.

Cindy sipped the wine after she finished her salad. When he offered her more, she held her hand over the glass. "No, I've still got to drive." The truth was she needed her wits about her. She watched as he ate, giving a slight smile when he caught her eye. Would he never be done, she wondered. She glanced at her watch. It was getting late. She needed to get this over with and be on her way. "Mark, I dropped off the papers at the office on my way here. I put them on my desk. I didn't think a restaurant was a good place since something could get spilled on them."

"You didn't?" Damn, he needed those papers.

"I really don't want to talk business this evening. I want to talk about us."

"Me too," he replied. When he reached across the table for her hands, she quickly pulled them away.

"Cynthia, I don't know what it is, but ever since you've come home, you've been acting like I'm poison. You won't let me even get close to you. We used to have so much fun. You enjoyed being with me. But now…."

"That's why I called and decided to have dinner with you." She didn't know how else to say it so she blurted it out. "I'm not going to marry you. I don't have the feelings towards you that I apparently had before. It wouldn't be fair to you or me."

"I thought you said you'd think on it, give it more time. You can't call it off. We've made all the plans."

"Plans can be changed. I've called the church, the rehearsal hall, and caterers, after finding a list in the top drawer of Dad's desk. Please Mark, try to understand. If I suddenly get my memory back and realize I've made a mistake, well, we can work that out then, but right now, I don't want to marry you."

"You can't do this to me! I won't let you! I've worked too damn hard for you to suddenly change your mind," Mark said loudly, as he stood up and knocked his chair down.

"Mark, please be quiet and sit down. Everyone is staring."

"Quiet down, you say?" His anger at the boiling point now, he whispered between clenched teeth, "You'll be sorry, Cynthia. You don't know what you're doing."

Cindy tried to put on a pleasant face as he stomped off and everyone seemed to be looking at her. The waiter came up and asked if there was problem and Cindy said, "just the check, please." She realized he'd left without paying.

An hour later, as she drove along the highway, relief washed over her. She'd done it, called off the wedding. She'd soon be with Rip once again and everything would be fine. She smiled at Bandon who slept. She wondered if Rip would be pleased to see her.

Chapter 31

Mark sat on the edge of the bed. He'd just had a good romp with her in bed. It always helped clear his mind. The woman next to him had fallen asleep, exhausted. He liked that in a woman, one who did a man's bidding and at the same time knew her place. Not like some other women, he knew. Damn her all to hell, he thought. He had to work fast. Tomorrow would be her doom. With that thought, he picked up the phone.

"What do you mean she's gone?" Mark all but hollered into the phone.

"I'm sorry, Mr. Osgood, but she left earlier saying she needed a rest and was going to Buford," Grace said. "No, she didn't say when she'd be back, but if she calls I'll…." He'd hung up.

Oh well, she thought, I don't much like him anyway. She'd never understood what Cynthia had seen in him. Now Mr. Walker, he was a different story, she liked him. She thought she saw something in Cynthia's eyes when she looked at him and if she was any judge, she thought Mr. Walker liked Cynthia. She gave a sigh as the phone rang again. "I told you I don't know when she'll be back. I don't like being hung up on," she said.

"I'm sorry, Grace, but this is Rip Walker and I don't remember hanging up on you. Who is it that isn't home?"

"Oh! I'm sorry Mr. Walker; I thought you were someone else. Please forgive me?"

"It's all right. Now may I speak to Cindy, I mean Miss Bradford?"

"I'm sorry, Mr. Walker, but Miss Bradford left."

"Left, what do you mean left?" Now where could she have gone and at this time of night, he wondered. It was close to nine in the evening. He'd just left Sarah and needed to talk to Cindy right away. "Did she say when she'd be back? Please Grace; it is very important that I talk to her."

"I'm sorry, Mr. Walker, but she left saying she needed to get away. She mentioned the town of Buford. Do you know where that is?"

Did he, of course he did; it was his home. "Yes, I know where it is. Now please tell me what time she left." He couldn't for the life of him figure out why she'd go there unless she'd remember something and was scared.

"Mr. Walker, are you still there?"

"Yes."

"I thought you'd hung up on me like Mr. Osgood, but to answer your question, Miss Bradford left around six this evening, but I did hear her on the phone saying she was meeting someone."

"Please Grace, think. Did she mention whom she planned to meet? It's important."

"No, I never heard her mention a name. No wait, I did hear her say something about papers needing signed. Does that help?"

"Yes, thanks." He'd been about to hang up when she added, "She took that wolf with her."

Chapter 32

Cindy missed the turn and had to back up, thinking it was further down the road. As she turned into the lane, she felt the excitement all the way to her toes. It wasn't too late and he should still be up. When she reached the clearing the dark prevailed, the only light coming from her headlights. He must have retired earlier or gone into town. Feeling better, she stopped the car and cut the engine. "Well, we're here," she said to Bandon as she got out and opened the back door to let Bandon loose. He began yelping and running around. "Don't go far," she called, as he was chasing after something. He too felt at home here. She went to the door and knocked. She waited a while and knocked again, but no answer. She tried the door and found it locked. Well, she'd just have to wait for him to come home. She decided to sit on the back porch that looked out over the river. The moon was full and she wished Rip was here to enjoy it with her. She wondered what he'd think when she told him she'd called off the wedding.

She pulled her jacket tightly around her. She was getting cold. If Rip didn't come soon, maybe she'd go into town and get a room for the night, come back in the morning. Then they could have breakfast together like old times. She started to call for Bandon when she heard a vehicle coming up the lane. Rip, she thought as she hurried around to the front. Her heart dropped. It wasn't Rip. She'd been outside for sometime and her eyes were well adjusted to the dark. She couldn't tell what color the car was, but knew it to be dark in color. She watched as two men got out and started walking toward the door. One was tall and skinny, the other tall but quite heavy. Bandon had started growling at them and one of them picked up a rock and flung it toward him. She saw him fall over.

"You've killed him," Cindy screamed as she ran towards Bandon. "How could you?" She knelt before him and could see the gash on the side of his head. He lay so still. "You will pay for this." She stood with hands on her hips. "Please, Miss Bradford," they said in unison. They knew her name, and where had she heard these voices before? She turned towards the house. The door was locked. She had nowhere to go. The woods, she thought. She began to run. She was thankful that she'd thought to change into jeans and tennis shoes after the restaurant. She didn't know the woods, but Matt's place was over the rise. If only she could reach it in time. She heard them huffing and puffing as they chased her. Where had she heard that before? Her own breath labored and she could hear her heart beating. The leaves swatted at her face and hands as she tried desperately to push them out of the way.

"Damn it lady, stop or we might have to shoot," one of them hollered.

They're going to kill me, she thought, but she wouldn't stop because she had a feeling that if they caught her she'd be dead anyway. She tripped and swore as she got back up. It's like before, she suddenly thought. Matt had said she'd been running. Had it been like this? No, please, don't let them catch her, she cried to the heavens. She needed to rest, just to catch her breath. She hid behind a tree, as her breath was short and harsh. She heard footsteps; they were close by, just like before. Her head began to pound through flashes of another time.

"Oh no," she gasped and put her hand over her mouth to suppress a scream that had lodged in her throat, wanting to escape. She knew! Oh God, she knew! They would kill her. Daddy, please help, she whimpered as tears ran down her cheeks. Her dad was gone now, gone to heaven. She had no one. Then she saw the light. Matt's place. It stood about a hundred yards away. He would help. She broke out into a fast sprint. She had to reach the cabin. Safety loomed ahead. Her lungs were ready to burst and she thought she wouldn't make it, but life meant more than death and with life there was Rip. Rip, why weren't you home? Please help me. She ran blindly now, the need to survive giving her strength.

When she reached the clearing and saw Matt's cabin she knew she'd made it. She made a last dash for his door. When she pounded on his door it opened, but it wasn't Matt. She spun around just as they grabbed her and put something over her mouth. Not again, she thought, as blackness engulfed her.

Chapter 33

"Hi Boss," Hank said into the phone. "Jake and I thought you'd like to know we have the package all wrapped up nice and tight just like you ordered."

"Good, how did it go? Any problems, anyone see you?" Mark asked. He sure didn't need someone seeing them and he didn't trust these two as much as he once had, especially after they bungled the job the first time. It'd been nothing but a big headache ever since.

"Everything is fine. The package was by itself. We are at the abandoned ranger station now. It's nice and quiet here, not another living soul around for miles. What do we do next, Boss?"

"Sit tight for a few days. I've a few loose ends here to finish up and then I'll call you. When I do, be ready to dispose of the package."

"How do you want it done?"

"I want it burned and the ashes scattered about. I don't want a thing left. Now, did you get someone to drive her car with her purse and suitcase into Chicago and park it where I told you?"

"Yes, did just like you asked. As a matter of fact, it should be there by now."

"Good, I'll call you in a few days. Hold tight and don't do anything till I call. Is that clear?"

"Boss, there is one problem."

"Jake, is that you? What happened to Hank?" Damn them anyway, Mark thought as he ran his fingers through his hair. They were bumbling idiots, but the best he could find.

"Yes, it's Jake. Hank had to go and give her another shot, she started to wake up."

"Damn it, don't let her wake up!" He screamed between clenched teeth. He didn't want her seeing them, but then thought, it wouldn't make any difference as she'd be dead soon. He lowered his voice and said, "I mean it, keep the package contained." He had to be careful here at work, the place had ears and now wasn't the time to screw up.

"Boss, Hank and I've been talking and we think a little more money is due. We need an extra fifty grand to finish the job."

"What the hell do you mean?" He spat. "You botched it up the first time. Now do as I say." Damn them, he wanted this done now and didn't have time for their games.

"I think we've got a problem here, Boss. This is the second time around and the first time we had a flat. You can't hold that against us, besides, the drug you gave us wasn't strong enough, she woke up. This woman is worth a mint. She might be willing to offer us some of it to let her go. See what we mean, Boss?"

"Yes." He saw what they meant. They were blackmailing him. He couldn't get hold of that kind of cash, not now with the lawyer overseeing everything. "Okay," he said knowing he had no choice. "But you won't get a penny till the job is finished. Do I make myself clear?"

"Yes Boss. We will be waiting for your call."

"One other thing," Mark added, wanting to cover all bases. "Don't try and trick me, because if you do, you're both dead. Do you hear me, dead?" He slammed the phone down. He looked up as his secretary walked in.

"What is it?" He asked louder than he meant to. "I'm sorry Beth; I'm not feeling well today."

"I just wanted to remind you of your meeting in five minutes," she said as she closed the office door.

Let them wait a few minutes, he thought as he leaned back in his chair. Soon, he thought, I'll have the office across the hall with a sign marked President on the door. First he had things to take care of, and one of them would be out of the way soon. Cynthia may have called the wedding off, but he had a plan. They would elope. With the bitch dead, it would all be clear sailing. Relieved and feeling much better, he grabbed the files Cynthia had signed and headed off to the meeting.

Rip had been on the road for a few hours when he decided to place a call to Grace. He knew it was late, but he had to have some answers.

"Grace, its Mr. Walker. I know it's late, but I've got a few questions. Would you mind?" When she said no, he asked, "Grace, could Mrs. Bradford have children?"

"Mr. Walker, what a strange question, but I'm afraid I can't answer that."

"Thanks, Grace, that's all the answer I need." He heard the intake of her breath. "One other thing," he asked. What car did Miss Bradford leave in?"

"She left in her red convertible. Why?

"In case I see her on the road. I'm headed home now. If Miss Bradford calls, please tell her I'm on my way."

Rip pulled into the lane leading to his home a few hours later. He hadn't seen her car. He didn't know if she'd be here. Maybe she'd gotten tired and stayed in town. He hadn't thought to check. Well, it was late, and it had been a long drive and he was exhausted, especially after seeing Sarah. He'd been shocked by what Sarah told him. He had to find out if Cindy knew. It just might jog her memory.

As he got near the clearing, he saw there wasn't a light on in the house and no sign of her car. Then he saw Matt's truck. His headlights were shining on something on the ground. The only thing he saw was hair. Rip stopped the car and went running, "Cindy, oh no, not Cindy." He came up alongside Matt to see Bandon lying very still. A small cut on the head had blood oozing out. "Is he dead?" He asked.

"I don't know, I just arrived," Matt said, bending down to touch the small wolf. "His breathing is shallow, but he's still warm." Matt took off his jacket and placed it over the wolf cub.

Rip looked around for Cindy. Not seeing her, he turned to Matt. "Where is Cindy? I don't see her."

"I don't know. I just got here. Came to check the place out and found Bandon hurt."

Rip knew she had to have been here because of Bandon. She'd brought him. That's it, he thought. "She's probably gone for help," Rip said as Matt held Bandon and headed toward the house. "Put him on the rug by the fireplace."

Later, they sat in the kitchen drinking coffee. "I can't understand it," Rip said, running his finger around the rim of his coffee cup. "Where could she be?" Then hearing a small whimpering sound, they rushed to the living room where Bandon lay. "He's moving Matt, he's coming around." Rip started to pick him up, but Matt touched his arm.

"I wouldn't, he could have broken bones. Here, let me have a look see." Matt began checking the cub.

Rip stood watching Matt. The man had helped more stray animals than anyone he knew. Besides, he knew these woods like the back of his hand. Then Matt turned to him, beaming.

"I think he's going to be fine. If he could talk, he'd be complaining of one big headache."

"Yes, if only he could talk. He could tell us what happened here and where Cindy is," Rip said as he reached down to pet Bandon. "Yes boy, you know, don't you?" He could have sworn Bandon tried to bark.

"He's lucky, that's for sure. That rock wasn't small," Matt said. "Yeah, you're one lucky wolf."

"What did you say?" Rip asked.

"I said he's one lucky…."

"No not that, the other. You said something about a rock."

"Didn't you see it? It was lying by his head with blood all over it."

"Matt, how can I be so stupid? If someone hit Bandon intentionally, then…." He didn't want to think about it, but it could be the only explanation, "someone has taken Cindy."

They looked for signs of a struggle, but the black night outside made it difficult. They sat in the house with Matt attending to Bandon and Rip pacing back and forth wondering what had gone on there. The idea of her going into town to get help for Bandon suddenly didn't make sense. "Matt, when you arrived did you seen any other cars on the road?"

"Yeah, come to think of it I did. I saw a dark sedan and a red convertible. Sharp looking car, the kind you don't see around here, but I didn't think anything of it, figured someone had got off the beaten path by mistake. Why?"

Grace had said Cindy had driven her red convertible. She'd been here and left, but why hadn't she taken Bandon, unless she had no choice. The thought of her having been taken sent shivers through him. He turned to Matt as Bandon started to come around. "I think he's going to be okay," Matt said.

"Good. Matt you said you saw two cars. Were they close to one another or a mile or so apart?"

"The convertible was right behind the dark sedan. Oh Rip you don't think--you mean...."

"Yes, the red car belonged to Cindy and the other vehicle, I'm suspecting, held those wanting to harm Cindy."

Matt asked. "Why would someone want to hurt Cindy?"

"For the same reason they did the first time. I'd stake my police reputation on it. These people want her out of the way, why, I haven't figured out yet, but I will. First we've got to find her."

"But find her where, Rip? The area is enormous; hills, mountains, not to mention the numerous woods. It's hard for animals to make it, let alone a bunch of greenhorns."

"True, but maybe the people that took her know this area. She'd been in this area before when you found her." Rip could kick himself for not watching her more closely, especially since she had amnesia. He remembered the times they'd sat talking over coffee. They talked about the little things she'd remembered, wonderful times. Would he never have those moments again? No, he didn't want to think of life without her. So what if she's engaged? He'd fight for her, but first he had to find her. Besides, he didn't think it was something she wanted, to be engaged and married to Mark. Maybe once she had, but he didn't think it to be true anymore. It was something Mark wanted, not Cindy.

Thinking of Mark and the way he acted when Cindy first told him she wanted to call off the wedding, he remembered the man's face had turned ashen and then angry. Rip thought he would explode, but in the next instant, he all but begged her to postpone it, using strategy on her. A few things bothered Rip; Mark didn't act like a man in love, it was more like a business deal, and he wasn't very attentive towards her. Hell, if he were engaged to her, he'd be smothering her with kisses and more if he could.

He'd always had this strange feeling about Mark. He wondered if Mark knew what Sarah had just discovered about Cindy.

Chapter 34

Cindy's head throbbed and her eyes hurt when she tried to open them, but try as she might, they wouldn't open. Then she realized that she had a blindfold on. She attempted to move her hands and legs, but couldn't. She felt confused and wondered where she could be. Her arms and legs hurt as she tried again to move, only to cause more pain. She wished her head would quit throbbing. She felt so groggy and cold. The side of her face lay on scratchy material that smelled of mildew. She tried to move and realized that her wrists and ankles were bound together. Why? Then she heard voices.

"I'm tired of playing cards, why don't you sleep and I'll take the first shift since we both can't sleep at the same time." She heard a deeper voice reply, "Yeah, we can't lose the package again."

Again, what did they mean and lose what package? If only she could move. Then she heard one of them saying, "She's been out a long time. How much did you give her, Hank?" She realized they were talking about her. What had they given her? Whatever it was, it sure gave her one massive headache, not to mention how dry her mouth and throat were. "The normal dose and don't mention my name again. She might wake up and hear."

"What does it matter? In a few days she'll be gone." The deeper voice spoke again. "I hope the boss doesn't renege on the payment because I want to head to Canada after this is over with."

"Not me," said the higher-pitched voice. "I'm going where it's warm, like Mexico, but first we've got to finish this job. We can't wait for him to call and tell us to get rid of her."

Cindy sucked in her breath with the reality of what they planned to do to her. They planned to kill her. Who wanted her dead? Who were they taking orders from? What had she done to make someone want her out of the way? Who were her enemies? Grace had said she seemed stronger since coming back home. Tears stung her eyes behind the binding. She didn't know what to do, but one thing was certain, she needed to lie quietly, and let them think that she was still asleep. She didn't want anymore of whatever it was they had given her. She lay there motionless, wondering how she could get away. Something bothered her. If they were getting money for her, ransom, she guessed, why would they still want to kill her? Then she heard the deep voice say, "It's too bad about her dad. I bet he'd be willing to pay a lot for her return, a lot more than the boss is paying."

Chapter 35

Rip hadn't been able to sleep. He'd made a few calls; one to Sarah to keep her abreast of what was going on. He'd called some friends he knew at the State Police and the Chicago office. He didn't want her reported as missing but asked them to keep an eye out for her car. He hadn't known where to start, but figured the car was as good a start as any. He wished Matt had paid more attention to the sedan, but then he hadn't been looking for anything out of the ordinary. He looked over at Matt lying on the couch with Bandon at his side. Rip whispered to Bandon, "where is Cindy?" To his surprise, Bandon started whining. "You miss her too," he said as Bandon howled, waking Matt.

"What the hell?" Matt asked, sitting up with a jerk. "Is something wrong?"

"No, Matt, but it looks like Bandon has had a full recovery. I'm glad you're awake. It's almost daylight. I want to run into town and do some asking around. Would you mind staying here and taking care of Bandon? There is plenty of food and beer in the refrigerator." With Matt agreeing, Rip gathered the information Sarah had given him and started out for town.

He stopped at the end of his lane and leaned his head on the steering wheel. "Cindy, where are you?" He asked, out loud. He could picture her face, so beautifully innocent in one-way, yet worldly in another. She had gotten to him, his heart and soul. He'd wanted to help and protect her, but he had done nothing.

What kind of a detective was he? A very good one or at least he had been. "Cindy, I'll find you."

He started to pull out onto the main road when something bright from the morning sun caught his eyes. A scarf caught on a tree branch. He got out and retrieved the silk scarf. He'd seen Cindy wearing it the day she came in from horseback riding. She'd had it tied around her neck. He put it to his nose and recognized the perfume she'd started wearing after returning to the estate. He now knew for sure that she'd been here.

Chapter 36

"What do you mean it's not signed?" Mark stared at the committee. He watched as the file folder found its way to him down the table to where he sat. He opened it and couldn't believe it; the bitch had attached a note. He'd been so busy all morning that he hadn't gone through the file. He'd assumed she'd signed it. Damn her to hell, he thought, as he read the note.

"I, Cynthia Bradford, have read the enclosed document and being new to this don't quite understand it all. I wish to have the items tabled and brought up at the regular monthly board meeting. I will have had more time to evaluate these items and many more."

Mark stared at the note that she had signed, 'Miss Cynthia Bradford, President.' President my ass, he thought, but put on his best smile and said, "Well, the lady has spoken. I will set your minds at ease. Since receiving the injury to her head and losing her father, not to mention the wedding plans and all, I can understand her hesitation. I will talk to her and have this matter settled soon." With that said, they adjourned the meeting.

When they all had left, Mark got up and began pushing chairs around. If she'd been there, he'd have strangled her. Then a smile played on his lips as he calmed down knowing that he wouldn't have to worry about that for long. His thoughts were interrupted, when the door opened and Beth entered.

"Mr. Osgood, there was a man here while you were in the meeting. He said to tell you that Miss Bradford's car is back."

Great, now he could get going on the next step of his plan. "Thanks Beth. Did he leave the keys?"

"Yes, I put them on your desk, and I gave him a twenty dollar tip as he stood there with his hand out."

"Thanks again," he said reaching for his wallet and handing her a twenty. Another scoundrel, as his men probably paid him handsomely in the first place. Oh well, the car was back. He turned to Beth as she started to leave. "Since it's Friday, and I've got a few errands to run, it'll be late, so I won't be back. If needed, you can reach me on my cell." He looked at his watch. It wasn't even noon yet, he had plenty of time before the courthouse closed.

"I now pronounce you husband and wife," the man said. "You may kiss the bride." Mark leaned over and whispered, "Nice going, Mrs. Osgood. You're doing fine."

"Oh, Miss Bradford, I mean Mrs. Osgood, would you be so kind as to tell me what made you decide to elope," a lady from the news media along with others called out, as they came down the court steps.

"Please everyone, can't you leave us alone? It's our wedding day. As for your question, we decided that with the death of Mr. Bradford and the strain Cynthia has been through, a quick and quiet wedding would be best. Now if you'll excuse us."

"Thank goodness that is over with," said the beautiful woman sitting next to Mark. "I think it went well. I don't think they knew."

"Darling, you were terrific, but we've still got a long way to go. Quit slouching, you must sit erect and poised. You're a lady now. If this thing is going to work you're going to have clean up your act."

"I know sweetheart. I wish I could see her, just once. She is my sister. You know I've always wanted one."

"I don't give a damn about that. What you have to remember is that she has it all while you ended up with rags. Now the tables are turned. So get any notion of seeing her out of your mind."

"I don't know, Mark, I'm so nervous. I mean, what if I mess up? I haven't gotten the knack of riding a horse as good as you wanted, and these artificial nails are driving me crazy. I'm sorry Mark, but Sharon Miller Osgood is nothing like Cynthia Bradford, or I should say Cynthia Osgood. Since we were already married, the Osgood part shouldn't be too difficult, but I miss biting my nails."

"Damn it woman, why do you think I've had you practicing this past year? Now I want you to forget the name Sharon as well as any fears you may harbor. Your name is Cynthia. Is that understood?" When she nodded, Mark reached over and patted her on the knee. "Now get yourself prepared to meet the house staff."

Chapter 37

Cindy had fallen asleep, until the smell of bacon reached her nose. When had she last eaten? Then she heard one of the men say, "I hope he calls today." Had she slept that long, causing another day to go by? It was hard to tell with her eyes covered. Rip would be worried and poor Bandon, he looked dead. He'd wanted to protect her. She'd miss him. If only Rip had been home, she wouldn't be in this mess now. One she didn't know how she would get out of, but she needed to or she'd be dead. Who wanted her dead? Why? What had she ever done to deserve this?

Rip would be frantic, she knew, especially after finding Bandon. Would he be looking for her? She hoped so. She'd told Grace she was going away for a few days. Why hadn't she told her that she was going to see Rip? She knew why, because she didn't want Mark to know. He'd sounded so angry when she'd told him she was calling off the wedding that she didn't want him following her. Let him think she needed a few days away. A lump developed in her dry throat as she realized no one knew where she was.

Then she heard a scrape, which sounded like a chair moving. "Well, I'm going outside for awhile to look around," she heard one of them say. Then, she heard a door close and figured that one of them had left. She could hear the other moving around. Then, the door closed again.

The quiet reached her and she waited to make sure she was alone. Sensing that both men had stepped outside, she shifted to relieve a cramp in her back. Something sharp jabbed her right hip. She lay on her back and wondered what it could be. Then it came to her, she'd broken a nail on the way to Rip's place. It was her fingernail file. The metal file was in her jeans pocket. If only she could reach it. Then the outside door opened and she went limp. She lay there thinking of a way to get at the file and free her hands. Every bone and muscle in her body ached, and her head felt the same as the time when she'd woken up after having her tonsils out. That time, her father had been at her side, telling her all would be fine. This time she had no one but herself. If only she could get hold of the file.

The door outside opened again and the man with the deep voice came back saying that he'd found the perfect spot for the package. She heard a phone ringing and then the other man said, "This evening? Sure, that's no problem. Yes, we'll bring it to you and then we'll expect the payment. Right, okay."

She didn't hear anything for a while, and then felt someone standing over her. His breath smelled sour and Cindy felt nauseous, as he got closer. She felt his foul breath on her face. What were they going to do to her, not another shot? No, not that, she prayed. Then, she felt someone push her over onto her stomach. It was a relief to be in a different position, but she wondered what he was doing as he pulled at her hands.

"Damn it, Hank, when you taped her hands you covered the ring hand," Jake said. "I'll have to take the tape off and do them up again."

Cindy's hands felt as if the skin was coming off, as he pulled on the tape. She felt the tears and swallowed the scream that developed in her throat. Then he began pulling on her left finger. Why?

"Damn it, there is no ring. What did the boss mean? That ring was supposed to get us the money and now that money is gone too."

The ring, she'd found the ring in the jewelry case. She'd put it on with intentions of giving it back to Mark when she told him the wedding was off, but he'd been so upset she didn't have the opportunity. She'd thrown it out along the highway somewhere between Chicago and Buford.

"Tape her back up. I'll give him a call," she heard one of them say.

She had to do something and quick, but what. Then she heard one of them say he had to go to the car and get the tape. She had a few minutes; it would be her only chance. Hearing the door close and the other man talking on the phone, she quickly reached up and pulled the bands of tape from her eyes and mouth. She could see that the man, whom she guessed to be Hank, had his back to her. The door was about six feet from the cot. Did she dare? She could hear the man on the phone saying that it was important that he call as soon as possible. It is now or never, she thought, and swung her feet onto the floor. She made a dash for the door as she heard the man on the phone say, "Shit." She opened the door and ran smack into what felt like a boulder, but it wasn't. The big man picked her up and carried her back to the cot. Then he hit her across the face. She fell back as darkness came over her.

Her father, her happy-go-lucky father, her head began to pound as memories of her life flashed before her. She remembered her beautiful mother being ill and sitting with her father at her side after her mother's death. She missed her mother. Her father became mother and father, he taught her everything, how to ride a bike and then a horse, how to cook, how to be a lady. Now he was gone, she thought, as suddenly, everything came rushing back to her.

She remembered her father going on a business trip. She'd gotten ill, thinking it was something she'd eaten. She'd told Mark she wanted to lie down. Mark, knew her father's business, and after a short period of courting, had asked her to marry him. She hadn't loved and didn't love him. He dated her because of who she happened to be; the daughter and sole heir to the Bradford fortune.

At first, with Mark, she'd felt different. He had his own money and always bought her expensive gifts. She'd asked once why he worked for her father if he had money. He'd told her he needed to work for fulfillment. She remembered her father really hadn't liked him, but he wouldn't go against anything that she wanted. Her headache had gotten worse. She wanted to scream from the pain, but knew she must lie there quietly and remain still.

After a while, the headache started to subside and at the same time, her mind started to clear. Oh my, oh my, her mind played like a picture show. She remembered running, then falling, and oh my, it's true. It wasn't a dream. Now these men had her again and memories of the past weeks became clear.

Her father, her wonderful father was gone! She'd never see him again. She felt her tears as she remembered the last time she'd seen him. He'd left for an overseas trip and they'd dinner together the night before. He wanted it to be just the two of them. They'd discussed everything from the weather to the stock market, to her riding in the upcoming state fair, something she did every year. When she'd tried to talk about the wedding, she could now envision how he had always changed the subject. She remembered something he'd said the next morning as he left for the airport. She hadn't thought much of it at the time, but now his words came back to her. "Cindy," he always called her that when they were alone, "this marriage with Mark, I want you to be sure that you truly love him. It seems as if you're not yourself when you're around him, not happy. So while I'm gone, think hard, for your old dad's sake."

She'd hugged him and said not to worry, but she could see in his eyes that he was. She knew he'd begun to have second thoughts about Mark, but had never said why.

Now he was gone and she'd never know. She remembered teasing him when he'd called himself old. "You're not old, Dad. You've more energy and spunk than a lot of younger men." It was true. He could work circles around Mark. Then she remembered something else he said as he hugged her for the last time. "There is so much I haven't told you and need to, but if I never get the chance, everything is in the safe at the office in a brown leather case."

She remembered seeing the case the day she'd gone to the office and removed some things. She'd taken it and placed it in a dresser drawer in her room, to examine its contents later, but she never had the chance. Had her father known or guessed he wouldn't be coming back? No, that was foolish; one doesn't know when they're going to die. But she did; these men planned to kill her.

Who would come to her aid? No one, she thought. Mark, no. She'd finally called off the wedding, and now knew that her father had been right, she'd never loved him. He'd been convenient and wasn't after her money, but now she knew she couldn't marry him because she didn't love him. She loved another, but he did love her? Rip what a wonderful, kind and caring man. She felt so happy around him, something her father had said was important. Would he worry about her? Yes, but he hadn't known she had plans to go to his place. It might be days or even weeks before he called or checked on her. She was sure he had a date the night she'd left. There wasn't a soul who'd be searching for her, at least not in time; she'd be dead before anyone even missed her. Suddenly a voice inside her said, "You've always liked a challenge, just like riding a horse. It will take cunning, skill, and courage to get away. So what are you waiting for?" Then she heard the two men in the room arguing.

"Don't yell at me, Jake. I had to take a leak. Besides, you took forever out there. You only went to get the tape."

"I was checking for a good area for the fire. Don't want the whole woods to catch fire now, do we? We can't take any chances. The fog will start rolling in a couple of hours from now. Smoke and fog blend in good together, won't draw attention. We need to get some firewood stacked up. Why don't you go and see what you can find," Jake said. "I'll tape her back up while you're gone."

Cindy tensed, with her eyes still closed; she heard his footsteps as he came near her and stopped. "You won't get away anymore," he said, as he put tape over her mouth. A chill ran through her body as she looked up into his evil, bloodshot eyes, eyes that were as black as his skin.

"So you're awake," he said.

Cindy stared at his snarled grin as he taped her hands in front of her, and then taped her ankles. He must have seen the fear in her eyes as he said, "Don't worry. You won't feel a thing. You'll go to sleep and it will all be over." Cindy shook her head back and forth, as she tried to talk through the tape. Then to her surprise, he reached up and ripped the tape from her mouth. She sucked in air, and her mouth burned, as she ran her tongue over her lips to soothe them. She asked, "Can I have some water?"

"I guess I can give a dying lady a drink," he said.

She watched him go to get her a glass. During her kicking episode, she'd caused the fingernail file to fall from her jeans pocket; she now scooted over to cover it with her bottom.

The man came back and lifted the glass of water to her lips. She'd begun to feel dehydrated and the water helped. She looked up at the man and asked, "Why are you doing this to me? What have I ever done to you?"

"For money, that's what it's about. Of course, you wouldn't know. You never needed it. You were born rich. It's nothing to do with you personally."

"If it's money, I've got plenty. I'd pay you to let me go, just tell me how much you want. I'll get it for you, just let me go," her raspy voice pleaded.

"That all sounds great, but now that you've seen us, I don't think that would be such a good idea. Now why don't you just lie still, and if you'll be quiet, I won't tape your mouth. As for your eyes, well, you've already seen us."

Cindy nodded and he walked back to the table, and sat down and began playing solitaire. She rolled to her side and felt for the file, which she grasped between her thumb and forefinger. With her knees bent, she placed the file between her knees and held it tight. She looked toward the man, but he kept playing cards, not interested in her. She began running the metal file back and forth in a sawing motion over the tape that held her hands together. She kept her eyes glued to the man at the table and to the door, in case the other returned. She worked slowly, planning her next step once her hands were free.

Chapter 38

Rip had stopped and seen Martha and Frank to see if they'd heard from Cindy. No luck and he hadn't wanted to worry them, so he left. He asked them to call his cell phone if they heard from her. He felt like he was on a wild goose chase. After finding the scarf, he knew she'd been to his place and hadn't left of her own accord. He knew there was no way Cindy would have left Bandon unless she had no choice. Damn it, where was she? He banged on the steering wheel as he stopped in front of the hardware store.

"Hi, Dan," Rip said to the owner. He'd been here a lot during the building of his place and Dan had always been helpful with supplies and his knowledge of the surrounding area. Now Rip hoped that he could help him again. "What can I do for you, Rip?" Dan asked as Rip walked up to the counter. "It's been a while since I've seen you around."

"I hope you can help," Rip said. "I've got a few questions for you."

"Shoot."

"Have there been any strangers around lately? Like anyone wanting camping supplies, like rope and kerosene?"

"Come to think of it, there was," Dan said, running his right hand over the top of his smooth head. "They were the same two fellows who were in here a while back asking about property. I remember asking them how things were going. The short, heavy one just grunted. I didn't ask them anything else. There was one thing that I thought was strange; they bought three rolls of duct tape. Now why would anyone need that much duct tape for camping?"

"Did they say where they were going camping?"
"No Rip and I didn't ask. Why, is it important?"
"Yes, but…." He turned to the man who had joined them at the counter. He didn't recognize him, but there were a lot of the locals that he hadn't met yet.

"You two wouldn't be talking about the same two guys who asked me to deliver a car for them, would you? They paid me well. Said it belonged to their sister, and she would be angry with them if it wasn't returned."

Rip all but pulled the skinny man up by his shirt collar with his fist. "Where, when did this happen?" He screamed into the frightened man's face. "Damn it, man, tell me!" He continued to hold on to the man's shirt until Dan came and pulled him away.

"Rip, what's gotten into you?" Dan demanded, holding him while the other man stood shaking.

"Dan, this is important," Rip said, trying to slow the adrenaline down that rushed through him. "It could mean someone's life." He looked over at the shabbily dressed man in dirty bib jeans. "I'm sorry." He truly was. It wasn't like him to lose his composure. Taking a deep breath, he turned to the man. "I didn't mean to be so harsh, but it's very important that I know where these men might be." Rip knew he'd frightened the man. "Please, you aren't in any trouble, but what you know might save a life."

The man put his grubby hands in his baggy pants pocket and said, "I don't want any trouble. I just did them a favor. They paid me five hundred dollars to deliver a car." Then he pointed at the television. "That's the car. I know it's the same convertible because of the license plate. Same name as my favorite candy bar."

The camera operator had turned to focus on the 'just married' sign on the back of the red convertible. The license plate read Snickers. Then the camera turned on Cindy and Mark as they came down the courthouse steps and got into her red convertible. "Dan, turn the set up!" Rip hollered.

"There they are, everyone, the newlyweds," said the news reporter, "Mr. and Mrs. Mark Osgood. It seems that Miss Cynthia Bradford has finally decided to tie the knot." The reporter put the mike in front of Cindy. "Miss Bradford, I mean, Mrs. Osgood, why the sudden decision? Why at the courthouse?" Rip stood there dumbfounded at what was transpiring before his eyes.

She responded, "For love, why else does anyone marry?"

Then the camera switched to the reporter. "Well, folks, there you have it, another love story." Then it returned to the regular broadcast, as his cell phone rang. "Hello," he said.

"Rip, it's me, Sarah, I've just seen the most incredible thing. Cindy and that Mark fellow got married late this morning."

"I know, Sarah, I just saw it myself, but I don't believe it. It looked like Cindy, but the voice. Something about the voice isn't right." He saw the man in the bib overalls leaving. "Listen Sarah, let me call you back. I've got to talk to someone about a car." He snapped his phone shut.

"Please wait," Rip called, as he followed the man outside. It had started to rain, with a light mist. He saw the man turn the next corner. He would soon lose him as fog had begun to roll in. Rip called, "Hey, I'm sorry about what happened in there, but if you could answer a few questions for me, I promise, I won't lay a hand on you and I'll make it worth your while." This seemed to get the man's attention as he stopped, turned around, and headed toward Rip.

"How much are you willing to pay?" The man asked, approaching him.

Rip had a little over a hundred in his wallet.

"That depends on the information."

"A hundred dollars, nothing less, or I'm not talking."

Rip looked at the man and guessed him to need a fix or a drink bad. After being a cop so long, he'd come to know the signs. He didn't like catering to those habits, but Cindy's life--he still couldn't believe what he'd seen on the news. Besides her voice, there was something different about her. He couldn't place it, but it was there. "Okay, one hundred bucks it is." Rip pulled out his wallet and held the money in his hand. The man's dirty hands were shaking as he reached for the money. First Rip needed some answers and fast. Rip folded the two fifties in his hand. "Information first, and then you get the money."

Rip saw how the man kept staring at his closed right hand with the bills. He wanted the money bad. What he said next surprised Rip.

"I can't yet."

"Can't yet what?" Rip asked. He didn't have any more money. "If it's more money, which I don't have, I'll haul you over to the sheriff and let him handle you." That seemed to frighten him as he started to run. Damn, why'd he say that? Rip ran after him, caught up with him a block away and grabbed his arm. Out of breath, he said, "Okay, I won't turn you over to the sheriff."

"Please Mister. I can't tell you much, and I promised them not to tell anyone about anything. They said I'd be sorry if I spoke to anyone about this. When I heard you and Dan talking back there, I forgot. So please Mister, let me go. I've already said too much, but I sure could use some cash."

Rip loosened his grip, but didn't let go. "Just answer one question. I won't tell a soul where I got the information. I promise." He knew the man was scared. "Tell me, was one of the men tall and black, and the other white and short?" The man nodded, "one more thing, where did you pick up the car?" He knew that to be more than one question, but he opened his hand, showing the money.

"Okay, but you promised. They had two cars, a dark sedan and the red convertible. I'd just come out of Harvey's saloon at the end of town when they approached me."

So, they'd been looking for someone, Rip thought. Rip handed the money to the man. "Thanks." He turned and started walking away. He hadn't found out a lot, but enough to know that Cindy had been here, at least her car had. He'd turned and had taken only a few steps when the man said, "I know where they were going."

Rip turned around to see the man's hand out. He wanted more money. "Sorry fellow, you took all the cash I've got."

The man must have believed him, for he went on to say, "I heard the heavy guy say something about it getting dark soon and they had to hurry or they wouldn't be able to find the tower."

He thought of Cindy in the hands of those two men who had come to his place asking questions. He went directly to the sheriff's office after talking to the bum. He'd known back then that those two were up to no good. He'd dealt with their type before. Why hadn't he done something? He knew why, because Mark came along and said they worked for him. That's it, he thought as he addressed the sheriff.

Chapter 39

Cindy knew that it would be dark soon, but she kept filing away at the tape. It wasn't easy as she had to stop every few minutes as when one or the other glanced her way. She had her eyes closed, but not entirely, keeping them opened just enough so she could keep an eye on them as they played cards. Her fingers had developed cramps, but she knew she had to keep sawing. She didn't know where she was, but knew it had to be high up, for the men had commented on the steep steps. Also, when she'd gotten to the door, all she had seen was sky and treetops. It's like I'm on top of a mountain. How would she ever find her way back to Rip's place? Thinking of Rip had her wondering if he'd come home yet. Had he found Bandon? Tears welled in her eyes as she thought of Bandon lying there next to the drive, his head bleeding; she just knew he had to be dead. He tried to protect her and now he was gone. She'd loved that baby wolf just like she loved Rip. Yes, she thought, I know now that I could never have married Mark. Had she ever loved him? Yes, she did at one time. Then it all came back to her with a picture of a woman kissing him in his car. She was sure it was the same woman she'd seen him with at El Rico's restaurant. Then she Jake say, "I'll go out and get everything ready. It'll be dark soon. You keep an eye on her. She seems to be sleeping. Soon she'll be sleeping forever."

Cindy's body turned cold at the thought. What did he mean by getting things ready? She began sawing even harder as the heavyset man continued playing solitaire. She felt the tape give a little and knew she'd have her hands free shortly. Would she have enough time? Then what? She didn't know. She let her eyes roam the small ten-by-ten area. There was the cot she was laying on, the small table the men sat at and four windows, one on each side of the wooden structure. She saw nothing that she could use for defense. She scanned the area again. That's it, she thought, as her fingers moved the file back and forth. She had a good weapon and she'd use it, but she had to wait for the right moment. She ran her thumb over the point of the file.

Continuing to file at the tape, she thought back to the argument she'd had with Mark that day over kissing that woman. She'd gone to his place to confront him, she'd been so mad. He tried to shrug it off as nothing, but she knew a passionate kiss when she saw one. She now remembered telling him that the wedding was off. He'd gotten angry, no, more like violent, as he'd grabbed her around the neck and said that would never happen. Then he'd slapped her and she must have blacked out.

The next thing she remembered was being in her own house in her bedroom. Her head felt woozy, like she'd been drunk. Afterwards she'd fallen into a deep sleep. She remembered seeing Mark, but he too was fuzzy as he lifted her head and forced her to drink. She knew something was wrong, and the next time Mark lifted her head and poured the liquid in her mouth, she pretended to swallow it; some dripped down her throat, but not much. When Mark turned his back to place the cup on the nightstand, she tipped her head away from him and let the liquid slowly drain out the side of her mouth. She could hear Mark say, good girl. She didn't know when it was, but her father came in to say good-bye and that he'd call to see how she was doing, saying he was sorry, she had the flu, as he reached down and kissed her forehead. She'd remembered how she'd tried to speak, to tell him that something was wrong, but nothing came out, and then he'd left.

The next day, Mark came and took her away in the car. She remembered being in a different car with two strangers and she'd run from them. A shiver ran through her as she suddenly realized these two men were the ones who kidnapped her earlier. The nightmare was beginning all over again. Would Rip come to help her this time? Why would he? She'd told Grace she'd be gone a few days. Had she told her where she was going? She couldn't remember. Her only hope was that Rip came home and found Bandon. Then he might think she'd dropped him off before going away for a few days. She had no one.

Chapter 40

Rip examined the field map the sheriff had on the wall. "If the man said tower, then the only towers around here are the ranger stations. They aren't in use yet. It will be another month before the campers and hikers start invading the place, when the rangers have to be on the lookout for fires," the sheriff said.

"How many are there?" Rip asked, afraid that there would be too many. He sighed in relief when the sheriff said three. Rip had him draw out a map to each and thanked him. The sheriff wanted to know why he'd shown so much interest in the towers. Rip had only waved and headed out the door. He didn't have time to explain, and besides, this was all based on a hunch. He had to make a few calls before he'd know for sure, wanted to have all his bases covered.

"Hi Grace," he said as she answered the phone. He didn't give her time to say anything. He started right in. "Grace, is Cindy there?"

"Yes, they came in sometime yesterday. I wasn't here. I had some errands to run. I haven't seen her though, but the car is here. I must say, I don't know what's gotten into her, running off and getting married like she did. I mean, with her telling me one minute she was going away for a few days and the next, well, it's more than this old mind can handle. You want to know something funny?" She didn't wait for him to answer but went on. "Jacob was walking Snickers when Cindy and Mark got here and when

Jacob and the horse got near her, Snickers became all testy and it took all Jacob had to get him under control."

He didn't want to cut her short but said, "Please, Grace, listen to me. This is very important. I believe that the woman in the house is an imposter."

"Mr. Walker, you don't mean…."

"I do, now listen."

"I'm listening."

"I want you to act like you don't know. Cindy's, the real Cindy's life depends on you carrying this off."

"I'll do whatever I can for Miss Cynthia."

"Good, now I need you to see if this woman has a birthmark behind her left ear? I'll call you within fifteen minutes. Do you think you can handle that?"

"I don't know, but I'll try."

"You need to more then try, it's a must. Now I want you to call her to the phone. It will give you a good opportunity to look then."

"Rip, I'm sorry, but Cindy doesn't want to talk to you right now," Mark said, answering the phone. "She said to tell you she'd call you later. I suppose you've heard we got married. Sorry fellow, it looks like she's made her choice. We are getting ready to go on our honeymoon, leaving first thing in the morning. Bye."

Rip sat in his car staring at his cell phone and was sure his suspicions were right. He'd thought it was a wig when he'd seen the news broadcast. Now he was all but certain. It wasn't like Cindy to not want to talk to him. Why would Snickers get upset at seeing her?

He waited the fifteen minutes, and then he dialed the house. "Grace, thank goodness you answered, I thought Mark-- never mind---did you do as I asked?"

"Yes, and you're right. She doesn't have a birthmark. I know Miss Cynthia has one. Oh, Mr. Walker, I'm afraid. I don't know what…."

"Listen, you've got to stay calm. I think I know where Cindy may be. I need you to be strong. Don't do anything that you don't usually do or it will draw their attention."

"Okay, Mr. Walker. You just find Miss Cynthia."

"I will." He hung up his cell phone and pulled out the map he'd gotten from the sheriff, who had marked where the towers were on the map. After an hour passed, and finding the first two ranger towers empty, he worried that maybe his hunch had been wrong, but there was still one left, he thought, as he headed towards the last one.

He stopped his car about a half-mile from the tower as he had the others. As he climbed the hill, he thought back to all Cindy had been through this past month with the amnesia, and now, after what Grace had found out, knew his hunch had to be right. He'd just reached the crest of the hill. The fog had thickened and with night approaching, the visibility would be nil. Then he heard a phone ringing. He reached for his cell, and realized it wasn't his phone, but if it wasn't his, then that meant someone else was out here. He could feel the beat of his heart against his shirt. He stopped short of the hill as he heard a voice. "Yes, I'll call when it's done." Rip rubbed his eyes in hopes of seeing better, but it didn't help. "Bring her down," he heard someone say.

Chapter 41

Mark sat in the library after hanging up the phone. He propped his feet up on the desk and grinned smugly. This was all his now. He sighed as the door opened and his wife walked in and stood before him. Yes, life is good he thought. He'd worked hard at it and won. He saw Sharon, no Cynthia, and she seemed upset. How could she be when they now had it all? "What's the matter?"

"It's the help, especially that woman Grace. I think she's suspicious and I don't trust her."

"Don't worry, my sweet. I plan to let the whole staff go after we come back from our honeymoon. Then you can hire whomever you want. In fact, we can have and do whatever it is we want. I've been thinking of purchasing a yacht. I told you not to worry. Now run along and get packed like a good wife, because I want to leave as soon as I know everything is taken care of," he patted her on the bottom. "Soon you too will have what is rightfully yours just like I promised."

"I won't rest until she is gone and we are on the plane out of here."

"We will be, soon. You've nothing to concern yourself with but being the perfect wife." He heard her mumble, "Yes, mine, all mine." He would have to keep an eye on her, make sure she didn't make any mistakes in being Cindy. If so, well he would worry about that later. He wouldn't loose. Everyone is dispensable, especially with so much at stake. That is why Cynthia has to disappear. He glanced at his watch, her demise should be happening about now.

Chapter 42

Rip crawled closer to where he'd heard the voices. He bumped into something and when he pulled the brush away saw a black sedan. He'd hit pay dirt. He glanced up toward the tower, but couldn't see any light, and with the fog, he couldn't make anything out. He needed to get closer. He slid on his stomach like a snake as he approached the backside of the tower. He lay still as he heard a door open. Then he saw shoes, men's shoes, coming down the steps. Damn, he wished it wasn't so hard to see. Then there were two sets of men's shoes. One of them asked, "Is she still sleeping?" Rip's heart gave a leap. She was still alive!

Cindy watched through the slits of her eyes as the heavyset man went out the door. This might be the only chance she'd have. She pulled at her hands and they fell free from the small strip of taped left. Swinging her feet to the floor, she bent over and removed the tape binding her feet. She had no shoes. She stepped carefully and made her way to the window by the door. Her body swayed and felt woozy from whatever it was they had given her. Leaning against the wood wall, she steadied herself, trying to gain composure. She peeked out from the side of the window. She couldn't see a thing as the fog had thickened, but she heard voices. If she couldn't see them, then maybe they wouldn't see her. She stepped to the door and with ease opened it slowly, just enough for her body to fit through. She quickly moved out to the three-foot-wide wooden porch that seemed to surround the building. Where was she? She wondered, realizing the height of the small building reached the treetops. It had to be some sort of lookout. She could still hear the voices, and they seemed to be arguing. It is now or never, she thought, and started down the steps on her bottom. She took one-step at a time, very slowly. Once she reached the bottom, she didn't know what to do; she hadn't thought that far ahead. Her need was to get away from these men and away from-- she didn't know who else. Who wanted her dead? Not only had they tried once, but twice. Would she have to run for the rest of her life?

She would if she had to, but she wouldn't run from Rip. He was the only man who had said he cared about her, and not the Bradford name, or what it stood for. Then she heard one of the men say, "go get her and give her another shot while I start the fire." She had to hurry and get down. She had to run! Oh my God, she couldn't believe it, they meant to burn her alive! She continued to descend. If only she weren't so groggy; she couldn't think straight, but knew, she'd fight until the end. Oh Rip, where are you?

Rip felt for the gun that he'd strapped to his belt. After retirement, he'd decided to keep it, and acquire a permit. It had become a part of him after so many years on the force. Now it would come in handy. Not that he intended to kill anyone, only if it became necessary. It was for protection, and now Cindy needed protecting. He unsnapped the holster and waited to see if they'd heard the small sound of it opening. They were so deep in conversation that they hadn't. Good. He started to get up when he saw something move above his head. Someone was coming down the steps! He squinted to get a better perspective. He sucked in his breath as he realized it was Cindy coming down the steps on her butt. His heart went out to her; the woman had nerve. Once she reached to the bottom, he'd crawl closer. He needed to get her attention without spooking her. The thought had no sooner entered his mind, than he heard one of them say to go and get her. Damn, she wouldn't make it to the foot of the stairs.

Rip had to do something and fast. He picked up a good-sized rock and hurled it behind him. Perfect, he thought, when he heard them coming his way. Then he saw them! He didn't think of their size or if he could take them or not. He reached out, and grabbed the first pair of legs and watched as the man fell with a thud. He quickly reached for the next one, but the man was quick on his feet and gave Rip a hard punch in the stomach. He doubled over in pain, as he heard someone scream; Cindy, he thought, and turned to see the second man headed to where she stood frozen at the bottom of the steps. He saw that the first man he had pulled down had hit his head on a pile of rocks. He ran towards the other man, and just as he started to grab Cindy, Rip hit him over the head with the handle of his gun. Cindy fell into Rip's arms like a rag doll.

Cindy sat next to Rip on the drive back home. They'd gone to his place first and had called the sheriff in Buford to have the two men that Rip had tied up arrested. She'd been so happy to see that Bandon had only a small lump and cut on his head, and that he would be fine.

It all seemed like a nightmare, as Rip drove them back to Chicago and to her home, but as Rip had informed her, the nightmare wasn't over, not quite yet. She glanced over at him now as daybreak broke and the sun began to burn off the fog. He gave her a gentle squeeze on the shoulder and asked, "Are you okay?" She nodded and knew she would be, as soon as the fog she'd been living with cleared.

"Cindy, you don't have to do this. We've enough evidence that you don't have...."

"It's something I want to do, no, need to do for myself."

The house seemed quiet as they walked up the lane; one she'd gone up not long ago to find herself. Well, she'd found that person and that person had become stronger. She looked over at Rip as he walked at her side. He reached over and took hold of her hand, to give her strength, as they made their way up the house steps.

She didn't have her keys as they'd been in her purse along with the car. That car now sat in the driveway. She tried the door and found it to be open. They quietly entered. Then she heard Mark's voice as he hollered, "Let's get a move on, or we'll miss the plane." The voice came from the library.

She stepped forward with Rip at her side. She noticed he had his right hand on his gun. She hoped it didn't come to that. Besides, the police were out at the end of the lane. She had a small recorder in the watch they'd given her. The library was ten feet away to her right. Rip gave her a nod as she stepped into the library. Rip remained back behind the door where he couldn't be seen.

"It's about time. I swear you women take forever to get ready." Mark looked up from her father's desk.

"Well, I'm here, Miss Cynthia Bradford." She watched him turn to a ghostly white. She would have loved to have a camera right then. "Why, Mark, don't you have anything to say? Aren't you happy to see me? I'm not a ghost, if that's what you think." Then he surprised her.

"Oh! My God, Cynthia, I've been so worried. When Grace told me that…."

"Cut the crap, Mark," Rip said stepping into the room. "It's all over. We've got the two men and--tell him, Cindy."

"I have total recall. I remember everything now, the drugs, the company, everything."

"Not quite."

Cindy turned as her knees suddenly felt like jelly. She found herself gazing at herself and she wasn't looking in a mirror. Only the image she saw had a gun and it was pointed at her. She turned to Rip who, too, seemed shocked.

"Thank goodness," Mark said, coming from around the desk. "I thought you'd never get here. Give me the gun."

"What and let you screw this up like you've done everything else? Not on your life. I've waited two years for this, sister." She looked directly at Cindy.

"Sister?"

"Yes, sister, your twin that no one wanted. From one foster home to another, that's what I had, while you had all this." She waved her gun around. "Isn't it ironic, now that the shoe's on the other foot? You see, Cynthia, or Cindy, whatever they call you now, this is all mine. I've taken your identity with the help here of my good husband."

Cindy couldn't believe this was happening. She had a sister. That meant she'd been adopted. Her parents weren't really her parents. Cindy all but whimpered, "But why"?

"Why? How can you ask something so stupid? Look at what you have, all the things money can buy, notoriety, prestige, you name it girl, you've had it all, while I have nothing. Nothing, do you hear me, nothing!"

"But all you had to do was come to me. I would have helped." Her double laughed an insane laugh that sent chills up Cindy's spine.

"Don't call for anyone to help you. We've given them a vacation, since we'll be touring the world as soon as I get rid of you."

"Sharon, I don't think that's a good idea. I mean, the gig is up. We need to take what we can and get the hell out of here. I'm sure they've called the cops."

Sharon, Cindy thought, I've a sister named Sharon. She'd always wanted a sister or brother, but one never came. Why hadn't her parents told her? Did they know she had a twin? Tears developed as she gazed up at her own flesh and blood. She had to try.

"Sharon, please, it's not too late. Please let us go. I'll get you the best lawyer's money can buy. I'll be with you every step of the way." She saw a flicker in Sharon's eyes, but only for a second as her sister suddenly aimed the gun at Mark.

"Sharon, what are you doing?" Cindy asked as Rip lunged towards her, but before he could get to her, the gun went off and Mark fell to the floor, blood gushing from his head. Sharon had killed him.

Cindy stood frozen, unable to move as the woman, her identical twin sister, had suddenly gone mad and was pointed the gun at her. She was going to kill her own sister. Then she heard the words, "Duck, Cindy, damn it, duck." She fell to the floor as a gun went off. She didn't know if she'd fallen on her own or if she'd been shot. She lay motionless, afraid to move, and then she remembered Rip. He'd been the one to tell her to duck. The next thing she knew she was in his arms. She leaned into him, safe and secure. "Is she--." Cindy looked at herself, no, not herself, but someone who looked like her, lying on the floor. She had a bullet hole in her chest. Her sister was dead. Cindy's eyes gazed up at Rip and she saw the truth in his face. He'd done the only thing he could have. He'd shot her sister to save Cindy's life.

EPILOGUE

Cindy sat on the verandah sipping on a glass of lemonade, as she reflected on the past year's events. A lot had happened. The investigation into Mark's stealing from the company had revealed his true character. After some deep thought, she had turned the running of the company over to the accountant, her father's best friend of many years. She remained on the board, but only as a figurehead. Maybe someday she'd be more involved, but right now she needed to get a handle on her life. She'd lost a father, the only one she knew, and a sister she never got to know. She'd found out from Grace that her parents had tried to tell her many times that she'd been adopted, but had never mustered up the courage. She couldn't blame them. She'd also found out that her parents hadn't known she'd been an identical twin. In her heart, she knew if they had, they would have adopted both of them. Yes, a lot had happened in the past year, but some good had come out of it all, she had Rip.

She stood now, facing the stable where he was loading up Snickers and her father's gray mare that he now rode. She chuckled as Bandon jumped up and down, yipping at them. Her family, she thought, as Rip spotted her and waved. They'd gotten married after everything had cooled down. Everything happens for a reason, she thought. Happier than she'd ever remembered, she waved back and called, "I'm ready whenever you are."

They were going to Buford for a summer, getaway. A place where Rip could start on his new book, as he'd sold the first one. It was a great place to relax away from the city, in the tranquil hills, the place where she'd met the man of her dreams. They would soon join their friends, Matt, Martha, Frank and their children. They had two now. Soon Rip and her would be adding to their family, she thought, as she rubbed her swelling stomach. She had her memory back, along with the happiness and love of being married to Rip.

Made in the USA
Charleston, SC
22 May 2013